ANNIE NICHOLAS

Not His Dragon

Annie Nicholas

Published 2016
Copyright by Annie Nicholas

I love hearing feedback. Email: annienicholas@ymail.com

BOOKS BY ANNIE NICHOLAS

Vanguard Elite
Bootcamp of Misfit Wolves
A Taste of Shifter Geekdom
Blind Wolf Bluff

The Vanguards series
The Omegas
The Alpha
The Beta
Omegas in Love
Sigma
Prima

The Angler series
Bait (Free)
Catch
Hunting Colby
Release

Chronicles of Eorthe
Scent of Salvation
Scent of Valor
Scent of a Scandal

Lake City Series
Ravenous (Free)
Starved for Love
Sinful Cravings

Stand Alone Books
Not His Dragon
Irresistible
Koishi
No Refuge
Boarded

Annie Nicholas

For more information on coming releases go to
http://www.annienicholas.com

Not His Dragon

CHAPTER ONE

The sudden blare of the fire alarm startled Angie enough to drop her favorite coffee mug with the words *I owe. I owe. Off to work I go*. Scalding coffee cascaded over Angie's tits and the cup shattered at her feet. Thankfully, the earsplitting noise masked her shriek of pain. Otherwise her partially senile neighbor would have been dialing nine-one-one already. The old sweetheart must have them on speed dial.

Angie yanked off her only clean work shirt and tossed it to the kitchen floor among her almost unpacked boxes. It had only taken her a year to get this much done. She kicked one out of her way and ran over to the sink, then splashed cold water on the singed girls. They went numb but as soon as she stopped wetting them the burning sting returned. She wanted to fill the sink and let her breasts soak but she was late for work.

Smoke billowed from the toaster she'd bought from a garage sale last weekend. The timer apparently was stuck on burn-to-a-crisp. She crossed the room and manually popped the button, ejecting the charcoal that used to be bread. The spring was broken as well and she watched the flaming piece of toast land on yesterday's newspaper. Or was that last week's newspaper?

The *New Port Times* instantly caught fire and the headlines vanished in mere seconds. Angie cupped water in her hands, tossing it on the flames, and smashed the burnt toast with a black dishtowel. When did she get a dishtowel? She unfolded the mess in her hands. Her yoga pants. Nice.

Half-naked, boobs scorched, she coughed and opened the only window in her crappy studio apartment. Inferno averted. Building saved. Her neighbors didn't even know how close they had come to being on the six o'clock news. She'd probably also flashed the old guy across the alley from her. She hoped his heart could take it.

She grabbed the same pair of yoga pants and waved it under the fire alarm until it stopped drilling into her eardrums. The noise faded but the sound of ringing continued in a new tone. She did a slow blink, staring at the alarm. Was this a new setting? Then she noticed the light flashing on her cell phone by the crispy paper. She answered it. "What?" All she wanted was to get to work. Her appointment book was full, her bank account was empty, and she had plenty of hides to scratch.

"Your eight o'clock is here. Tell me you're around the corner," her receptionist spat back.

"I'm around the corner." And five blocks down. If she ran the whole way, she could be there in twenty minutes. Her receptionist would have to call the paramedics to revive her though. She hoped they were cute. It had been weeks since anyone had given her proper mouth to mouth.

"You're lying, aren't you?" Beth whispered and ground out the words at the same time. She had many hidden talents and she'd make some werewolf an awesome mate one day.

Angie grabbed a t-shirt from the "bedroom" floor, sniffed and pulled it on. Only a paper screen wall dividing her apartment made it a separate room. Even though she mended freakishly fast for a human, she didn't have time to wait for her burning tits to heal. In a rush, she grabbed a fistful of ice from the freezer to tuck inside her bra. "Oh God, that's so good."

"Angie!"

"Get off my back. I had to stop my building from burning down. Keep your panties on and offer them a cup of coffee. I'm on my way as we speak." Who was her eight o'clock appointment?

"Keep my pan—" Beth's voice faded.

Angie tugged her apartment door closed using all her weight to fit it in the crooked frame, and locked it in place.

"Hey." A male voice purred in her ear. "Why am I here and you're not?"

She grimaced and dug deep for her inner professional businesswoman. "Ryota, I'll be there soon. I set my place on fire."

"Again?"

"The last time wasn't my fault. The building has faulty wiring." She took the steps two at a time.

"That's what happens when you live in a dump." He hung up on her.

She stuck her phone in her back pocket and hit the streets at a run. One shouldn't keep the local werewolf pack alpha waiting, especially when one had dumped him a few months ago and didn't want to get bitten.

She weaved her way through the sea of pedestrians suddenly flooding the sidewalks. Had aliens landed on her rooftop? Was Godzilla rampaging through the city? Where had all these people come from?

Turning the corner, she spotted the farmer's market. Oh yeah, not a grand disaster. Just a hoard of fresh produce junkies needing their fix.

Of all the times for her to be surrounded by vegans, this was not the day. Ryota Ken'ichi didn't wait on anyone. He was her best customer, and more importantly, he encouraged the pack to use her services to incite more shifter-based businesses. She couldn't afford for him to storm away in a hissy fit. The pack was her bread and butter—well, more like noodles and Pop Tarts. Her money vanished back into her business quicker than she could make it.

Finally treading past the last shopper, she took off like a lone gazelle at a lion convention. Who said a woman couldn't sprint in flip-flops? She pumped her arms, feet driving into the concrete—eat your heart out high school track team. Good thing she lived close to her small shop.

"Whoo wee, shake it, mama!" some ass in a truck heading past her shouted.

She twisted to give him the one-fingered salute without breaking stride. There weren't many people she'd run for, since it was against her religion, but to keep Ryota happy, she'd make seed sprout in a salt mine.

The barista wouldn't meet Eoin's gaze. Not many shifters would, since dragons topped the food chain. "A large black coffee and a triple…" He glanced at the note in his hand. "Venti, half sweet, non-fat, caramel macchiato." Was that really a drink?

She smirked but still avoided his stare.

"That last one is not for me." He crumpled the paper and tossed it in the trash.

"No doubt." She busied herself with his order.

The gallery manager had obnoxious taste, but Eoin couldn't really complain. The fop had great connections and had helped Eoin break into the art world. Now his work was touring Europe while he worked on a new series at home.

Dragon art sold well and paid the bills.

Eoin sank into the closest chair and picked up the latest edition of Art World. The gallery was across the street, so it was no wonder the magazine had landed in the coffee shop. He flipped through the pages, not really reading anything but absorbing the pictures until a familiar painting caught his eye.

The small image accompanied a review of his latest exhibit in Germany. He couldn't go on tour like other artists. If he left his territory, someone might try to take it from him. Leaving his city for an extended period of time wasn't an option. He scanned the article. Comments like *lacks emotion* and *poor depth* jumped off the page.

The edges of the magazine crumpled under his grip. This was the third similar review in less than a month. He tore the page out and stormed across the street.

Inside the gallery, three of his paintings hung on display. Lorenzo, the gallery manager and art dealer, stared at Eoin's latest masterpiece and adjusted the lighting to something more somber before reassessing the work.

"Read this." Eoin pressed the review against Lorenzo's chest.

The manager stumbled back and caught his balance. "Where's the coffee?" He unrumpled the page.

"Fuck the coffee." Eoin stood by a table covered in marketing material for his new show and leaned against it with his ankles crossed. Taking a deep breath, he settled his predator/prey instincts. Lorenzo wasn't the enemy. He rolled his head to relieve the strain in his shoulders. The art critic, on the other hand…

Lorenzo suddenly stank of fear. "You can't please everyone."

"He says people only buy my art because they want something made by a dragon." Even if that were true, sales had dropped in the last six months. Which had driven him to create this new series of paintings.

"This one is quite exceptional." The dealer pointed to the abstract Eoin had titled *Storm*. With different shades of grays, he'd tried to show the world rain clouds through his eyes, but he'd failed.

Not His Dragon

"You know I can sense when you're lying, right?" Eoin picked some dried yellow paint from under his nails, and held in his growl.

"N-no." The dealer swung around to face him, the whites of his eyes showing. "I don't mean to offend you. I—"

"It's all right, Lorenzo. I haven't eaten a human in decades. I need an honest opinion from someone I trust. Please, give me one. How else can I grow as an artist?"

Lorenzo straightened his tie and met his glare. The human's bravery was noteworthy. He was the best dealer on the East Coast, so he should have an educated opinion. He returned his attention to the dragon's work. "I don't think you're moving in the right direction by going abstract."

"What?" Eating Lorenzo would be a tragedy.

His whispered question sent the art dealer's hands a-flutter. "I m-mean…" He sighed. "If you want my honest opinion it would help if you stopped trying to intimidate me."

"I wasn't trying." Eoin massaged the bridge of his nose between his fingers. Now the scent of his lie filled the room. "Continue."

"Your technique is flawless…"

"But."

"But I don't feel anything when I look at your work. I should have a gut reaction." Lorenzo tossed him an amused glance. "Like I just had with your question."

Eoin snorted. "You want my paintings to terrify you?"

"Not exactly, but at least I'd feel something when I looked at them. People partake in art for entertainment. They want to feel. That's the key to any successful artist. They evoke emotion."

Eoin straightened and joined Lorenzo in front of his paintings. The dealer was right. Eoin stared at his art and felt nothing. That wasn't new, though. At his age, it took something extraordinary to move him. He wanted to feel something as well. With unnatural speed, he grabbed the painting off the wall and snapped it in half.

Lorenzo made a noise of part protest, part startled fear. He probably imagined his neck in place of the painting. "Eoin, don't do that. It's still good work."

Tossing the broken pieces on the floor, Eoin gave him his back. "'Good' isn't my goal." He ran his hand over the stubble growing on his head. He'd have to shave it off again soon. "I want to be known as great. I just don't know how to achieve it."

"What would you like them to sense when they look at your paintings?" At least the annoying human was trying to help him, but Eoin wasn't in any mood to express his gratitude.

"I don't know. Anything besides terror. I can do that without the help of paint." He twisted to glare at Lorenzo. "What do you want to feel when you look at them?"

Lorenzo frowned. "Something good."

"Like?"

"Try love. That works for everything. Everyone wants to be loved."

"Fuck." He kicked the closest easel and sent another of his paintings to the floor. "Might as well ask me to paint faith or God." He stormed toward the exit.

"What about your paintings?" Lorenzo called after him.

"Burn them." Burn them all. He pulled a cigarette from his shirt pocket and lit it with his breath.

CHAPTER TWO

Only one block separated Angie from her workplace. Her lungs burned. No matter how much air she sucked in, there didn't seem to be enough oxygen.

A tall, slim man smoking a cigarette watched her from half a block away.

How did she notice him in her state of asphyxiation? Because his pale, blue gaze cut across the distance and met hers with such intense fury that it scorched her retinas.

She slowed her pace, glancing over her shoulder, but saw no one. Why was she the focus of his death glare? Maybe he was friends with the jackass in the truck who'd cat-called her and didn't appreciate her attempt at sign language? If so, he could take a number and get in line with all the other things wanting to destroy her life today.

As Angie jogged closer, she couldn't help but notice the brightly colored tats peeking out from under his long-sleeved dress shirt. His business attire looked out of place with his shaved head and a cigarette hanging from his lips. He'd never be the poster boy for GQ *Magazine,* but he sure fit her bad boy fantasies.

He strode into her path, blocking her way. "What are you doing here?"

She tried to brake, but flip-flops weren't made to stop on a dime. The front ends folded under and she scraped the tips of her toes along the concrete sidewalk. "Mother fucker, son of a bitch…" She hopped on one foot to rub her bloody toes, then repeated the process on the other foot. "What's wrong with you?" She planted her hands on his chest and shoved, propelling herself backward.

Pinwheeling her arms, she caught her balance. Great, a supernatural. She had a better chance of pushing the Hanover Tower.

He grabbed her upper arm and yanked her kissing-close. "Don't do that again."

Her blood smeared across his white shirt where she'd laid her dirty hands. She couldn't help but notice a small blue symbol tattooed by his left eye. From this angle, she couldn't see the design completely.

Try as she might, she couldn't jerk her arms free. Her heart hammered. "Let go." She glanced around for help, but no one seemed to want to meet her desperate stare. They crossed the street, gazes glued to the ground. The pedestrian population thinned out quickly as many of them found stores they just had to enter. The scent of fear filled the air and only some of it was hers.

"What are you doing in my city?" His whispered question sent chills down her spine.

"Your city? No one owns New Port." Oh God, she couldn't stop her mouth. All she had to do was apologize profusely for whatever imagined transgressions and he'd most likely let her go. Angie stared at the shaved dark stubble on his head, since she couldn't take his penetrating glare. He kept his hair cropped real close. Almost like velvet. She caught her hand before she reached to touch him. Her senses said he was some sort of shifter, but she couldn't tell what. She suspected she had a little supernatural blood in her lineage, so her skills were limited. Definitely not werewolf. Her ties to the pack were close enough that she knew them at least by sight.

Unfortunately, humans didn't hold the monopoly on criminals. Supernaturals had them too and Ryota had shown her how to best defend herself. She slid her free hand into her front pocket. "I said, *let me go*." She gave her arm another jerk.

He gave her a condescending smile that would have frozen the Eastern Ocean. "Or what?"

She withdrew her hand, aimed at his face, and pulled the trigger on her pepper spray, remembering at the last moment to close her own eyes and mouth.

He let go and roared an inhuman sound. The noise rattled the windows. She thanked God that she'd emptied her bladder before setting the kitchen on fire.

Shit, shit, shit.

She geared her ass to holy-shit-it's-going-to-eat-me speed and didn't think the soles of her flip-flops hit the ground until she reached the door to her own little business. Like a hurricane, she swept into the waiting area and crashed onto the first loveseat. "Water."

Not His Dragon

Beth hovered over her and touched her cheek. Her fingertips came away covered in soot. "You weren't kidding about the fire."

"What the—?" She rose onto her noodle-like legs and took a gander at her reflection in the gilded mirror on the wall. Ew, she had grey soot on her cheeks and forehead. The t-shirt she'd pulled on was the one she'd dripped ketchup on yesterday, and now fresh sweat marked her armpits. Great, she'd forgotten to put on deodorant, when one hundred percent of her clientele were shifters with ultra-sensitive noses.

"The light in room three isn't working again. I changed the light bulb and checked the circuit breaker." Beth handed her a paper cup of water.

Fantastic. She had a rent-to-own deal with the landlord that didn't include repairs. The building was turning into a money pit. Every extra cent she made went right back into the business. "Call the electrician."

"Already done, boss. He'll be here in the morning."

Angie rubbed at the soot on her cheek. "Can I die and start my life over now?"

Ryota's face joined hers in the mirror. "Wait until we've done our business first. Then you can throw yourself off the roof if you'd like."

She hung her head. "Go to room two and shift, alpha. I'll be there in a minute." Her day couldn't get worse, right?

The inferno in Eoin's eyes continued even after he tried to dispel it with a healing spell. It was made neither of magic or fire, so he didn't have much resistance. He needed to rinse the poison from his eyes before he could heal them. Cracking his eyelids open, he saw the direction in which she escaped. The she-dragon could run, but now that he had her scent, she couldn't hide.

He wiped his eyes with his sleeve but the burning only got worse. Sniffing his fingers, he identified what she had used. Pepper spray, of all things. A laugh rumbled from his chest, rusty and unexpected. Eoin, harbinger of smoke and darkness, taken down by table spice. He could already hear the bard's songs of mockery.

The door to the art gallery crashed open. "What was that noise? Eoin?" Lorenzo laid his hands on him. "Let me help you."

"Water." Wait until he got his hands on that female. She wouldn't be able to sit for a month once he was done with her. A plastic container was placed in his hands.

"It's my water bottle." The sound of Lorenzo's retreating footsteps followed his fear-filled words. Pepper spray was mixed with an oily substance. Water by itself wouldn't wash it away but it would ease the pain long enough for him to find her. He could take the pain until he washed it off later.

Eoin tilted his head back and squirted the cool liquid in his eyes, flushing the chemical burn away. The sharp discomfort faded and a dull ache settled under his eyelids. This would take at least an hour for his spell to heal completely. He drained the bottle, taking what relief he could. The water soaked his shirt until it clung to his shoulders and chest like a second skin.

Pushing from the wall, he blinked to clear his vision. His bellow had emptied the streets. Let that remind them who truly ruled the city. Hopefully the she-dragon's mate had heard it. He should come face Eoin instead of sending his female to do his dirty work.

Eoin never would have thought one of his kind would stoop so low as to use pepper spray. No matter how effective it may be, where was her dignity? He inhaled deeply and caught her scent.

Yes, there she was. How long had it been since he'd seen a female of his kind? Not since he'd moved to New Port over a hundred years ago. It shouldn't matter. Her mate wouldn't be far. Females of his kind didn't stay single for long. They were too rare. He'd have to drive them from his territory before their clan arrived to support their claim to a home. He didn't like his kind and had chosen to live alone for a reason. How had they crossed into the city without him knowing? He'd better reset his spells.

He jogged, following her trail. Cars lined the street, parked and waiting for their owners to finish work. The sidewalks were bare of pedestrians, which helped him ease into a faster pace. It would be awhile before the humans found the courage to resurface.

Two blocks from the site of their encounter, her scent ended at a storefront. He squinted at the sign to be sure he'd read it properly.

Scratch Your Itch.

Not His Dragon

Scratching for shifters? Ingenious idea. Once he escorted the she-dragon from the city, he'd have to come back and see if they did scale care. He walked into the full waiting room.

CHAPTER THREE

Ryota was good looking even in beast form. Glossy black fur covered his bipedal form and muscles rippled under his soft coat as he settled on Angie's workbench. She used modified massage tables to scratch her customers' backs.

Lots of Hollywood movies had confused the general public about shifters. Growing-up, Angie had always thought of them as people who could turn into animals, but that wasn't the case. They were a race who could change shape but not as the actual animal. So a werewolf was a mix of man and wolf. Ryota walked on two legs and could talk like he did in human form, except now he had fur, sharp teeth, and the face of a wolf. There was no mistaking one for the other, but underneath his skin, no matter the shape, he was still the same insufferable person.

He rolled onto his stomach. "The usual."

She rolled her eyes, glad he couldn't see her. The alpha had more faults than appeal, in her opinion. She was glad she'd discovered the size of his ego before their relationship had grown serious. Dating a shifter was a huge mistake and something she wouldn't repeat. Their concept of love was mostly biological and possessive. She didn't want a mate. She wanted someone who loved her for who she was, not because of a biological imperative. She needed to start hanging out with her own kind, but humans grew twitchy around her after a while. Her friends never stayed around long. Not unless they were supernatural, like Beth, but she couldn't help wonder if to them she was only prey. Or maybe, whatever genes gave her sharp nails also instinctively frightened humans. She'd rather believe in the latter.

Ryota, on the other hand, only thought about anatomy and he was very good at it. She lightly ran her sharp nails through his fur. It was the only thing she missed about him.

He shivered. "Stop teasing me."

Not His Dragon

She smiled at his reaction and put more pressure into the scratch. Six months ago, she'd been penniless and on the verge of being homeless when she'd met a flea-ridden leopard shifter who'd paid her to scratch his hide until he'd almost passed out in relief. The idea for Scratch Your Itch had been born. Genetics had blessed her with very sharp nails, something that must have come from a very distant shifter ancestor. She'd decided to put them to good use and make a living as a scratching service.

For the first time in memory, she had a steady job and a boss she loved. Herself.

The alpha's back leg quivered as she focused on his sweet spot over his lower back.

She moved to avoid being kicked.

"Right there. Don't stop. Please." He arched his back slightly to give her better access. She'd never been able to make him plead like that in bed.

New Port's shifter community had opened their arms and wallets when she'd opened her shop. Ryota and his pack were her best customers. Who needed a security system when she had a werewolf pack?

And a lion pride. And a lone tiger. And a bear family. She was knee-deep in shed fur and loyal customers. At this rate, she would need to hire help soon. If she could keep her repair bills down.

"You smell weird." Ryota angled his hips to the left, leaning into her nails. "Like a combo of burnt toast, BO, and fear. Was the fire that bad?"

"No, having the worst morning of my life will do that to me."

He inhaled deeper then sneezed. "With a dash of pepper."

His comment caught her off guard and she laughed. "Yeah, some asshole shifter grabbed me on the street. I pepper sprayed him like you taught me."

He rose to his elbow and turned his amber gaze on her. "Good girl."

Slapping her best customer across the muzzle was bad for business, no matter how satisfying it would have been. Instead, she ground her teeth and gave him a flat smile. He had shown her the secret defense to most shifters. They didn't want their vulnerability to pepper spray becoming public knowledge. Even though shifters were faster and stronger than humans, the mortals outnumbered supernaturals a thousand to one.

"What kind of shifter? I'll have a word with his leader."

She shrugged. "I don't know. I wasn't in a position to ask questions."

Ryota settled back on his stomach, making happy wolf noises as she dug her nails into his back again. "Can I tempt you into a full body scratch?"

"No."

"You didn't even think about it."

"I didn't have to." Those days were over. Full body scratching led shifters to wanting to rub naked skin together. She'd learned this lesson the hard way when she first opened shop. Come to think of it, that was how she and Ryota had started dating.

"No more full body scratching. Shop policy."

"You write the policies."

"Yep."

A knock on the door saved Angie's ass and she gave thanks to heaven. "Come in." She didn't cover Ryota. Shifters didn't have a nudity complex.

Beth stuck her head in the room. "Sorry to interrupt, alpha. We've got a problem in the waiting room, Angie, demanding to see you." Beth was part of Ryota's pack and instinct drove the werewolves much harder than most shifters. Beth would always defer to her alpha before anyone else, even her boss.

"Tell them she's with a customer," Ryota answered. He flinched as Angie dug her nails even deeper.

"I'll be right out, Beth. We're done."

"We just started," the alpha replied.

"Consider it a freebie. I've had a rough morning and can't take your shit."

Beth hadn't moved.

Angie tossed her a questioning look. She was an omega of the pack. They were rare, since their goal in life was pleasing others and most werewolves were jerks by nature. The pack spoiled Beth rotten. Angie had placed her friend in a predicament, though. She couldn't please both her and Ryota at the same time.

The alpha sat on the edge of the table and assessed the smaller female. "Why do you smell like fear?"

Not His Dragon

"Because it's the dragon."

Angie stepped back as if Beth had slapped her. "The dragon?"

The omega nodded.

"I wonder what he wants?" Ryota began to shift back to human form.

"Yeah," Angie whispered. Rumor had it the dragon didn't leave his castle often. He was a recluse who lived on the mountain by the edge of the city. If a person drove on Route 38, they could see the towers over the tree line. There was even a sightseeing spot where tourists gathered to get a glimpse of him flying over his lands.

"Maybe he's here to get his back scratched?" Beth's giggle held an edge of hysteria. She clapped her hand over her mouth. "Oh, that wasn't funny."

"There's only one way to find out what he wants." Angie led Beth out of the room, leaving Ryota to finish his shift.

The waiting area was empty. Where had all her clients gone? In the center of the room stood a familiar figure. "You!" She set her hands on her hips and met his bloodshot glare, determined not to flinch this time. "Beth, call the police. This jerk assaulted me on the street." She didn't even feel bad about the blisters forming around his eyes.

His grin froze her soul. "Yes, Beth. Call the police." He made it sound like a dare. His wet, semi-transparent dress shirt clung to his body like a second skin and she glimpsed multi-colored tattoos over hard flesh.

Angie twisted her head to look at her friend. She was motionless by her desk, the whites of her eyes showing. Angie set her hand on Beth's. "What's wrong?"

"He's the dragon," Ryota answered as he entered the room. He bowed his head. "Eoin." The alpha gathered Beth behind him. "Forgive Angie. She lacks any manners."

The dragon crossed his arms. "She sprayed chemicals in my eyes. I wonder where she learned that trick?"

Ryota sniffed the air. "This is the guy you pepper sprayed?" He slapped his forehead with the heel of his hand, leaving a vivid red mark. Japanese fell from his lips in either swears or prayers; he spoke so quickly she couldn't distinguish the words.

She jabbed a finger in the dragon's direction. "He grabbed me for no reason." How did she become the bad guy in this situation?

"I had reason." Eoin's voice ricocheted off her shop's walls from the volume of his shout. "She's trespassing. I'm here to escort her and her mate off my land." He bared his teeth. "Peacefully."

Ryota eyed her as if seeing Angie for the first time. "Trespassing?"

"Mate?" She asked at the same time. "Why would you think I'm mated? Do I look that stupid?" Angie crossed her arms. "Never mind that, I'm not going anywhere." Her chest tightened. This was the first true home she'd had since her parents died. She'd worked too hard creating her niche in the shifter society. Nobody was driving her away. Not even a dragon.

Ryota let out a frustrated growl. "Stop antagonizing him." He shoved her behind him with Beth. "Obviously there's been a misunderstanding."

Angie touched her now clean cheeks. "The soot on my face didn't come from my apartment fire. It came from you when you yelled in my face." That was a different version of 'say it, don't spray it,' but Angie kept this thought to herself. Though Ryota probably wouldn't believe her, she did have a brain-to-mouth-filter and she did want to survive this encounter.

The enormity of her situation finally grew clearer and Angie understood Beth's fear. If the dragon wanted to kick her out of the city, who would stop him?

Sure, people put up a fuss when supernaturals broke human laws but she had to have someone in the city to tell her story to the press and the police. She was an orphan, a survivor of the state system. The only people who cared about her were in this room and they weren't human.

"Angie is allowed to live in our territory. Humans are exempt from our laws." The alpha appeared calm and cool, even though he faced something that exhaled smoke without a lit cigarette in sight.

She, like most people, knew a few details of territory laws between species and that they considered them important. Like Ryota and his pack could co-exist with a dragon in the same city, but if another werewolf pack tried to move in there would be bloodshed. However, humans didn't count. They lived everywhere. Supernaturals have co-existed with humans as far back as recorded history, but they kept secrets and little of their cultures were shared.

Not His Dragon

Eoin cocked his head to the side and took a deep breath as if tasting the air. "I want a word with her in private."

Angie gripped the back of Ryota's shirt. Her throat had gone dry. He wouldn't leave her. Right? She knew she wasn't pack but they'd been lovers.

The alpha shook his head. "She's under pack protection."

She released a breath she'd been holding. Abandoned before, she couldn't stop wondering when it would happen again.

"We value her services."

The words stabbed her in the heart. She released her hold on Ryota and stepped away from the werewolves. She was just a service?

"I give you my word no harm will come to her while we talk. You seem correct in assessing that this is a…" His gaze traveled over her but the anger in his eyes still burned. "…misunderstanding."

Ryota glanced at her. The alpha wouldn't fight for her. Why would she ever believe he would? She had been just a piece of ass and she'd burned that bridge. Now, she had to figure out how to apologize to a dragon while keeping some of her dignity intact.

Apparently her day could get worse.

The wolf alpha left the shop with Beth in tow. They crossed the street and watched the building. "You've got good ties in the shifter community." Eoin returned his attention to the she-dragon pretending to be human. How had she pulled it off with the other shifters?

"Like he said, I provide them with a valuable service." She held up her hand and he caught sight of her nails. Glossy and long, her nails appeared sharp.

"Those don't look like human nails."

"They are genetic leftovers from some distant ancestor. I can't shift, so I'm classed as human." She stuck her hands in her pockets as if suddenly ashamed of them.

And that's why the werewolves treated her as human. His nose said otherwise. "What species?"

She shrugged. "I don't know. No family tree to speak of."

Could her ancestor have been dragon? Even if that were possible, her scent sang to him. He leaned closer and there it was—the scent of she-dragon. He closed his eyes as it curled around him in seductive coils.

Wait.

He shook his head. She'd said something about not being mated. "Are you okay?"

He pulled away toward the exit before his body started acting instinctively to her unmated scent. "I'm fine." The last thing he needed was to become hormonal over a human. She wasn't even his type. He liked them sleek and slutty, with names like Bambi or Lola. "What's your name?"

"Angie."

Damn. She was petite and curvy. Her short hair allowed him to admire the strong line of her jaw, and the delicate bone structure of her face gave her character.

"What did you want to discuss?" Angie met his gaze and stood her ground. He admired a woman with backbone. Those who cowed to him, like Beth, broke too easily.

He could scoop Angie in one arm without any effort. How long had it been since he'd smelled an unmated female of his kind? Obviously, too long. Except she claimed she wasn't his kind. He cleared his throat and glanced around the empty room. "I've never met a human who smelled like dragon. I didn't mean—well, I did mean to scare you, but I thought you were trying to infringe on my territory." He rubbed his head. It was starting to ache. Apologies tended to give him migraines, which was why he avoided them. "We good?"

Her big, dark eyes grew impossibly wide, softening the hard edges of mistrust in her expression. A male could drown in that kind of gaze. "So I can stay in New Port?" she whispered.

He nodded. "Just stay out of my way." Turning his back on her, he left her shop. He ignored the werewolves as he strode down the street and shifted to his dragon form, tearing through his clothes. This would make the evening news, but after this shitty morning all he wanted was to be alone in the refuge of his castle.

CHAPTER FOUR

Warm updrafts carried Eoin over the city. He spotted a few humans on the rooftops, cameras aimed in his direction. On better days, he'd do a few acrobatics to appease them. It was good PR, but today he wanted to burn things to the ground. He swallowed his flame but let loose a roar that rattled the windows.

A few screams followed. Reminding them he was a black-scaled predator would keep the paparazzi away for a few days. Better for everyone that way. He felt on the edge of biting things in half.

Seeking solitude would ease his temper and a dip in the glacier-fed lake would sooth his eyes. He blinked them clear. The shift to dragon form hadn't healed him as he'd hoped. Modern technology affected magic this way. He glided toward his mountain home, flapping his wings to gain more altitude. The aerial view of his castle soothed his fury.

Poor review from a critic he couldn't eat, sales plummeting, then beaten by a little human girl. Viktor would demand he turn in his dragon card. His vampire tattoo artist always had a flare for the dramatic, but he would be right. Eoin enjoyed a good scrap or a hunt like the next dragon but, unlike his kin, he appreciated the challenge of creating something.

Humans had a natural knack for crafting new things and ideas. Most long-lived races didn't have the capacity to value this gift.

He dipped his left wing and took a leisurely turn around the turrets, only to come to a mid-air stop.

A black Cadillac was parked in the courtyard by the front door. His agent waited by the car, waving his arms at him, as if he couldn't see the human from the sky. This day couldn't get much worse.

Eoin dived toward the car and back-winged at the last minute so he could land right next to Roger.

The human covered his head and crouched. "Fuck Eoin, I hate it when you do that."

He settled on his stomach so he could better view Roger's face. "I know." They'd worked together for the last two—three—six

23

years? Time moved differently for dragons, so he had trouble keeping track in human manner. "What drags you out to the mountains on such a lovely day? Good news, I hope." He'd made Roger a very wealthy man. The agent worked for him exclusively now.

Roger held up a copy of Art World. "Why would you have Lorenzo read this? Are you trying to sabotage all my work?" He rattled the magazine in front of Eoin's snout. Not many humans would yell at him. Roger had balls made of brass, which made him a great asset and a better agent.

With sharp claws, Eoin scratched his chin. "It seemed like a good idea at the time." In retrospect, he could have done better by ignoring the review. The critic had hit a nerve though. "Do you think people buy my work just because I'm a dragon?"

"Who gives a shit?" Roger tossed the magazine on the ground. "As long as they buy it."

Eoin shot a small fireball from his nostril and watched the offensive review burn.

Roger retreated and blinked at the flames. "You should have done that to begin with." He frowned. "Lorenzo wants to postpone the show."

Shooting to his feet, Eoin spread his wings for balance. "For how long?"

"Indefinitely."

"I was just there. He never said a word." Lorenzo had been one of Eoin's biggest supporters. He'd introduced him to the art community and done a yearly show since his debut.

"I think this latest review combined with your newest work has him doubting your viability as a selling artist. We all have bills to pay, Eoin."

He dropped his wings to his sides and they hit his flesh with an empty thud. Just like that, his career as an artist ended. Without a gallery to back him it would be almost impossible to contract more tours. He'd left his clan to pursue this lonely path.

Most dragons lived isolated lives high in the mountaintops where only the craziest of creatures would dare tread. He'd been painting for as long as he could remember, but his kind loved things that sparkled like gems and gold. Art held little interest to any of them.

Not His Dragon

He fisted his clawed hands. "What now?" No matter the consequences, he wouldn't give up. He'd fought too hard to be recognized for his work.

Roger crossed his arms and stared at his feet. "Try something different. A new medium."

"You mean stop painting?"

"I mean, create something to wow Lorenzo."

"Just like that." Eoin snapped his fingers.

"I know you have piles of paintings in that castle." Roger pointed at Eoin's home. "Let me see them. Maybe you have something amazing hidden in there."

Eoin shook his head. "It's trash." He didn't like strangers in his home. It was part of being a dragon. He'd come down off the mountains, but that didn't mean he was social. "Give me a few days to think things over and I'll get back to you." He moved toward his front door.

"Eoin!" Roger shouted. "Come on, buddy. Don't give up."

"I'm not giving up. Not yet."

"Sort through your work. I'll bring Lorenzo in a couple days to look at what you have. Together, we'll change his mind."

Eoin hesitated by the entrance. "Did you want me in dragon form so I can coerce him?" It wouldn't be difficult. Lorenzo feared him in human form. He couldn't imagine the art dealer's reaction to him in his beast form.

"No." Roger met his glare. Another reason why he liked his agent. "We do this based on your work."

"Very well." He left the sunlight by entering his castle. The doorway barely accommodated his size. Most of his home did, though. That was the point of living in such a huge building by himself. Just the bedrooms and bathrooms were too small. He rarely used either. He swam in the lake to bathe and slept under the stars on the rooftop.

Taking the curved staircase, he climbed the tower to his workshop and glared at the stacks of unframed paintings piled against the wall. Monet, Da Vinci, Rembrandt, Van Gogh, even that fart Picasso had surpassed him with their work. What did they possess that he lacked besides their humanity?

One by one, he flicked through the stacks, stabbing his paintings with his claws and tossing them over his shoulder into a huge pile. Sceneries, portraits, abstracts—crap, crap, crap. Others had described his work as flat, emotionless, and one-dimensional. Of course it was one dimensional and flat. He painted on a smooth surface. How did one inspire emotion when inside he felt dead?

Heat rolled within his chest. He spun and blew fire over the pile of trash. Now, this was art. He sat by the window and watched the last century of his work turn to ash. When his agent brought Lorenzo in a few days, Eoin would have nothing to show him. Maybe he should return to his clan. They didn't understand him—no one did—but at least he would be among his own kind.

He reached behind him and scratched his lower back. The flames licked over the surfaces of the canvas as if tasting the dried paint. They reached high above, almost touching the ceiling. The castle was made of stone. Fire would scorch the wall and maybe burn the roof. All could be repaired if he cared to.

The heat grew until his scales sizzled. In the corner of the room a mound of empty paint and soda cans sagged, melting in the presence of the intense heat. He snaked over and smashed the heap with his fist.

Fuck them.

Fuck the critic, fuck Lorenzo, fuck Roger. He spun around, whipping his tail to slap-shot the accumulation of melted scrap out the window. He breathed heavy and watched the flames lick over his scales. The red and orange contrasted nicely over his black hide. So much color in just this room.

Eoin shifted to human form and dressed in a pair of stained jeans he kept here for this reason. Grabbing a brush and pallet, he picked a blank canvas. The light from his fire flickered over the flat surface. The differences in the shadows gave it depth. He watched the shades of light change until they blurred. With a little confidence, he traced this new inspiration.

The shadows moved from dark to light so quickly it took his shifter reflexes to follow. He paused to observe once more. The violent nature reminded him of his not-quite a she-dragon who liked to scratch backs. A smile almost tugged at his lips.

Pepper spray. That's what he'd call this painting.

CHAPTER FIVE

Eoin grew more aware of his surroundings as he woke. The hard stone floor bit into his soft skin. He hated when he slept in his human form. It left him vulnerable. Where had he been last night? He cracked open an eyelid. A pile of ashes filled the center of the room except for his latest painting drying on the easel.

He rose onto his elbows and wiped the drool from the corner of his lip. He'd been so exhausted that he'd fallen asleep next to his easel. He stretched and worked on the knots in his shoulders and legs.

Reaching around, he scratched his lower back but his blunt nails didn't ease the itch this time. Withdrawing his hand, he glimpsed blood on his fingertips. What the fuck? He glanced over his shoulder and could see a bloody smear where he'd itched, but not the source of the injury.

Eoin left the room and moved down the hall. The cold stone made him step quickly since he was still barefoot. He slammed the bathroom door open and a flock of pigeons flew out the open window. Stunned, he watched them take flight before seeing the mess of bird shit everywhere. The birds must have been living in here. When had he opened this window? It must have been years since he'd used this bathroom.

The birds didn't matter. The wound on his back did. He twisted to look in the full-length mirror. "Fuck." He must have a bad case of scale rot for it to have manifested to his human form as a scabby rash. Real sexy.

He grimaced at the mess. Once the rot got this bad it would take some real elbow grease to pick it out. He ran his hand over the short buzz on his head and snarled. If he ignored it, his scales would fall off and wouldn't grow back, leaving a big weakness in his best defense.

Scale rot. The trouble with being so big was the inability to care for his own hide. If he'd mated, his female could do it and likewise he'd return the favor.

In the old days, he'd train a human squire for his scale care and other needs. His last squire died recently at the ripe old age of ninety-eight. Eoin hadn't been prepared. He'd been in denial of his friend's mortality. Training someone new, so soon after Jasper, his squire, had died, seemed like a betrayal.

He rubbed at the dull ache in his chest. Where would he look for a new squire? The modern authorities would bomb his home if he swooped upon a playground and chose one of the many urchins running around. Things had changed quickly over the last century. Maybe he could buy one on eBay? No, he'd never seen that category while browsing.

Absentmindedly, he scratched his lower back and paused. The pretty little not-dragon girl who scratched backs for a living. He wouldn't have to keep her or feed her. He'd just have to pay her on an as-needed basis, and he'd better do it soon. Hurrying to his sleeping chambers in the next tower, he paused in the center of the room. Where had he left his cell phone? The fucking thing needed a bell or an app that would beep when he clapped. He barely used the bed and kept this space to store his clothes and gadgets. Tearing his drawers open, he dumped the contents until something shattered on the stone floor. He blinked at the cracked screen. Fuck, he swiped it on but it refused to respond. He hadn't plugged it in for days. Stupid technology. These things were worse than babies. As soon as he turned his back they died.

He searched through a pile of clothes on the floor, sniffing at them until he found something that wouldn't knock out a shifter from the stench. When he returned home, he would order more clothes online. Much easier than going to a Laundromat. Whenever he went to one of those there was always so much screaming.

Angie eyed the box of muffins a regular customer had dropped off on his way to the office. Her stomach growled. She'd skipped breakfast.

"Wow." Beth bit into one. "These are fantastic. I think he added pineapple chunks with the blueberries." She pushed the box closer toward Angie. "You have to taste this."

Shaking her head, she retreated a few steps, the hunger plaguing her suddenly replaced by nausea. "I'm watching my diet."

Beth frowned. "Don't be silly. You're perfect."

"Not diet, as in weight loss, but what I put in my body. Eating healthy." Yeah, that sounded sane. Better than the truth. What would Beth think if she found out Angie couldn't eat anything cooked by a man? Ever since her parents had died, she couldn't stomach food touched by male hands. Didn't matter what race. That had gone over well with the foster homes when she was growing up.

"Okay, more for me." Beth hugged the box to her chest. Werewolf metabolisms were incredible. Her best friend could out-eat a high school football team and still remain a size five. Part of Angie hated her for it.

The electrician waved good-bye through the storefront window.

She held his recent bill in her hand for a new light fixture, the second one in a month. At this rate, she should keep him on retainer. The inspector she'd hired to check out the building before signing the contract had given her the thumbs-up. The landlord must have paid him off. Otherwise, she was the unluckiest businesswoman in New Port.

The shop door chimed as it opened. Her first appointment was a little early. That was a good omen. It would help the day go by faster if she could keep to her schedule. She twisted around and stumbled against Beth, who had jumped to her feet.

Her receptionist curtsied. "Mr.—Mr. Dragon, nice to see you again." The scent of Beth's fear almost choked Angie. "Would you like a muffin?" She squeaked out the last word.

Angie moved around the desk between the dragon and the omega werewolf. Without Ryota here, she would have to play protector. She fingered her pepper spray. If she had to use it again, she doubted her survival. "Eoin, what can I do for you?" His eyes appeared less bloodshot than yesterday and the blisters had healed.

He glanced at Beth. "Go away."

The chair clattered to the floor and was followed by Beth's retreating footsteps as she hurried to the back of the shop. Hopefully, she'd think to call her alpha for help.

"That was rude." Angie fisted the sprayer.

"It was necessary." He stared at her for a moment and a crushing silence filled the room. "You scratch backs for a living?"

29

She held up her chin. "Yes."

"Do you know scale care?"

"Uh…" She released her hidden weapon and scratched her head. "No."

"That's not a problem. I can teach you. The process would usually take a few hours but I have a bit of an issue that might take a couple of days to fix. Clear your calendar."

"Just like that." Angie snapped her fingers. She'd thought Ryota had an ego issue. Eoin put him to shame.

"Is this a problem?" He leaned toward her and inhaled.

"Are you smelling me?" *That* wasn't creepy. She moved behind the desk.

A blush tinged his cheeks and highlighted his sharp cheekbones. "No." He broke eye contact and stared at his worn boots. "I can compensate you for your inconvenience."

"It's not good business for me to cancel appointments. Your needs aren't greater than anyone else's. I could possibly fit you in on the weekends until we're done." That would suck away all her free time, but she would like to stay off the dragon's menu.

He shook his head. "That won't work. It has to be done soon." Shoving his hands deep in his jean pockets, he dropped his chin to avoid her stare and muttered something.

"What?"

"I've got scale rot."

She took an involuntary step away. "Is it contagious?"

He shot her a hard look. "No." The word snapped with contempt. "There are many steps to curing it and they can't be skipped or done far apart."

"I can maybe take care of this issue in patches?"

"I'm not a car asking to be waxed. This is my skin." He twisted around and lifted his t-shirt. His back was completely inked. At first glance it appeared like some hipster tribal tattoo thing she'd seen on Pinterest a hundred times, but on closer inspection she noticed they were words in a different language intricately woven into a pattern.

"Nice tat." She moved around the desk to get a better look. "What does it say?"

He followed her gaze. "Rash."

"What? Why?"

He pointed to the red sore spread across his lower back. It looked infected. "Rash."

"Oh." Fine, let him be that way. "Can't I care for you in this form? It would take less time." She'd never actually seen a dragon up close. She half hoped he'd say no. Television reporters did their best to catch them in flight but dragons were a very private race, and a very violent one as well.

"I wish it were that simple." He settled his t-shirt back.

"How did you normally have it done?"

A pained expression flashed across his face, so quick she wasn't sure if she'd truly seen it. "Someone from my clan would have helped, but since I've moved away from them I usually have a squire." He moved within her personal space. "They're in short supply nowadays."

She tried to move away but her traitorous legs wouldn't respond. The oxygen seemed to have vanished from the room as Eoin's heat enveloped her.

He touched her hair, running his fingertips through the short strands.

A wave of dizziness crashed over Angie. Danger! Danger! Her proximity alarm rang in her head.

He pulled something from her hair and set it on the floor. It crawled away.

"I had a spider in my hair?" Her voice rose to an octave close to breaking glass. She sat on the desk and pulled her knees to her chest. "Oh my God."

He smirked. "It's smaller than you are. I think you'll live."

"That's not the point." She shook out her hair to make sure it hadn't laid eggs or made a nest. "I'm going to have to shave my head like yours."

His laugh sounded rusty and unused. The way he tilted his head gave her a better view of his eyes with their corners crinkling in mirth.

Her stupid heart beat a little faster.

"That would be a shame, Angie." The way he said her name, as if he savored it, sent a shiver along her spine.

She wanted to slap herself. How many times had she witnessed broken hearts when shifters found their true mates and dumped their human lovers like yesterday's trash? This was the real reason for her leaving Ryota. Dump him before he dumped her.

"I'll triple your fee if you take care of my scale problem this week."

Angie slid back onto her feet, eight-legged invaders forgotten. "Triple?" That would give her a nice cushion. Business had been good, but what if the novelty of back-scratching faded? She needed some savings if she ever wanted to move out of her crappy apartment. "I'll do it in the evenings after my appointments are done. Will that do?"

He nodded. "Do you know how to reach my castle?"

"Wait, what?" The isolated, desolate stone building way outside the city where no one could hear her scream? Luckily, she'd remembered to wear her brain-to-mouth filter today. "All—all my equipment is here."

The smile he'd worn not seconds ago vanished, replaced with a sterner version of a frown. He crossed his arms. "You can't possibly think I'll fit in here." He leaned in so close his lips brushed her ear as he spoke softly. "I'm much bigger in dragon form."

She needed air. And a cold shower. "How big are you?" Apparently, her filter still let stupid questions slip out.

A spark of mischief glinted in Eoin's gaze even though his expression never changed. "Very."

The tips of her ears ached from blushing so hard. She wanted to cover them with her hands. How had she let Beth convince her to go for a pixie cut? Her short hair left her ears vulnerable for all to see her embarrassment. "I don't have a car."

"I'll pick you up. Where do you live?"

The last thing she wanted was for Eoin to see her rat-infested apartment building. "I'll get a ride. What time should I be there?"

"Seven."

"Should I bring anything?"

"I have all the tools and oils. I just need a pair of reliable hands."

ℭHAPTER SIX

Angie leaned face-first against the shop door and peered out the window at Eoin's departing form.

He sauntered along the sidewalk like a creature who knew he could eat anyone who bothered him. With one swallow.

Whose cornflakes had she pissed in lately to deserve this tsunami-sized wave of misfortune? Sure, cleaning dragon scales could open a new branch to her services, but did she really want to deal with dragons, with their teeth and hair trigger tempers? Add in her pleasant disposition and she'd be dead by the end of the week. Tripling her fees was like hazard pay. She might as well offer dental care for great white sharks on her lists of services. If she'd wanted to place her life at risk, she'd have been a firefighter or a soldier. All she wanted was security, and Eoin was anything but.

A familiar, sunny-blond face blocked her view of Eoin and gave her a warm smile. "What are you looking at?" Ken, her next appointment, shouted through the door then looked over his shoulder.

She opened the entrance and pulled him inside.

"Was that who I think it was?" He pointed toward Eoin, his eyes wide.

"Yes."

"You think he'd give me an autograph?"

"After he bites you and uses your blood as ink." Did Eoin deserve that? No, he'd been rather polite for a dragon, she imagined, but anything that big and deadly deserved to be treated with caution. Something Ken didn't know how to do.

"Really?" He took a step toward the exit.

She shook her head. Werewolves. "You have an appointment." She gave him a playful swat on the shoulder.

"You're in room three, Ken." Beth had returned to her desk. "Go in and shift. Angie will be right there." Her best friend must have heard Eoin leave, and probably their whole conversation. There was only so much *privacy* with werewolves in the building. Beth hugged herself, her face pale and drawn.

Ken's gaze moved from Angie to Beth and back again as if trying to decide whether he wanted to be caught in the middle. He shook his head and departed for room three in the pregnant silence.

"Are you okay?" Beth scanned Angie from head to toe. Angie didn't blame her for leaving when Eoin told her to. The omega didn't have a drop of fighter's blood in her veins.

"I'm fine." Angie held out her arms and spun. "See, not a nibble."

Beth's frown grew deeper. "Except you agreed to go to his castle tonight."

"What would you have me do? At least he's offering me danger pay." Angie grinned to take the sting out of her words. She didn't want Beth fretting about Eoin all day and night.

Beth's bottom lip quivered. "I don't like this." She hurried around the desk and into Angie's waiting arms. "You should call Ryota. He won't let you go alone."

"Oh my God, Beth. Tell me you didn't call him."

She shook her head. "I was too afraid Eoin would hear me. We should call him now. I don't like this dragon's sudden interest in you."

Angie pushed the omega away to look her in the eye. "He's not asking me out on a date." Beth's worries were settling her own doubts about going to Eoin's castle. This was just business. "He needs help and he'll be a new paying customer." Eoin hadn't threatened her. As long as she kept her mouth shut everything would be fine.

"You shouldn't go alone."

Sighing, Angie mentally went through her short list of friends and only one seemed likely to calm Beth. "I'll ask Ken." He was part of Beth's pack, and unbelievably, Ryota's second.

Beth took a deep shaky breath. "Okay, that seems reasonable."

The click of claws on the shop's tiled floors drew their attention. Ken stood in the hallway in his glorious bipedal beast form. White-tipped grey fur covered his body as he leaned against the wall and crossed his arms. "Ask me what?" A claw tipped finger glinted in the dim morning light as he tapped it on his forearm.

Angie threw her hands up in the air. "It's a long story. I'll tell you while I work on your back. I can already see my next

Not His Dragon

appointment walking up the street." So much for being on schedule. "Offer Mrs. Gambindini a muffin while she's waiting," she whispered to Beth.

Ken scratched his shoulder. "I'm ready." His smile in beast form would have made the average human pee themselves. Sharp canines did not express reassurance.

She followed him into room three. "Lay on the table."

"Sounds like your lover's spat with Ryota is growing serious." Ken lay prone so she could examine his fur. Everyone got a quick flea check prior to scratching. She couldn't afford an infestation.

"We're not lovers anymore. I broke up with him."

"He agreed to that?" She wished he didn't sound so surprised.

"I can't believe you just said that. Doesn't matter if he agrees or not." Besides Beth, Ken was the closest thing to a friend she had in the city. They had met at a fundraiser for the state orphanage where she'd grown up. She'd been handing out lemonade and he'd been spiking his. He'd lived at the orphanage until the local pack adopted him. He'd introduced her to Ryota when she'd opened the shop.

"That's how it works in the pack."

She snorted. "Thank God, I'm not pack." Something jumped in Ken's fur and startled her. "Shit, don't move."

He went rigid. "Did you see something?" His voice rose to an unmanly octave. Oddly cute on such a big shifter.

She parted his fur and she inched her way across his hide. A flea jumped from amid her fingers. "Fucker." She moved faster, chasing the parasite through the coarse strands of fur until she impaled it between her sharp nails. "Got it." She held it under the werewolf's nose. "You, Mister, have fleas."

"When I change to human form, shouldn't they go away?" He contorted his body as he tried to scratch his own back.

She shrugged. "You would think so, but I don't know anything about magic. I do know this is your second appointment this week." Bending over, she searched through her cabinet and pulled out a bottle. "Wash in your beast form with this. It should do the trick."

He scanned the bottle. "What is it?"

"All natural flea bath made with tea tree oil." She grinned as his lip curled. "Free of charge if you give me a ride up to the dragon's castle tonight."

"I would have given you the ride without the bribe." He made as if to lie back on the table.

"Uh-uh. Out you go."

"But you haven't scratched my back yet."

"You're contagious and until you fix your flea problem, no service."

With a snarling growl, he jumped to his feet.

She broke eye contact and stared at the floor. "It's not personal, Ken. It's shop policy. What if it gets out that there are fleas here? I'd lose business. I'm just starting to get out of the red." No matter how friendly she was with a werewolf, she'd never be able to let her guard down enough to be herself.

Beth was the only one. She'd taught Angie the right body language to use to avoid confrontations. Angie wouldn't be considered a threat if she made a plea to Ken's business sense.

"Is the money good enough for you to consider opening a second shop across town?" Ken leaned against the edge of the table as if nothing had occurred. Pack life sucked, in Angie's opinion. The roller coaster of emotions running through a werewolf was exhausting.

She breathed a sigh of relief. "No."

He sniffed the bottle of flea shampoo and grimaced. "Smells like shit."

"It'll leave your fur conditioned and silky. The females will want to roll all over you."

"If that's true, you might need to open a second shop just to sell this stuff." He chuckled. "I knew I shouldn't have run with that pack of dogs. That's probably where I caught the fleas."

Angie raised her eyebrow. The word *dog* had many meanings among the werewolves, so she wasn't sure what he meant.

"Running is part of my new exercise plan." He patted his flat stomach. "But I hate to run alone and most of my pack mates are early birds, where I'm a night owl. There's a pack of stray dogs roaming the alleys by my place." He stared at the shampoo. "Maybe I should buy a few more bottles."

"For the strays?"

He nodded. "Someone should watch out for them."

Not His Dragon

She rolled her eyes and pulled out more bottles. "On the house." She hated it when Ken strummed her heartstrings. He knew all her notes. As orphans, they'd both been considered strays of human kind.

He grinned. "Thanks, Ang."

"You better not come back with fleas. Wash those dogs good."

He set the bottles aside and started shifting.

She hurried from the room to give him privacy. Watching shifters change shape poured too much envy in her blood.

Beth sat at her desk, another muffin in hand. "Will Ken go with you?"

"Yes, Mother." Angie nodded to her next customer. "Room two is ready if you'd like to go shift."

Ken joined them and set the bottles on the desk. "Not one word about this to the pack, Beth."

She smirked and pretended to zip her lips. "My lips are sealed."

"Why exactly are we visiting the dragon?" He grabbed a muffin and wolfed it down in one bite. "You never told me your long story. Dragons are a bad idea."

How did he manage to speak with his mouth so full and not choke?

"We were interrupted by your tenants." Angie glanced at room two. She'd never get out in time to have dinner and a shower if she kept being stalled. "Beth can give you the details. We have to be there at seven, so don't be late, okay? I don't want Eoin greeting us with a bottle of ketchup in his hands."

"Hey Ang," Ken called.

She paused on her way to room two. "What?"

"The sink in room one is plugged up something fierce."

She rubbed her temples. Every day something different broke.

"Do you want me to call the plumber?" Beth offered.

"No, I'll look at it first." Since opening the shop, she'd collected small amount of tools. She owned a pipe wrench. Maybe if she whacked the sink enough it would unplug.

Eoin pulled up to his home and parked his Harley in the detached garage. The urge to itch had almost made him pull to the side of the road. Only the thought of hidden paparazzi taking photos of him kept him on his bike. It was the longest trip ever. He jogged inside the castle.

Once across the threshold, he came to a halt in the grand foyer as a breeze blew in from behind and stirred the loose leaves across the floor. A pile had gathered in the far corner of the foyer across from the broken stained glass window. Eoin took a step inside, his gaze following the sunlight to the cobwebs decorating the ceiling and the chandelier. The candles in the chandelier had melted away long ago, leaving piles of wax on the dusty metal. He'd forgotten to fix the busted window. That was—what?—five years ago when his roar had shattered it? He couldn't even remember what had upset him.

Crossing the foyer, he stopped at the entrance to the dining hall. Broken glass littered the floor. The remains of the charred table stood in the center of the room. He recalled how elegant his home had been not long ago when he'd first moved here. The local humans and supernaturals had wanted to meet with him. To ease their fears, he'd thrown a ball. Food and wine had flowed freely all night. That had only been a century ago.

Maybe he should hire a maid.

He rubbed his chin. The place had taken a beating over the last decade and had a whole retro-abandoned thing going on. The petite not-a-she-dragon might not return to finish treating his scale rot if she thought him poor. She would arrive later this evening and there were no second chances at making a first impression. He'd already failed, but his home didn't have to. Maybe *he* could clean before Angie arrived? Scowling, he turned his back on the dining room. He couldn't afford to alienate her. She held his health in her sharp-nailed hands.

She also possessed secrets. Shifter ancestry or not, her smell wouldn't leave him. She was in every breath he took. He liked secrets. Either way, he needed to not frighten her away until the scale rot was taken care of and he figured out why she smelled of she-dragon. Both were equally important to him.

Pulling out his cell phone, he dialed his tattoo artist and oldest friend. The answering service picked up since it was still daylight. "Viktor, I need you to gather what information you can on the human who runs the back-scratching service off Newman Ave. I need it as soon as possible." He cut off the call. The vampire ran a tattoo parlor but he also had a wide network of friends within the supernatural community. Viktor owed Eoin.

He stripped of his t-shirt and jeans, tossing them at the entrance before shifting to dragon form. The process wasn't painful for him like for most shifters. Or maybe, with age came tolerance and he didn't even register the discomfort anymore. Either way, the process didn't take long. Black scales covered his skin as spikes rose from his spine. Sharp horns grew from his head and his glorious wings extended from his shoulder blades.

With a swish of his thick tail, he cleared the broken glass from the foyer floor. He closed the double doors to the dining hall. She wouldn't need to go in there. A few strong beats of his wings had the leaves blowing out the front door.

He'd ready the ballroom. It had the space they needed. The architect who had designed the area had spared no expense. God knew what state that room was in at present.

CHAPTER SEVEN

Angie pulled out a work polo from her laundry basket and smoothed the wrinkles. Maybe she should iron it? She rolled her eyes. What was she doing? It wasn't a date. Actually, he'd seen her covered in sweat, wearing flip-flops and a ketchup-stained shirt, so clean clothes would be taking a step up. She'd made quite an impression on Eoin when they'd met. Looking professional wouldn't erase his memory of the pepper spray.

Using her apartment building's Laundromat after work had taken longer than she'd expected so she only had enough time for a quick peanut butter and jelly sandwich for dinner. Maybe she'd make another to go. Her stomach ached with hunger. She'd only had a bowl of cereal for breakfast, since her toaster malfunctioned yesterday, and she hadn't had time to run home for lunch. It didn't help that Beth kept trying to order in meals, but without knowing the gender of the cook, Angie wouldn't touch the food.

She set the polo on her bed next to her work khakis, the ones she should have been wearing these last two days if she'd done the laundry sooner. She needed to shop for more durable uniforms. Shifter fur was difficult to get off clothes. She'd tried everything from ice to hair spray to special pet brushes, but the small coarse hairs worked themselves into the fabric. What did employees at those grooming places wear?

Aprons…that was the ticket.

Before she could add the idea to her to-do list, someone knocked on her door. Damn, Ken was early! She glanced down at her outfit, the comfy yoga pants and worn t-shirt she'd changed into after work. The shifter would just have to take a seat and wait while she finished getting ready. If he could find a chair. She'd used them to separate her clean from dirty laundry.

She crossed her loft and opened the door and fisted her hands. "Ryota?"

The alpha filled her doorway. "You don't look ready."

"For what?" Angie recalled Ken's comment about Ryota *letting* her break-up with him. Her stomach knotted. Did he think they were still an item?

"To go to the dragon's castle." He brushed past her and grimaced when he saw her apartment. "You should have let this place burn."

She gave him a slow blink. "I don't recall discussing this with you."

He tossed her a smug look over his shoulder. "I'm alpha. You think either Ken or Beth would let you go there without letting me know?"

Traitors. She'd never get Ryota out of her life if she continued hanging out with werewolves.

"Don't be angry with them, Angie. They have to answer to me, they can't help it."

"Oh, I'm not angry with them." She crossed her arms and got in his face. "But I asked Ken, not you, to accompany me."

"Ken's busy with a flea bath. I offered to replace him."

"Out of the kindness of your heart?"

He ran his fingertips along her chin. "You own my heart."

She jerked away. "Don't give me that bullshit. Shifter hearts don't have room for humans. Our relationship is good the way it is."

"Which is?"

"You're my client." She stepped out of Ryota's reach. "Please, go home."

"You're brave enough to go to the dragon's alone?" He didn't budge.

"I'm fine. When you abandoned me with Eoin, he kept his word and didn't eat me." Ryota had enough alpha testosterone coursing through his blood to have resisted Eoin's demands for him to leave. If it had been Beth who the dragon had wanted privacy with, Angie was sure the fur and scales would have flown. "He was a gentleman today." She ignored the memory of Eoin sniffing her and the image of Eoin wearing his wet transparent dress shirt, the way it had clung to the hard muscles hidden beneath… Oh, baby…

She shook her head. Honestly, Eoin had better worry about her. Not the other way around.

Angie returned Ryota's glare. Ken would have been a more reliable ride. What if there was a pack emergency? She didn't want to be abandoned at the castle all night long. She didn't trust herself to be good.

Ryota pressed his lips together. "You're mad at me."

"No shit." She stabbed his chest with the tip of her fingernail, drawing blood. "You left me *alone* with a dragon. He could have barbequed me and had me for a snack."

"You just said you trusted him!"

"I do now, but at that time, I'd just fucking sprayed him in the eyes with goddamn pepper spray. Who knows what he would have done?"

"What would you have had me do?" Ryota snarled in her face. "Would you have had me fight him for you? He would have won and left my pack leaderless." He ran his fingers through his thick black hair. "I'm a gnat to him. He really wouldn't have hurt you. I smelled his honesty."

She glared at him. He was too big and strong for her to manhandle out of her apartment. Her jaw ached from clenching her teeth. She'd been around werewolves long enough to understand the way they thought. Their relationships were part possession. She might have walked away from Ryota but he hadn't walked away from her. Shit, that's what Ken meant.

If she let him win and take her to Eoin's, then he'd try to bulldoze his way in other areas of her life.

"Look." She bowed her head and rested her hands on her hips so she didn't try strangling him. "I'm not sure how to act. I mean, I'm an itsy-bitsy part shifter but I don't think it's werewolf and I *definitely* don't have the instincts to guide me in this situation." She glanced up at him.

He stood quietly, his eyes still human. All good signs.

"What do you want from me, Ryota?"

He tilted his head to the side. "To drive you to the castle." He pointed to the clock on her wall. "We're going to be late."

She tossed her hands in the air. "You taking me up to Eoin's will give him the impression we're still together. We're not." She should have shouted louder. Her landlord, who lived in the basement, probably hadn't heard. He'd feel left out. Why did she care what Eoin thought? Except she liked the way he said her name and the way his body heat enveloped her when he stood near.

"I doubt the dragon will care." Ryota gave her a small push toward the door. "Are you going to do this the hard way or the easy way?"

"I can't go dressed like this."

He eyed her, his gaze slowing over her breasts. "You look fine to me."

"I'm not going with you. I'll take a taxi." She waved him to the door.

"So the hard way. Why am I not surprised?" He lifted her by the hips and tossed her over his shoulder.

"Put me down." Angie pounded on his back.

"Oh baby, you know how I like it." He purred as she put more muscle in her hits.

None of her neighbors peeked out into the hallway. They were used to domestic disputes and this was mild in comparison to the Rodriguez couple in two-twenty-three. Angie squirmed and kicked and tried to bite.

"Fuck, Angie, keep this up and I'll take you back to my place instead. Fuck the dragon too."

She stilled. "You wouldn't dare."

He chuckled and slapped her ass.

"Ryota, we're through. Done. Caput. No more." She elbowed him in the back of the head.

"Ow." He rubbed the spot.

"You will not touch me again." She dug her claws in his ass with all her strength and punctured through his jeans.

"Whoa." The alpha half-shouted and laughed. He jumped and wiggled until they reached his car where he opened the trunk.

"You fucking wouldn't dare!"

"Well, I fucking wouldn't let a hell-cat like you loose in my new car." He dropped her inside, pressing her head down so he wouldn't knock it as he closed the trunk door.

What a fucking gentleman.

Clinging to the parapet on his castle, Eoin watched the silver sports car pull up to his front door. His black scales blended in with the night sky and as long as he didn't move the passengers wouldn't see him.

Angie had said she'd find her own ride to his home but Eoin bared his teeth when the werewolf alpha climbed out of the driver's side. He'd been at her shop yesterday. The alpha's reputation with females was legendary. Angie could do better.

Eoin leaned forward, stretching his neck toward the car. Where was the petite not-dragon?

Ryota circled to the trunk and popped it open.

Angie sat up. Even from this distance he could see the fury carved into her features.

Chips of stone tumbled from the castle as Eoin's claws jabbed deeper into the wall. The alpha had locked her in the trunk? Eoin roared and stormed down the side of the building head first, lashing his tail to release his battle spikes.

Angie clapped her hands over her mouth. Her eyes had gone so wide Eoin could see clear through to her retinas.

The alpha spun around. As he focused on Eoin, he shifted to his beast form in his clothes and pulled the torn rags off his furry body. "Peace, Eoin." He shouted and raised his hands, claws retracted.

Eoin landed next to the car, his wings extended fully as he loomed over them. His bedroom could use a fur rug and Ryota was the perfect shade of black. "How is it peaceful when you bring my new caretaker to me in your trunk?" Fire rolled within his chest and smoke drifted from his nostrils. He wanted to sear the alpha's body and suck the marrow from his heat-cracked bones.

Angie's scent coiled around Eoin and he shuddered as it filled his lungs. She made him react instinctively. That was dangerous for all of them. He needed a dunk in the glacier lake to cool off before he did anything stupid like leave New Port's werewolf pack leaderless. *She's not a dragon. She's not a dragon.* He glanced back at her and sighed. Fuck, she wasn't a dragon.

Angie climbed out of the car. "When did I become your caretaker?" Her question caught Eoin off guard and extinguished his fire.

"Uh, you'll being caring for my scales?" What other title could he have used?

"So that makes me your *official* caretaker?"

"It's not like we're married or anything."

Her eyes roved over his form, traveling over his shoulders to his wings.

Reflexively, he extended them fully and flexed his chest so his wings wouldn't quiver from the strain. A dragon's best asset was his span. Maneuvering his body between her and the werewolf, Eoin managed to guide her closer to him. "Are you injured?" He asked her without taking his eyes off the alpha.

"Slightly bruised."

"Why did you treat her this way?" He lowered his head to meet Ryota's gaze. The werewolf smelled of fear. Like he should. Even though the different races ruled themselves there was a hierarchy among supernaturals. A food chain of sorts, and Eoin's kind sat on top.

"She wouldn't come willingly." The alpha raised his chin and set his feet as if ready to fight.

"That's not true. I was willing to come here, just not with you." She moved around Eoin's arms and confronted the alpha, nose to muzzle. "I can't believe you put me in your trunk."

"I can't believe you kicked and clawed me." He pointed to his ass.

Eoin rumbled with amusement. "You clawed his ass?"

Both alpha and human turned to face Eoin at the same time. Their combined fury should have fried him; instead, it just made him laugh harder. Angie had the spirit of a she-dragon to go with her scent. "Go, Ryota." He shoved the alpha toward the car. "I'll keep her safe." He winked at the shifter over Angie's head. "I'll bring her home unmolested."

She jumped at his comment. "What's that supposed to mean?"

"That I won't take a taste." He swept her toward the front entrance, using his tail to herd her away from the alpha. He lowered his head above the car and the werewolf. "Don't come back here uninvited," he whispered. "I spared you for your pack's sake. I won't be so merciful next time." With the tip of his claws, he scratched the alpha's hood, leaving four distinct marks.

CHAPTER EIGHT

Angie scooted ahead of Eoin's tail before being impaled on the spikes. Just before touching her, they retracted inside the flesh. She halted mid-step with her jaw unhinged as his tail slid up along her legs to her hips and continued to push her farther from the car.

The scales felt softer than she'd expected, like hard, warm leather. Eoin hovered over the sports car and whispered something to Ryota, who went rigid before climbing back into his vehicle.

The alpha tossed her a sharp look, as if torn. She'd yelled at him for leaving her alone with Eoin and here he was being forced to do it again, except this time she didn't feel frightened or abandoned. "Ryota!" She leaned over so she could see around Eoin and meet the alpha's gaze. "I'll be fine. Go home." The alpha tended to act irrationally, at least in her opinion, when it came to his territory. She just hoped he would stop thinking of her as his. For everyone's sake, he needed to let her go.

"You have your cell phone?" he shouted.

She held it up.

"Call me when you get home or if you need anything."

Eoin made a noise that was close to a hiss that ran along her nerves like broken glass.

The alpha shuddered and gunned his car back toward the city.

"I will never understand werewolves." Eoin shook his head as he watched the alpha drive away.

"You and me both." She caught herself shaking her head as well. "He means well, in an asshole kind of way."

The dragon slowly turned, snaking around as if boneless, to face her. He lay on his stomach and held his head to the side so she could see his bright blue eye. The tattoo by his eye still showed in his dragon form. A quick scan proved that none of the other tattoos had. "Tell me, are you and he involved in some mating ritual?"

She took a step back and tripped over his tail. He'd curled around her so silently that she was good and trapped in the center of his body. "No." She cradled her elbows within her hands. "Well, not that I know of." Shifters took mates but she didn't know how. Those kinds of things weren't public knowledge, no matter how much the press speculated.

"That explains his recent behavior. Has he bitten you deep enough to scar you?"

"That's none of your business."

"Actually, it is. If Ryota has claimed you as his mate, then I am in the wrong and you have placed me in an awkward situation." He raised his scaly eyebrow, waiting for her to answer.

She stared at his feet. "No bite marks. I don't view biting as foreplay. It hurts and is gross." Ryota *had* tried the last time they'd been together and she'd elbowed him off her. It hadn't felt right and something drove her from his condo at warp speed. She'd refused to see Ryota socially since that night.

"That's just because you haven't met the right lover." His body uncoiled around her, leaving her a path to his home. "Ryota will have to soothe his own ego. Mating rituals are a bitch and I don't want to get caught in the middle of one."

"I wouldn't know." She led him inside the dark castle.

"It's hard to describe the instinctual urges to humans. The call is something to be felt, not discussed, and when it grips a shifter, there's no stopping it."

She opened her mouth but her question vanished as she crossed the threshold. It had been too dark outside to view the castle that sat on the edge of the mountain's cliff-face, but inside hundreds of candles burned in the foyer. The warm yellow light danced with the shadows against the stone walls. Her gaze traveled up, up, up to the dark ceiling above where the roof sections must meet at the crest. "Wow."

Eoin glanced over her shoulder with a confused look. "What?"

"I've never been in a castle before." She took the steps into the foyer one at a time. This could be her last visit here and she wanted to soak in Eoin's home. The thick, scarred stone suited the dragon. Scorch marks stained the walls and some of the windowpanes were empty. "How long have you lived here?"

"A hundred years, give or take a few. This castle has been in my clan for centuries though. It was given to me when I moved to New Port."

"People make it sound like you've lived here forever."

"For some humans a hundred years is forever." He continued moving.

She passed by a stone staircase carved out of the walls that led to different levels. What was up there? Not a single piece of furniture decorated the room, just a dusty old chandelier and candles.

"We'll work in the ballroom. Follow me." Eoin stepped around her and moved deeper into the shadows, almost vanishing into them if not for the candlelight.

Angie scurried after him, afraid of losing her way. The castle seemed like a maze in the dark. She stepped on something roundish and twisted her foot. Catching her balance with a hand to the wall, she spotted electrical extension cables the length of the hallway. She limped in the direction Eoin had taken and slowed as she discovered their destination until she made a complete stop.

Eoin had used electric spotlights placed around the walls to light the massive room. The stark modern, metallic fixtures didn't diminish the elegant beauty in the marble walls and ceiling. A huge dome carved with arches sheltered their heads.

Angie spun slowly. A terrace circled the walls just below the dome with intimate alcoves carved into the walls. Anyone who stood on those balconies could clearly observe those below. To her right, a long, heavy table held all sorts of antique metal pinchers and files. They would look more fitting in a torture chamber than a refined ballroom.

The open space and stained glass windows and the arching domed ceiling…the room was missing dancers and music.

"Angie?"

Or not, because a dragon stood in the center. She tried to blink but her eyes wanted to drink him in.

He rose on his hind legs, wings resting to the sides. His long muscular neck moved with a fluid grace as he bowed his head toward her. Teeth like daggers lined his mouth as he spoke eloquently. He was terrifying and strange and beautiful. "You will need to climb on my back."

Eoin watched Angie sort through his tools and get accustomed to them. The sour smell of fear didn't tangle with her natural scent this time. No denying it, if he closed his eyes, his nose would tell him a she-dragon was in the room. It made no sense. Even a halfling wouldn't have smelled this pure.

Something was wrong. *Angie* was all wrong. The werewolves swore she was human. They didn't smell the same thing he did. Eoin couldn't figure out Angie. How could she be both?

She turned around holding a saw. "What am I supposed to use this on?"

"Fractured scales need to be cut away." He answered with a calm voice, though inside he wanted to shift to human form and rub his scent all over her. The raw longing awakening in his body made it hard to breathe. How did she have such an effect on him? He'd only known her for two days and already he would disembowel Ryota to protect her.

"I don't want to hurt you, Eoin."

He blinked afraid he'd spoken his thoughts out loud. "What?"

"Won't this saw hurt?"

He drew closer to her. "My scales have no nerve endings. It's like clipping toenails, just a lot harder." No dragon would deny their true identity and pretend to be human. His nose must be wrong. Maybe the rot was so bad it affected his mind? "Angie, what do you know about your shifter ancestry?" He would get to the bottom of this.

Her gaze narrowed. "We discussed this already. Stop beating a dead horse."

"I can't help it. You're a puzzle and it's been a long time since I've met anyone as interesting as you are."

"Are you flirting with me again?" Her tone took on a dangerous edge.

"I don't think I ever stopped." As soon as he spoke the words he heard the truth. Well, well, looked like Angie really was his type after all.

"You've an odd way of flirting. All we've done is argue."

"From what I've witnessed, you seem to like my kind of flirting." He lay on his stomach and offered his wing to climb. "The patch you need to work on is on my lower back where I can't reach."

She glanced at the table. "What will I need first?"

"We'll start by tearing away any rot on or under my scales. Take some pinchers and scissors to start with. We'll use the saw as a last resort." Dragon half-breeds were extremely rare. Human lifespans didn't last more than a blink. He guessed it was possible for her to have a distant dragon relative. Genetics could do weird things. Either way, he should report her existence. She-dragons were in high demand. Maybe Angie could produce children with his kind? As long as they could shift they would be considered dragon.

When her slim fingers gripped the edge of his wing, desire flared in his blood. Angie was a hundred more times dangerous to his well-being than any knife forged. She didn't need a weapon to penetrate his scales. She was already slipping past all his defenses.

He snapped his teeth together and focused his gaze on the distant wall. Gods above and below, he wouldn't let the weakness of his flesh bring him to his knees. Dragons didn't fuck around with their own kind. It was disrespectful. If a male wanted a she-dragon, he mated her. If he wanted something to keep him warm at night, he found a human or a shifter. Not a vampire; they were never warm.

So what was Angie to him? Both? Neither?

Angie sat on his spine and kicked her flip-flops off. "I'll have a better grip on your scales barefoot." She padded over his back to the itchy spot.

He stared at the cheap sandals. Who wore flip-flops? All evidence pointed to the fact that Angie was as clanless as he. She *worked* for a living. She mustn't have any treasure.

"Eoin?"

He jumped. "What?"

"Whoa, take it easy. Don't knock me off. It's a long way down. I found the spot. It's like a black fungus has taken hold on your scales."

He sighed. "Yes, a fungus. Rip away. I can take the pain."

She ran her hand over his healthy scales. "Isn't there any way I can do this without hurting you?"

"No." He watched her over his shoulder. "I'm not human. This won't bother me like you seem to think it will."

She plucked gently at the spot with the pinchers and tossed the rot to the floor in a neat pile. She worked in silence, concentrating on each scale with meticulous care.

"Why aren't you afraid of me anymore?" Since her arrival, he hadn't gotten a single whiff of fear.

"Because who else would be crazy enough to care for your scale rot if I mysteriously disappear?" She smirked as she pried a particularly large piece of gray fungus from under his scale.

He snaked his head around back as far as he could and rested his chin not far from her. "Touché." He liked how her fingertips trailed over his scales as she searched for more rot. "Not to mention the uproar your absence would cause among the shifter community. I mean, they'd have to scratch their own backs, right?"

She snorted. "Says the dragon paying triple my price."

He narrowed his gaze. "Why did you break the alpha's heart?" Eoin couldn't imagine why Angie had left Ryota. The alpha had money, power, and youth. What more could a female want?

She dug the tip of her sharp nail deep into the tender flesh under his scale.

"Ow. What the fuck?"

"I didn't break Ryota's heart." She yanked out her nail and had the audacity to turn her back on him.

He swung his head around the other way so she'd be facing him again. "He sure looked heartbroken this evening." Eoin might be reading too much in the alpha's scent. He could have been grieving the scratches on his paint job.

"Ryota is possessive and hates that I dumped him first. It has nothing to do with love."

"You're absolutely certain he wasn't courting you as his mate?" If he was going to get Angie out of his system, he wanted to make sure of no prior claim. Fucking someone else's potential mate was tasteless.

"God no, we argued more than we made love."

"Some shifters would consider that foreplay."

"Not me. He's never had a relationship that lasted more than three months. Our time was up, and good riddance. He treated me more like a pet than a woman."

Eoin took mental notes. From his experience, a lot of women preferred to be taken care of, but he found independence was sexy as hell. This didn't bode well for Angie. "So…" He ran a claw over the ballroom's tiled floor, leaving a deep groove. "About your ancestry?"

"I'm *not* a dragon, Eoin."

He winced as she scraped a patch raw with her razor little claws. "Well, you have to know something about where you get your fucking nails of torture." His words came out gruffer than he intended.

"I was an only child and my parents didn't have any family. When they died in a car accident, I was ten, so forgive my lack of knowledge." She grabbed another handful and ripped it from his flesh with a vicious yank. "Satisfied?"

Eoin's eyes watered. "Yes." This possibly wasn't the best time to talk about her family.

CHAPTER NINE

Angie lifted a scale. The rot was a soft black moss-like substance. It seemed to take root on Eoin's skin and lifted his scales as it grew. This type of work should be gagging her but the stuff was dry and didn't smell. Actually, as she cleaned off an area a sense of satisfaction developed akin to when she cleared her kitchen counter and could actually see the gleaming surface.

With a set of metal pinchers, she plucked a few strands that had been left behind. The patch of rot measured about four by eight feet. She'd been at this for over an hour and had only cleared the big clumps. "This might take me more than a week."

Eoin lowered his chin to the ground.

"I've cleared the visible areas. Tomorrow, I'll work on the stuff deeper under your scales. Do you have a pen light I can use?"

"Buy one and I'll reimburse you." Thick muscles moved under his skin as he shifted his weight and he lowered his wing to the floor so she could descend. He felt so warm under her.

"I guess you don't have to heat the place in the winter." She landed on her feet, thank God. The last thing she wanted was for Eoin to see her fall on her ass. He probably thought her the biggest fool he'd ever met after their first encounter on the street. The whole dramatic scene with Ryota in front of Eoin's castle wouldn't have helped the dragon's opinion of her. What was she going to do with that alpha?

Eoin's body went hazy as if she were seeing him through a heat wave.

She wanted to rub her eyes, but not until she'd washed the scale rot from her hands.

The dragon's body shimmered and moved like silk as he shifted. Eoin, the man, stood in front of her. His upper body was completely tattooed with sleeves on both arms but the bottom half was *au naturel*, including his ass.

She dragged her gaze away from the hard-packed muscles of his behind before he turned around. After months of dealing with shifters in both beast and human form, Angie had grown accustomed to being around naked strangers. None of them had been Eoin, though.

He slowly turned to face her. "What do you mean?"

"W—what?" Oh God, had she said that out loud? Or worse, could he read minds?

"About heating the castle?" He strolled toward her, shoulders rolling like a predator on the hunt. "Most of my rooms have fireplaces."

She was giving off enough heat from blushing to take over any fires. "I didn't think you would get cold."

He drew closer. All she had to do was raise her hands and she could touch the deliciousness. "My human form needs to be kept warm." Those piercing blue eyes… It seemed like Eoin could see right through her, down to the core of who she was.

Her mouth went so dry, her tongue stuck to the roof of her mouth. She didn't want to know what he saw. Poor and alone, she had been left raw and scarred by her life. The last thing she needed was a dragon's pity.

He reached around her.

She held her breath, unable to move from sheer anticipation. Would he kiss her? Would he sweep her off her feet and carry her away?

Please.

He straightened, holding a robe that had been on the table behind her, and he dressed. It was an old-fashioned piece made of thick tapestry-type material. The sleeves were worn on the edges and elbows. The hem dragged on the ground and the belt didn't match. He looked thrift-store sexy as he settled the wide collar around his neck.

Clearing her throat, she returned the pinchers in her hands back to the table and kept her back to him. This was ridiculous. She'd broken up with Ryota because she didn't want a shifter relationship, yet here she was ready to jump in Eoin's bed.

No.

She learned from her mistakes. No boyfriends, lovers, or fuck buddies until she got her shit together. She needed a home. A knot formed in her gut. She wouldn't attain her goal if she had a man butting into her business. In Eoin's case, literally.

"Angie?" Eoin's hot breath caressed her ear.

She jumped and spun, only to stumble into his arms. Jerking away, she pressed against the table.

He gave her a shy smile. "You have such expressive eyes."

She dropped her gaze and clung to the edge of the table. A wave of dizziness threatened to send her back into Eoin's arms. What had he seen in her gaze? Likely too much. She liked him better when he was threatening. It was easier to hate him.

"Would you like a tour of the castle?"

"All of it?" The place suddenly seemed immense. She'd seen clips on television from helicopters but no one had ever filmed the inside. "I don't want to intrude."

"I wouldn't have offered if that were the case." He held out his hand, waiting for her to take hold.

She stared at it. His invitation was weighted with more than just a look at his home. The way his eyes caressed her face and his possessive proximity triggered her meager shifter instinct. How stupid was she? Not very. "Maybe another night. I'm pretty tired." She'd been up since dawn and hadn't eaten much. "It's time for bed."

His shy smile turned salacious.

"My bed." She edged away from him.

He followed. "Tell me more."

She set her hand against his chest, preventing him from closing in. "Alone."

"You're no fun, Angie." His words didn't sound malicious. He only teased.

A smile tugged at the corners of her lips and she fought the urge in vain. "I'm a lot of fun, but not tonight."

He entangled their fingers. "Then tomorrow, after our appointment. I'll make you dinner."

Like a crash of ice-cold water dumped on her head, the sudden grip of desire had her gasping and she jerked from his touch. She wanted to very much, but she didn't know Eoin. Hell, he was a *dragon*. What was wrong with her? "Uh, that's very kind of you."

His eyebrows rose. "Are you refusing?"

"Look, I just broke up with Ryota."

Eoin grimaced and crossed his arms. "I'm nothing like the alpha."

"Doesn't matter. I don't want a relationship."

He smirked. "Obviously, since you don't even want me to call you my caregiver. It's just dinner."

Her heart thumped. It wasn't that simple. Her gut told her this was much more than just dinner because the idea of Eoin cooking her food didn't nauseate her like it should. "I'm only dating my own kind from now on."

"We're partially the same kind."

She rolled her eyes and walked away from him. "This again. I'm human, no matter what you smell." She spun to meet his hot glare. "I'm human."

"On the surface."

"What the fuck does that mean? So what if I carry some piece of dragon DNA in my system?" She held up her nails. "This is it."

"I think there's more."

She blinked. "How would you know?"

He shrugged. "Instinct."

"Save me from shifter instinct. It's time for me to go home." She pulled out her cell phone to call Ken. The last thing she needed was for Eoin to raise any hope of her being more. It had taken her years to accept her humanity. She didn't need a dragon knocking down her confidence. She could manage that all her own if she wanted.

"Dragon genes are very rare. Not to mention skipping so many generations to occur in you. I might be able to help you find answers you are looking for."

Returning her unused phone to her pocket, she squashed the hope blooming within her chest. "So what if I have dragon blood. I'll always be human in everyone's eyes as long as I can't shift. It's not like *your* people will claim me." When she had first realized that she wasn't like other children, she'd done everything to hide her differences. It only grew worse and she couldn't keep it from her parents anymore. Their worried looks and late night whispers she wasn't *supposed* to hear isolated her even further. Her parents feared the shifters would take her away. She wished she could have told them their fears were unnecessary, but they died soon after.

She was caught between two worlds. Not really accepted in either. The last thing she needed was to recall her parents' disapproval or their passing. She knew how alone in the world she was. Eoin's claim only made it worse. "I don't have any questions that need answering."

"I didn't mean to upset you." He extended his arms toward her but she stepped out of his reach.

"But you did."

"I'll take you home then." He disrobed and shimmered to his dragon form. "Have you ever flown before?"

CHAPTER TEN

"I've flown in a plane." Angie eyed the dark dragon filling the ballroom. "Are you suggesting what I think you're suggesting?" Was it possible? Her heart skipped a beat.

He moved toward the far side of the room and climbed a set of wide stone stairs. "Follow me." The tip of his tail nudged her hand until she took hold.

This was how horror movies started. The bad guy would lure the idiot girl to his home using his charm and then show her his collection of torture tools. She chuckled. She was the one who had used those tools on Eoin though. Not the other way around.

She took a hesitant step but the tug of his tail in her hand propelled her faster. If she were smart, she'd call Beth to retrieve her and wait on the front steps. Nobody would accuse Angie of being smart though. She held the state record for running away from foster homes until they made the orphanage her permanent home. She'd also dropped out of high school only to return six months later to finish with a GED.

She wanted to belong, yet every time she started to fit in something drove her away. It was stupid.

Like following a dragon deeper into his lair.

But he'd said something about flying…

For as long as she could remember, she'd dreamt of having wings. Not a fantasy, but at night in her sleep she would often have sweet dreams of playing in the clouds. She had to take the stairs two at a time to keep up with Eoin so she wouldn't have to let go of his tail. The castle was a maze of stairs and halls. She'd be lost in minutes. Her lungs burned for oxygen as she climbed higher and higher until at last cold, sharp air hit her face.

Eoin stood on a balcony with no railings, a silhouette against the night sky blocking out the stars. "I like to launch from here."

Darkness blanketed the wilderness below so it seemed she stood above an ocean of nothing. The chirping of frogs reached her even this far up and reassured her that the world still existed. She released his tail and leaned against the wall, scanning the vast view. "The sky seems to go on forever." She spoke between gasps.

He made a pleasant rumbling noise that moved through the stone under her feet. "The sky does go forever, and everywhere. I can take wing now and go wherever I wish."

"It's freedom."

His tail wrapped around her ankle. "Yes, it's precious to our kind."

"Eoin, stop it. Not *our* kind. *Your* kind."

"You're so stubborn. Maybe you have distant relatives your parents never mentioned or someone's done a family tree. I've never heard of a partial dragon. I didn't think it was physically possible. That deserves some attention. Trust me, you'd rather have me looking into this than other dragons."

She laughed but it sounded bitter next to his excitement. "Because you're so sensitive?"

He growled. "No, because I won't snatch you away from your life and keep you as a pet. Don't let modern television blind you. Most supernaturals follow human laws because humans outnumber them. Dragons aren't part of that faction."

"I don't hear about dragons stealing people. You'd think that would make the news."

"That's because they don't, normally. We're a quiet species. Time moves differently for us and in the last century the world has changed so much it has made us even more isolated."

"You're one of the few that talks to the press." She'd known dragons didn't like living among humankind but she hadn't known why. With the sudden advancements in technology over the last century, it made sense that the old dragons hadn't caught on. "Why are you so social?"

"I haven't a choice. Someone has to do it." Smoke drifted from his nostrils and curled above his head. He gave her a crooked smile. "No extended family?"

"No grandparents, aunts or uncles, no fucking cousins. Sorry to disappoint you but my heritage will remain a mystery to both of us."

"What about the people who raised you after your parents passed?"

"You mean the state-run orphanage? Let it go." She wrapped her arms around herself. "Don't get me wrong. The orphanage and Mrs. Gracie were my salvation. Better than those crappy foster parents who only wanted my monthly check. But Mrs. Gracie doesn't know more about me than I do. My parents kept to themselves, they didn't have much money and they loved me with all their hearts. That's all that matters and now it's gone."

He lowered his body until he rested on his stomach then pulled her close by using his tail. "I'm sorry for your loss. I'm alone too." He pointed to the tattoos by his eye. "Do you know what this means?"

She couldn't resist touching the raised blue tinted markings. "No."

"When a dragon reaches maturity his clan places their mark to claim him or her. Their status determines the position of the mark on their body."

"Why don't any of your other tattoos show when you're in dragon form?" He was covered in them as a human.

"Magic, of course." He tapped by his eye. "This mark comes from my people. The other ones are done by a local vampire."

"Seriously? Your tattoo artist is a vampire?" She knew they were around but they were as elusive as dragons. Maybe more so, since they were rumored to still need human blood to survive. Prejudice still ran thick in mortals, and vampires bore the brunt of it. Who would cry foul over a pile of ashes?

"I'm his canvas." He said it so softly she had to bite her tongue on her sharp remark. There was a lot of pain behind those three words. The tattoos meant something more to Eoin than just ink.

She stroked his muzzle. "What does your clan mark mean?" Just yesterday the thought of being this close to a dragon would have made her stiff with fear. Amazing how her sense of preservation melted with Eoin around.

"Its proximity to the eye means I'm a forward scout for the clan military."

She'd read about the dragon wars in school. It had been one of the few subjects that interested her. The last battle had been fought over Iceland over a hundred and forty years ago. "Were you part of the Gálgahraun conflict?" The volcanic territories were quite a prize.

"No, my clan lives in the Andes."

Not His Dragon

The number of dragons in the world was unknown. A few scientists tried to keep track of the more public dragons like Eoin but everyone knew most of them lived in isolated pockets away from mankind.

"See the X over my mark?"

She leaned back to get a better view. "I thought that was part of the design."

Eoin shook his head. "It means I left my clan." He rose to his feet and lowered his wing until it brushed her hands. "Climb aboard."

Hesitant, she stared at his back. How could he drop a bomb like leaving his clan and not expect a thousand questions?

"Angie, are you afraid to fly?" The challenge was clear in his tone.

She'd been so wrapped up in her head, she'd forgotten his offer. Gripping his wing, she began the climb to his back. "There's nothing for me to hold. What if I fall?"

"Sit between my shoulder blades. I'll fly smooth enough that you won't need riding straps."

She swallowed a lump in her throat. How many times had she dreamed of flying? More than she could count. Could she trust Eoin not to drop her? After pepper spraying him yesterday, she gave herself fifty-fifty odds.

He twisted his head. "Shifters are simple people. We like someone, we go after them."

"Until your mate comes along and you drop the other person."

"Ah, the elusive mate. It's a much rarer occurrence than you think. Most shifters don't even aspire to ever finding one."

"You?"

"Never. Well, not actively. I mean, if she showed up on my doorstep, I wouldn't turn her away."

Angie finished her climb and settled where he'd directed her. Eoin wasn't what she'd expected. He was easy to talk with and he listened. Over his shoulders, she glimpsed the ground so very far away. "Uh." She squirmed and clenched her thighs uselessly on his thick neck. "I changed my mind."

"Don't be silly." He gently launched from the balcony with his wings extended so he easily slipped into a glide.

She clung to him and screamed from the bottom of her lungs as if she'd dropped from the top of a roller coaster ride. Running out of air, she let her voice fade.

"Done?"

Heat of embarrassment scorched from her chin to the roots of her hair. "Yes," she whispered with a hoarse voice.

His body vibrated with a chuckle. "I won't let you fall."

"The ground is telling me something different."

"Don't look at it. The earth lies." He leaned slightly and made a slow turn toward the city. The yellow glow of the lights haloed the skyline, a beacon in the night calling her home.

She sighed and relaxed into her spot. "It's so peaceful."

"It's one of the reasons why I choose to live here. I enjoy watching the city at night."

"You do? I don't think I've ever seen footage of you flying at night."

"I wonder why?" he glanced at her and winked.

When she gazed at his wings, she realized how well he blended in with the sky. She laughed. "The press can't see you."

"I'm sure with their fancy night vision cameras they could, but they don't know to look."

"You make a perfect scout." He'd be capable of flying anywhere at night unseen.

"I know." He sounded suddenly distant.

"If you didn't like your clan, why don't you join another?" She knew the answer as the question came out. It was difficult to become part of a new family.

"Clans are not like clubs where I can apply for membership." He shrugged, which was quite a feat with her between his shoulder blades. "I'm happy here."

She rolled her eyes. She didn't have to be a shifter to smell his lie.

Banking to the right, he flew over the neighborhood with her shop. "Where do you live? It has to be close to work since you don't have a car."

"Just leave me here. I'll walk home."

"No, it's not safe for a female alone at night."

"I can take care of myself." She'd left her pepper spray at home since Ryota had tossed her in the trunk unprepared.

"I noticed." He pointed to his eyes where she had attacked him. "I can glide all night until the sun rises, Angie. Or you can make things simpler and give me directions."

"You'll scare my neighbors." Which was true, but her neighbors were made of stern stuff. They lived among gangs and thugs. Eoin would give them something to gossip about for a week. She didn't want him taking her home because she wasn't proud of her address in a torn-up part of the city, where drug lords ruled and the police turned their backs on crime. Angie didn't want Eoin to see where she lived. Bad enough the werewolf pack knew.

He snorted and a small flame shot from his nostrils. "Then get comfortable. It'll be a long night. Unless you want to return to my castle?"

"Eoin!"

"Another option is to land by your shop and I'll shift so I can walk you home."

"Naked?"

"Sounds like the best option, doesn't it?"

"I live in an apartment building on the corner of Fifty-fifth Avenue and Elm Street. Land on the roof and please don't roar or shoot flames."

His rumble sounded suspiciously like laughter as he winged toward her neighborhood. "Is this it?" He hovered over the red brick building.

She leaned forward to peek over his shoulder. "I think so." She'd never seen her home from this vantage point."

"Careful, don't fall now." He circled the roof slowly until he landed soft as a butterfly.

Before he settled on his stomach, she slid off his back and hit the rooftop hard enough to snap her teeth together.

Whipping around faster than Angie's eyes could track, Eoin steadied her with a clawed hand. "What's the rush? You'll hurt yourself with stunts like that."

Her jaw hurt and her knees protested. She leaned against Eoin even though her ego refused to admit she was being a dumbass.

"I'm fine. Really." She limped a few steps toward the roof entrance. "You can go now."

"Are you dismissing me?"

"Oh my God, don't tell me you're the sensitive type." All day long she had to deal with one type of shifter or another. They all had their idiosyncrasies that she had to tiptoe around and she'd had it. Seeing Eoin in the evening was a terrible idea. Her shit-o-meter for dealing with shifter crap was full.

CHAPTER ELEVEN

A shiver of anticipation ran down Eoin's spine at the wrath flashing from Angie's eyes. Very few people stood their ground with him. He'd grown so accustomed to complacency that he'd become numb inside. Until now…

He hissed and pressed his snout against Angie's lower abdomen, pushing her against the exit door. "After living for three hundred years, I think I have the right to be a little sensitive."

She went very still. "No you don't. Shifters all seem to think that letting their emotions rule them is a fine way to act. It's not. A little self-control could go a long way in relationships with humans."

Lowering his head, he viewed her stubborn, furious, beautiful face. "What do you mean?"

"This." She pointed at him and her. "Humans don't regularly pin each other to doors. Most of us can get a handle on our tempers before it goes that far."

With a small snort of smoke, he pulled his head back. Was she that naïve? Maybe she really was human at the core. If she were shifter, he wouldn't have to explain. "Being part animal means that kind of control is very difficult for us to reach. The fact that I haven't eaten you yet is evidence that I have a better handle on this than you think. Same goes for all the other shifters you know and probably antagonize." Eoin smiled, showing her his long sharp teeth. "Try to remember that when you have to avoid eye contact with the alpha tomorrow."

"Ryota doesn't have an appointment."

"Oh, he won't need one. Humans tend to think of shifters as people who can change shape, but we're not. We're at least half of that animal inside. Instinct is a huge drive and I've crossed a line on mutual territory."

"Me?" She pulled her hair and growled at the night air. Something in Eoin's gut stirred and it had nothing to do with the goat he'd had for dinner. From what she'd told him, Angie didn't

65

have anyone. She was alone like him. "What do I need to do to get him to leave me alone, Eoin?"

"Keep telling him no. He hasn't begun the mating ritual with you, so you're safe. Once it's started it's almost impossible to stop." Her scent suddenly filled his head. He wanted to toss her on his back and return her to his castle where Ryota would never reach her again. With a sudden backpedal, he retreated from Angie. What the fuck?

"What is it?" She stared at him as if he'd lost his mind. For a moment, he almost had.

"Uh…" He scratched his chin and fought the illegal urge to kidnap Angie. "Don't sleep with him again. No matter how tempting Ryota makes it seem."

"Don't worry. That bridge is burned."

The vise around Eoin's chest eased so he could breathe again. "Good."

"I don't plan on ever sleeping with another shifter."

The vise squeezed twice as hard. "Be careful what you wish for." She meant werewolves. She couldn't mean him. The ache in his chest kept getting worse with every breath. He had to get away. Her scent filled his head until his pulse pounded through his veins. Dormant hormones would drive him mad, trying to make him mate with a human. He hadn't been around females of his own kind for so long that his stupid body was reacting to Angie as if she were full blooded, single and ready for mounting.

He wanted to give her a present. Something tangible that would remind her of him. The need thrummed along his nerves until he took a shaky breath and removed the tiny earring from his ear. He held it between his claws. "I have a gift for you." Earrings were the only thing he could wear when he shifted from human to dragon. The hole in his earlobe remained the same size. Light from the bare bulb glowing above her head shone onto the ruby and fractured into a rainbow of different shades of red, sparkling on the rooftop.

"What is it?" She drew closer as if unable to resist the gem's call.

"It's a ruby." He lowered his hand so the gem hovered in front of her face where she could properly admire the stone.

"It's beautiful." The awe in her gaze transformed her from pretty to heart-stopping. On an instinctive level she sensed the magic in gems like all their kind did. It was plain on her face. She just didn't

66

know it yet. Eyes half-lidded and lips slightly apart, she reminded him of the wonder he had lost. Her sleepy gaze met his and for a moment it sparkled with joy.

"Do you have a favorite gem? I could bring you others." What the what? It was if his tongue was possessed, but as soon as he made the offer the ache in his chest vanished. He wanted to lavish her with gifts.

This neighborhood left a bad taste in his mouth. Nobody *wanted* to live here so that meant Angie had no choice. He could give her those choices though. The ruby could give her the means to move out of this dangerous area.

She gave him a slow blink. "Is this a trick question? Because I've never given it much thought." Her expression remained grave except for a hint of laughter in her eyes. "I guess it would be a ruby since it's the only gem I've seen in the flesh."

"Not surprising. Not many deal in such currency anymore. Hold out your hand."

"That's not a good idea." Just like that, she retreated back to the door. "I can't accept your gift."

He held up the ruby and scrutinized the crystal. "What's wrong with the earring?" It was top quality. No visible flaw and the color as deep as blood. His tattoo artist had been trying to buy it from Eoin for decades.

"Nothing. It's gorgeous but I can't accept a gift like that from a client."

"Don't they ever tip you?"

"Not in gems."

"Consider this my tip for tonight's excellent service."

She folded her arms and stared at her feet. "About that…"

He sighed and set the earring back in his ear. Maybe he could find something else she'd like. What did modern women want? Usually the tables were turned and the females vied for his attention. The last time he'd tried wooing a female was in the eighteen hundreds. Women's ideals had changed drastically. He'd really have to ponder this.

"Tonight was on the house. You don't have to pay me."

"But I want to pay you." He rubbed his temple where it pulsed. A frustrated noise escaped him. Nothing was going according to plan. All he wanted was his scale rot taken care of and somehow that turned into him trying to—to what? Seduce her? Nah, he could have taken care of that before they'd left the castle.

Angie was more than a woman he wanted to fuck. Looking at her was like looking in a mirror except she reflected only noble things.

"I don't think it's a good idea if we see each other again." She clicked the door open. "It shouldn't be too hard for you to find my replacement. The work is tedious but not difficult."

"No, we made a deal." He had to stop her.

"I know and I've never let a customer down but you seem to want more from me than just scale care and…" She swallowed hard. "I'm finding it hard to say no."

"This is a bad thing?" Maybe her small bits of dragon DNA were driving her to him. He restrained his grin. But wait, if she'd always thought of herself as human and was raised by humans then those instincts would be confusing. No wonder she ran from Ryota, and now him.

The only way to know was to test his theory. He angled his wings and swished them to create a gentle breeze in her direction. When his body began reacting to Angie it created pheromones. Every male dragon could produce them. They didn't stimulate sexual interest or cloud their minds like an incubus' pheromones, but sent a clear mating message of interest. They wouldn't be strong since he'd just begun producing them, but if she was dragon then she'd react in some manner. He wouldn't try this trick with most she-dragons because they would slap the snot out of him.

He released his scent slowly so it wouldn't overwhelm her. A human wouldn't have the sense of smell to detect what he advertised.

Angie rubbed her nose. "For me it is. The last thing I want to do—"

"Who burnt your heart so bad?" He'd find the bastard and char him to coal.

"None of your fucking business." The passion he'd seen in her returned. She could set the world on fire with that look. Taking a deep breath, she fluttered her eyelids then sneezed. Not the cute dainty kind that most ladies attempted. This came from her gut and he half expected flames to scorch his hide. She wiped her mouth on the back of her arm. "Sorry." Then sneezed again.

"Bless you." Could this be a reaction to his pheromones? "Do you have allergies?" Please let her say no.

She sneezed again. "Not until now. Are you wearing cologne? There's a weird smell."

"No." Technically, he wasn't wearing it. He was producing it. What the fuck did this mean? The pounding in his head grew worse. She obviously could sense the pheromones but if he made more she might sneeze to death. He laughed. Nothing about Angie would be solved easily.

"I don't see the humor." She continued sneezing. "God, I gotta get out of here." She opened the rooftop door and descended the stairs at a run.

Eoin kept the door from closing and shouted after her. "See you tomorrow."

Annie Nicholas

CHAPTER TWELVE

Angie rubbed her eyes and yawned as she walked the quiet streets the next morning. She'd slept like a rock after taking an antihistamine and eating half a box of cereal. God, she'd been starved. She'd eaten only a peanut butter jelly sandwich today.

Today would be different. Breakfast had consisted of eggs and burnt toast, then she packed a lunch. No more fooling around with missed meals. She had a bottle of *Liquid-Plumr* in her bag with a pipe wrench in case unclogging the sink in room one became nasty. Keeping a normal routine would be today's goal along with not having to spend what little money she had left on a real plumber. She needed a standard, customary, boring, regular day.

The only thing missing so far was coffee and that would be remedied in a moment. She climbed the stairs to the java shop, so she could grab a cup to go, when from the corner of her eye she spotted sexy in physical form leaning on her shop's window front.

Her heart skipped a beat. Smoke drifted above his head as he blew lazy rings, as if a dragon had nothing else to do but lounge. She noted the lack of cigarette in his hands. His lean form appeared relaxed but he watched the coffee shop where she stood with intense interest.

Tingles ran over her skin in anticipation of seeing Eoin again. No, no. She'd specifically told him, and herself, he was to seek help somewhere else. Maybe he wanted a referral. She could think of a few shifters who could use the extra cash.

All of them male, of course. Her gaze traveled along his long legs. His jeans clung in all the right places. Mixing business and pleasure would lead to terrible things like broken hearts, especially when her client filled her head with wicked thoughts.

Angie wiped the thin coat of sweat from her forehead. She could better deal with Eoin in his dragon form. She entered the shop. "The usual, Margie."

The barista gave her a welcoming smile. "Heard about the excitement at your place the other day." She handed Angie the cup of coffee with a shot of espresso, black like Satan's heart.

70

"Everything okay? You look stressed. Maybe we should make that a decaf."

Angie took a swig. "No, I'm fine. Do you have a back way I can use?"

"Sure, because people having fine days like you always need an escape route." Margie gave her a concerned look. She'd been making Beth's and Angie's coffee regularly since the back-scratching shop opened. "It's by the bathroom."

Before Margie started asking more questions, Angie hurried and exited into the narrow alley that connected all the shops on this side of the street. Facing Eoin first thing in the morning while her head was still foggy from antihistamines seemed too unfair. He'd starred in her dreams and occupied her thoughts. Couldn't he just give her a break?

She'd sneak in her shop, start her day and maybe he'd go away without making a scene. She was allowed to fool herself for a few more minutes.

Trash bins blocked her path though. Dump trucks couldn't fit into the alley, so shopkeepers were expected to drag their bins closer to the road behind the java house. It was trash day and the bins made it difficult to navigate to her building.

Of course, it was trash day. She pushed through the cans, careful of what she touched and to be sure not to knock one over. Any other day this alley would be easy to walk. The only time she *needed* to use it a garbage gauntlet had formed.

From the side, she spotted a trash bag move inside the bin. Her heart rate rocketed in a flashback of the horror movie marathons. Against her better judgment, she stepped closer. There could be a doorway to another universe developing in the trash. God, she was stupid. She pushed it aside.

An orange cat jumped to the ground in a blaze of hisses and high-pitched screeching.

Angie tumbled back, knocking over one of the fullest cans and spilling her coffee. "Fuck, fuck, fuckity, fuck fuck."

The cat took off, back legs churning faster than its front as it turned the corner, heading toward the street.

She kicked the closest bag and tossed her empty coffee cup against the wall. With careful steps, she traversed the rest of the gauntlet to the clear part of the alley behind her shop.

Unlocking the door, she swung it open and heard the warning beeps of the alarm system. That meant she had ten seconds to punch in the code before it went off. Why was the alarm still on? Beth usually arrived earlier to open the shop, which meant shutting off the alarm.

Angie tossed her bag on the closest chair. "Beth?" She hurried to the front of the shop to the empty receptionist desk. "Beth?" she called out louder.

The beeping responded instead of the omega. Angie sat at the desk and punched the code into the control pad. Silence filled the shop. Beth still hadn't responded.

A flashing light on the phone caught Angie's attention. She dialed in the appropriate numbers to access the messages and played them on speaker.

Beth's voice played. "Angie, I'm at Ryota's office."

Angie rubbed her temples and glanced out the window at Eoin's back.

"The dragon was waiting outside the shop and I didn't want to confront him by myself. I—"

"What the fuck is going on between you and Eoin?" Ryota's voice interrupted Beth. "I have a meeting that I can't reschedule. Once I'm done I'll walk Beth over." He hung up.

Ryota's office wasn't far. Couldn't he have another pack mate walk Beth? No, the alpha wanted to butt his nose in her business.

Beth had run to her alpha, as she should when frightened, but why hadn't she called Angie's cell? She pulled out her phone from her pocket. Dead; that's why she hadn't received any warnings.

She glanced at the window again and met Eoin's gaze. Her heart beat a little bit faster.

He grinned and waved.

Those blue eyes seemed capable of seeing right through her barriers into her soul. He stripped her naked every time their stares met, and she didn't like it. Not one bit. She tried to blink but her eyelids refused to work. She couldn't break contact. Even though Eoin was in human form, his presence crowded her shop waiting room. "What do you want?" she shouted.

His grin became crooked and he shrugged.

Not His Dragon

Angie blew out a frustrated sigh. What did she expect? She wouldn't be able to avoid him as she'd hoped.

Unlocking the shop's front door, she came face to face with the gorgeous dragon. She rubbed the bridge of her nose and counted from ten. "Eoin."

"Good morning." The smoke drifting from his nostrils faded. He handed her a cup of coffee. "Thought you might need some after last night."

Butterflies took over the acid boiling in her stomach and left her lightheaded. She accepted the coffee and took a sip. "Thanks." How did he know to keep it black?

He wore a threadbare Pixie Cunt t-shirt. They were an old punk rock band that had broken up a couple years ago. She fingered the hem of his shirt. "You've good taste in music." As if burned, she yanked her hand away. That would only encourage his behavior. Whenever Eoin was around all she wanted to do was touch him.

"The band wasn't mainstream. I'm surprised you know them." He ran his hand over his chest in a nonchalant fashion. Angie couldn't help but notice how the motion caused the material to mold to his hard-packed pecks. Those muscles had to come from all the flying; otherwise it just wasn't fair.

"Do I look like a mainstream girl?" She always marched to the beat of her own drum.

He traced the short strands along her hairline. "You look beautiful."

Her lungs forgot how to work. Clearly, he was blind. People used words like cute or pretty when describing her. Hellcat on occasion, but not *that* word.

Eoin hooked a finger in the belt loop of her pants and drew her against him slowly. "Are you feeling better?"

She took a deep breath, doing her best not to gasp like a fish in a net. "I took some allergy medicine." And dreamed all night of Eoin wearing things like whipped cream and Nutella. That's what happened when she mixed drugs and a stomach full of sugared cereal. "I'm fine." Being this close to Eoin made her head feel stuffed with cotton candy. All her angry scripted speech shriveled as her brain went dead and images of Eoin wearing only lamplight filled her imagination. Her throat went dry. "Must have been some weird pollen in the wind." She sounded hoarse.

He gave her a secretive smile. "Sounds possible."

"Eoin, what are you doing scaring my only employee away?" She tried to back away but his finger locked and she didn't want to tear her best non-stained pants. "Is it for a referral for my replacement?" Please, let that be the reason. "I'll need at least a day." She didn't sound half as confident as she wanted.

"I'm here to find out what time to pick you up tonight."

Maybe he hadn't heard her. She'd been in the middle of a sneezing fit. "I can't see you anymore."

His smile faded. "Can't or don't want to?"

"Why does it matter?"

"We had a deal."

"And it's not working out. Time to compromise. I'll find a replacement and they can care for your scale rot."

Eoin let go and spread out his arms to gesture at the empty street. "Good luck."

"You scared everyone away."

"Without even trying. All I did was lean against a window and smoke." The depth of sadness in his voice struck her hard.

"It would help if you turned down the intimidation factor."

"Doesn't seem to affect you any."

Her teeth snapped together painfully, stopping her response. He was right. She wasn't afraid of him anymore. Things were worse. She wanted him.

He returned to his spot against the storefront window and set a cigarette in his mouth. The dragon didn't even light it before blowing smoke. The tight muscles along his jaw popped as he blew more rings. He glanced at her. "I'll wait right here while you make calls to find someone brave enough to replace you."

Those last two words stung more than they should. She blinked at the sudden moisture in her eyes. "You'll scare all my customers. None of them will enter my shop." Her voice came out raw.

"Not my fault they're cowards. I'm not even in dragon form." He showed his teeth in a grim smile. "I can't even take a decent bite."

"I'm sure you could barbeque them," she muttered under her breath.

"I heard that." He took another drag from his cigarette but didn't look in her direction.

"I can't afford to play this game. My schedule is full and I have rent to pay."

"So seven o'clock again?"

She set her hands on her hips and glared at the sidewalk. Beth had all the contacts. The omega would know which shifter would be desperate enough for cash to work for Eoin. Beth wouldn't come to the shop with Eoin staked out front in that mood. He may as well be in dragon form.

"You could make three months' rent by finishing the job." Eoin made small rings float through a bigger one. Her nails dug into her fisted palms. He knew exactly why she didn't want to return. Their mutual attraction would destroy her. To Eoin, she'd be a short distraction but he'd ruin her for any other man because they'd never compare.

He turned toward her still leaning against the building. "You still want me to leave?"

She hesitated then whispered, "Yes."

He sighed. "There's more to you than just your scent, Angie." He pushed off the wall to leave.

Her stomach plummeted. She'd never see him again except from clips on the television. "Eoin?"

He tossed her a questioning glance over his shoulder.

"Pick me up at seven."

"Flying or driving?"

"Driving. No trunks."

Eoin smirked. "Never." He strode toward her, pulling at his earlobe. "Here." He held the ruby earring between his fingers.

"I won't accept that."

"Consider it a down payment." He fingered the fake gold loop hanging in her ear and grimaced. "This is almost blasphemy." Removing the piece of jewelry, he replaced the loop with the ruby stud. "Now you can't break our contract."

He knew she wouldn't renege on their agreement; otherwise she would have done so already. Angie twirled the gem in her lobe, sensing the new weight. Words flowed from her so easily when angered, but at the slightest kind gesture they vanished.

"I'll see you tonight." He bent closer.

Angie held her breath.

He hovered where her neck met her shoulder and inhaled. "Still smell like she-dragon."

Eoin couldn't resist the urge to take a lungful of her scent. The prickly spice stung his nostrils and made his mouth water. She smelled better than two days ago, even though a trace of garbage clung to her scent. What had she been doing in the back alley?

Angie cleared her throat. "Stop that." The offense in her voice was a lie. She didn't make any effort to distance herself from him. If she truly wanted nothing to do with him, then she would have let him leave.

Purring, he stroked her cheek. "It's okay to like me. I won't be offended." She had reacted to his pheromones last night. Not the way he'd expected, but she sensed them nonetheless. A human wouldn't have flinched. Dragon traits ran stronger in Angie's blood than he'd suspected. He wouldn't test it in this manner again unless he wanted her to run away.

Maybe she owned other undiscovered characteristics like producing smoke or breathing fire. She said she couldn't shape shift, which was a magical process. Her link to those powers could be blocked by her human DNA.

A flush of color brightened her face. "This is why I don't want to return to your castle. No matter what attraction you are imagining, I'm not looking for a boyfriend."

"That's good." He breathed a dramatic sigh of relief for her benefit. "I'm terrible boyfriend material." Pinning her against the wall with his body, he relished the way her breasts pressed against him as she breathed in deep. "I've been told I'm very selfish."

"This is sexual harassment." She didn't sound convinced.

"Two days ago you called it assault. I don't think you know what these words mean."

"What would you call it then?" A cute snarl followed her question.

He chuckled. "Flirting."

Not His Dragon

She set her hands on his chest and did her best to push. He had to admit she was stronger than a human, but he didn't budge.

With a distressed noise, she flopped limp between him and the wall. "Does what I want even matter to you?"

He scratched his chin. Of course it did, but why was she misunderstanding him? He was only responding to his instincts. Was she this capable of ignoring hers or was she playing hard to get? The relationship with Ryota had left deep scars and Eoin would need to help her heal before she'd let him close. Tact and sensitivity would be needed and he owned neither of these qualities. It looked like they'd be in for a hell of a ride.

He backed off from Angie, giving her space. "No flirting." Raising his hands in the air, he took another step away toward the shop door and opened it for her. "I promise to be a gentleman."

"And you always keep your promises?"

"I have to. A dragon is nothing but a beast without his honor."

"Thank you." As she passed into the shop, he couldn't resist smacking her heart-shaped ass.

That felt way too good. "See you at seven, toots." He let the door close on her squeal of shock. Grinning, he strolled along the street and popped another cigarette in his mouth. They didn't affect his health like humans. If anything, the cigarettes made him more socially acceptable since he produced smoke even in his human form. Smoking just made humans see him as less of a monster.

Light on his feet, he made his way to his Harley. He'd parked his girl a block away to avoid any trouble. He half expected Ryota to appear at Angie's shop and after the mark Eoin had left on the alpha's car, well, let's just say his bike didn't need a scratch. The werewolves seemed protective of Angie. From Ryota's behavior, Eoin suspected she could be made honorary pack as his mate if she wanted. Yet, it seemed she pushed the alpha away. What drove her? Not greed, not power, nor status. Well, maybe a little greed. He chuckled recalling the way her gaze riveted to his ruby when he'd offered the gift. It was exactly how a she-dragon should react. Treasure made their world go round, after all. It was the definition of treasure that changed from dragon to dragon.

The bright morning sunshine warmed Eoin's face. Oddly, it didn't bother him. He preferred the night for obvious reasons, but this morning found him anxious to convince Angie to reconsider her resignation.

She really didn't *want* to quit and she admitted to needing the money. Her fear of him drove her away. He had twelve hours to figure out how to bypass this dread and show her he wasn't just a dragon shifter. He could be a man. She needed to see beyond his scales.

He took a deep pull on the cigarette and blew it out in a slow stream. Pausing in the street, he looked around the buildings and empty sidewalks. When had he felt this animated? He'd grown stale living alone all these decades. Recalling his emotional state a few days ago, he had seemed dead in comparison. Empty of everything. Hollow inside. Angie had ignited his soul and sparked a new interest in the world.

Was this what the art dealer had tried to tell him?

For the first time in a long while he felt young and alive, like he had a purpose, yet the source wanted to escape him. He had tried luring her with money and that had worked until he'd crossed a line, making his personal interest in her too obvious. Threatening her clientele had worked but it would lead to negative feelings.

He rubbed the short stubble on his head. Well, fuck, he cared what she thought. He had one night to fix this so she could see that he wasn't an asshole like Ryota.

Speaking of which, the alpha was waiting for him by his bike. Eoin approached, keeping his body loose and relaxed. "Ryota." He flung his cigarette at the alpha's expensive-looking shoes.

Ryota startled at the toss. "Hey, watch it."

"What do you do again for a living?" Eoin couldn't imagine having to wear something so uncomfortable all the time.

Ryota pulled out his wallet and handed Eoin a business card. "I'm a lawyer for the supernatural community."

"Huh?" Why did they need a lawyer? He pocketed the card. "I suppose you're here because of Angie."

"That and you frightened my omega."

"Please, give Beth my sincerest apologies. She ran off before I could assure her of my intentions. I would have let her inside the shop." He would have let any customers in as well.

"What do you want with Angie?"

Not His Dragon

Eoin didn't like Ryota's possessive tone. "To thank her for last night. She has the most exquisite touch."

The alpha growled. "Leave her alone."

"She told me you haven't marked her."

"Yet."

Eoin blinked his nictitating membranes, the ones that moved horizontally, and enjoyed Ryota's flinch. Shifting his eyes to his dragon's, with the vertically slit pupil, he met the alpha's uncertain glare. "Angie belongs to me now, little dog." Eoin patted the alpha's head. "She made it quite clear that you are no longer part of her life. You've done enough damage. Now run along before I forget my manners and eat you in public." He'd never had issues sharing a female, but the thought of anyone hurting Angie boiled his blood.

Ryota didn't love her. Werewolves wanted to claim their mates. A female like Angie should be cared for. Pampered. Cherished.

The alpha scowled but turned his back to Eoin and made his way to the office building across the street.

That's what Eoin would do for Angie. He would pamper her. Starting with a meal. His gaze traveled to his bike and the deep, grooved scratches carved into his paint job. "Fucking wolf."

He jumped on his bike, refusing to let petty werewolf tactics wreck his good mood, and drove home. A familiar black Cadillac blocked his courtyard. His gut twisted. He'd forgotten all about Roger and Lorenzo. What would he show them? He'd flash-fried all his paintings the other night. Parking next to the car, he noticed they were examining the lump of metal he'd thrown out the window in a rage. "Gentlemen?" He joined them.

Lorenzo shook his hand. "This is fabulous." He gestured to Eoin's trash. "Why did you keep your sculpting secret?"

Eoin raised an eyebrow. Speechless, he turned to Roger, who stood behind the art dealer.

His agent rolled his eyes. "One can't rush art. Eoin wasn't ready to share this side of himself with the public yet." This was exactly the reason why he'd hired Roger. The man could think fast.

"Yes, that's eloquently said." Eoin stared at the molten mess with jagged claw marks seared in to its element. He couldn't even distinguish the cans.

Lorenzo joined him. "It's visceral. Like a kick in the gut." He fingered a sharp edge and hissed. Bright red blood seeped from a thin cut on his fingertip. "And dangerous." He glanced at Eoin. "Just like you."

"It's what you asked for." He wanted to pound the statue into the ground. This wasn't a medium he was familiar with.

"May I see the others?"

"Others?" Eoin's voice rose an octave.

"They're en route from Berlin and will be here in a few days," Roger interrupted.

"A week," Eoin countered.

Roger gave him a tight-lipped smile. "Five days at the most."

Lorenzo watched their exchange with interest. "Then you can deliver them in time for your show."

"I thought that was canceled." Eoin eyed Roger.

"I hadn't finalized the cancellation yet. Roger had promised me something spectacular first and this is beyond my expectations." Lorenzo clapped Roger on the back. "I'll wait for you in the car."

His agent faced him quickly and whispered, "I bought you five days and a show. Don't let me down." He turned and marched to his car without a backward glance.

Eoin watched them depart. Five days. Where was the closest scrap yard? He needed metal of all types, and his fire. It would be a long night.

Not His Dragon

CHAPTER THIRTEEN

Eoin's acute vision helped on the dark roads as the streetlights flickered. Those that worked. His fingertips ached from molding molten metal all day. So far everything looked like car wrecks. He could hear his future art career going up in flames. The only thing that helped him through the day was his appointment with Angie.

She lived on the fringe of the industrial area of the city. Her walk to and from work was not safe. She needed a car.

Parking his bike in front of her building, he gazed at the chipped red brick. Some of the windows were cracked. Before he could get off his bike Angie ran out the door. She'd been waiting for him.

The warmth spreading in his chest had nothing to do with his flame.

Worn jeans clung to her shapely legs and her tits strained against the plain gray t-shirt, leaving him sucker-punched. She set her hands on her hips and the motion exposed a thin line of midriff, just enough to draw his attention and tempt him to run his tongue along the edge. Her chest heaved as she caught her breath. "Ready." She glanced at his bike. "Wait, you expecting me to ride on this death trap?"

He ran his hands over the gas tank. "Don't listen to the mean girl. She's just jealous."

Angie's lips quirked, struggling not to smile.

"It's a beautiful night for biking." He handed her a helmet. "I didn't think you'd be afraid."

With her fingertips, she traced the scratches Ryota left on his paint job. "Looks like you've taken a spill."

"Nah, that's vandalism. Cold, calculated vandalism." He didn't mention Ryota's name. The alpha's invisible presence would only stain their evening together. He wanted Angie all to himself, no sharing her with a memory.

"Whoever did that must have balls the size of watermelons to touch a dragon's toy."

Eoin enjoyed the sharp edge of her teasing. "I'm sure he does, but his dick must be pine-needle-size to do it while my back was turned."

She laughed, the sound deep and throaty rolling from her belly.

"I've never crashed." He held the helmet out and dared her with his gaze. Where was the hellcat who'd pepper sprayed him?

She snatched the helmet from his hands. "Being cautious is not the same as fear. Remember, I'm frail in comparison to big boned dragons." Swinging her leg over the seat, she sat as far away from him as possible with just her hands holding his waist.

He reached under her thighs, pulled her against him so her breasts pressed against his back and her legs cradled his hips. "That's better." He guided her hands to rest on his chest. He could think of a better place to set them but he had promised to behave. Well, mostly.

Her gasp was audible through the helmet.

He pulled away from the curb before she could change position. Not long after, her body melted against his as he drove out of the city and toward his mountain home.

The castle loomed into their view and he sensed her tense. In the night, his home could appear foreboding. Dark towers rose, blocking out the stars and not a single inviting light was left burning in the windows. He had done it on purpose to dissuade the press and tourists from trespassing. The rumble of the engine crashed over the quiet of the forest and the single headlight of his bike parted the night. He coasted to the front entrance and silenced his bike. The calm of the evening rolled back in place.

A welcoming cool breeze ran over his skin. People thought dragons sought out heat but the opposite was really the truth. The volcanoes they prized were for hatching eggs and raising their fragile young. Adults preferred the cold since they produced enough heat on their own.

Angie swung off his bike, landing hard on her legs. Her knees buckled at the sudden motion.

He steadied her by the elbows and dismounted. "Whoa. Your legs aren't used to clinging on to something for so long."

She shot him a daggered look but didn't respond to his innuendo.

"Do you think if I provided enough light we could work out here?"

"Why?" She shifted her gaze to the dark forest.

Not His Dragon

He followed her stare. "I guess you didn't camp as a child?" Modern society was losing its edge by turning away from nature. If a squirrel jumped from a tree, Angie would probably scream.

"I've spent my share of nights outdoors, except mine were in boxes or under bridges. No tents for me." She gave a weak laugh as if haunted by those memories.

He'd been wrong about Angie. If something jumped out of the forest, she'd slay it. He rested his arm over her shoulder. "A beautiful night shouldn't be wasted staying indoors." He resisted the urge to gather her in his arms. "Nothing in those woods could harm you. Not with me around."

She scooted out from under his arm. "I wasn't worried." She stood taller. "I just don't see how you can light the place enough for me to see."

"My resources to create fire are limitless." He strode to the garage. "With enough torches I can light the general area." He came to a sudden stop. Maybe they were stored in the dungeon?

Angie walked full force into him. "Ouch." He hadn't noticed her following. "Warn a girl." She rubbed her nose.

"Are you all right?" He leaned close to check her injury and inhaled deeply, taking in her addictive scent. He suspected she wouldn't complain even if she'd broken it.

"Yes." She retreated. "I'll be fine. I was more surprised than hurt." She kept avoiding his touch.

"You should have waited by the bike."

Toeing the ground, she wouldn't meet his gaze. "It's creepy."

Smiling, he turned his back on her and unlocked the garage. If she was going to be jumpy about the dark, then he shouldn't bring her to the dungeon. That would send her screaming out of his life forever. He'd make do with whatever stuff he found in the garage.

He flicked on the overhead light and searched the shelves.

"Wow." The breathless word made him spin around. Angie turned a slow circle in the middle of the room surrounded by his cars. "Some of these are antiques." She ran her hands over the Aston Martin with reverence.

"I am the original owner of most of them."

"Why do you drive the motorcycle?"

He chuckled. Of course she liked the Aston Martin. "I like the wind in my hair."

She pointedly stared at his shaved head. "Yeah." What could he say? It was easier to care for if he kept it short.

Behind her, in the far corner leaning against the wall were some tiki torches he could use. He gathered those, a hard hat, and a handful tools.

She followed on his heels. "If you're the original owner, that makes you much older than me."

"Does it matter?" He set the hat on her head.

"No." She removed the hard hat with a puzzled expression. "Really none of my business."

He flicked the headlight on and she jumped. "You'll see my scales better." He set the hat back on her head. She was much, *much* younger than him and she'd never met another dragon. He took a step nearer. The need to possess and claim her uncurled in his gut. She'd be *only* his.

Angie stared up at him with her big, brown eyes. She'd given him her trust when she agreed to return tonight. Oh, how he had misjudged the depth of his desire for her. Her thin t-shirt would tear with one hard yank and he could be upon her within seconds.

With a jerk of his head, he stormed from the garage before he broke his word and her trust. In the clear expanse of grass, he'd used for naps, he jabbed the torches one by one into the ground with single, hard strokes until they circled the area. Fire burned in his chest and he lit the wicks by spitting small fireballs.

Angie stood in the center of the circle still wide-eyed. "I didn't know dragons had such good control over their fire."

Feeling smug, Eoin took off his shirt. "It's a practiced skill." He and his brothers used to toss them at each other for fun. Either they learned to dodge or they improved their aim. He tugged off his jeans and sensed Angie's gaze caressing his flesh. Desire blazed thick in his blood.

He lowered his gaze as he marched toward her. If he saw even a hint of interest in her eyes, his control would vanish. Better for him to look away and avoid her gaze altogether. He shifted to dragon form in a pop of silken magic. Lying down in the circle of light, he offered Angie a wing to climb aboard his back.

"What tools will I need tonight?" She rummaged through the things he'd carried out of the garage.

"After you finish cleaning out any missed spots of rot, use the coarse file and the handheld garden clippers to cut off the edges of any chipped or cracked scales. The scales need to be smooth to heal properly."

She gathered what she needed and climbed on his back.

He liked her slight weight on his spine, the feel of her fingers gently prying his scales. Sighing, he closed his eyes while she worked in silence. The cool breeze soothed the smoldering heat growing inside him. No female had ever affected him like Angie did.

CHAPTER FOURTEEN

Angie worked through Eoin's damaged scales with blind focus. He didn't chitchat like last night. His back rose with each slow, deep breath as if he were meditating.

He snorted and shifted his legs as he moved to roll on his side.

"Hey, take it easy. You're going to make me fall." She clung to his scales as she slid. The sharp edge sliced through her palm and she hissed with pain.

Eoin swung his head around. "Sorry." He righted her with a nudge from his nose. "How long was I asleep?"

Blood pooled in her palm. "I don't know, but I've been working on your scales for over two hours." She was tired and hungry. "I'm actually done. There was very little damage to the scales and the rot is all plucked away."

He lowered his wing so she could climb down easily. His gaze darted to her hand. "You're hurt. Let's tend to your cut." He shifted to human form, grabbed his jeans and cradled her hand within his. "Follow me to the kitchen so I can clean the wound."

"It's nothing." Her skin tingled where they made contact. She should struggle against his hold; instead she let him lead her deep into his dark castle. He hovered close enough to envelop her with his heat. No matter how she tried, her gaze kept wandering back to his naked flesh.

Hard muscles covered in inked skin. The images flowed nicely from wrist to solid shoulders, over well-defined chest, to lick-able abs, to… She yanked her gaze from his semi-erection and met his self-satisfied smirk. "Stop that." She gave him a shove.

"Stop what?" He laughed.

"Yes, you're my type but that doesn't change things." Eoin was *every* woman's type. That ripped body came from plenty of activity and she'd bet his endurance would make his lovers weep. She shook her head. God, she'd need an ice cold bath when she returned home.

And she *would* go home. Without taking her clothes off. Or touching him. "Get dressed already, Eoin."

Not His Dragon

"As you command." He flourished a fancy bow and pulled on his jeans.

She turned her back to him. How long could she fight her attraction to Eoin? Would one night in his bed be such a bad idea? Most of the time she considered herself a grown woman, and accordingly a one-night stand could be fun. But she should wait until the job was done. Mixing business and pleasure had never been a good idea. She'd learned this firsthand with Ryota.

"You know," he whispered by her ear making her jump. His strong hands grasped her upper arms from behind. "It would only be polite if you took off your clothes and let me stare in return."

A brush of desire fluttered in her lower abdomen. She turned just enough so their gazes locked. "Too bad I'm considered rude."

All he had to do was lean a bit closer and their lips would mesh. "Let's clean your cut and make sure you don't need stitches." He kept her injured hand cupped within his as he guided her through the castle's many hallways towards the far back of the building. He still wasn't wearing his shirt and his shoulders rolled with each step.

"Stitches won't be needed. I heal fast." She'd been knifed in the gut, during one of her many attempts to run away from the foster system. The mugger had stolen her backpack and left her for dead in the alley she'd been using as her home. The next morning she'd awoken almost healed with a scab on her stomach and an ache when she walked.

"More shifter traits?" He raised an eyebrow. "Ever consider that maybe there's more shifter in you than human?"

"My parents were both human. That would be impossible." Unless they'd lied to her, which they wouldn't have done. How many times had they told her she was the most important thing in their lives?

They entered a kitchen where Eoin guided her to the sink and ran cool water over the cut. On the black granite counter rested a plate filled with cut vegetables. Her stomach growled.

"Hungry?" He dried her hand and wrapped his shirt around it. "No stitches required. It's not even bleeding anymore." Staring at her bandaged hand, he remained quiet as if struggling with something.

"Eoin?"

His gaze rose and trapped hers. "My scales are sharp. I should have warned you."

"I noticed the first time I worked on them. It was just an accident."

"Sorry. Again." The words came out stiffly like a cramp had seized his throat. "I shouldn't have fallen asleep."

She chuckled. "I'm used to it." Many of her clientele slept under her care.

"You don't understand." He pulled out some pans, and set them on the gas stove and pointed to a stool by the counter. "Sit."

To her surprise her ass made contact with the stool before her mind registered his order. She clenched her teeth to hold the sharp words on the tip of her tongue. He didn't even gloat at her obedient move.

Instead, he pulled out plates of raw steak and a bowl of potato salad from the fridge.

Her gut seized. He wanted to cook for her. How would she excuse herself when she had admitted to being starved? Except that sensation plaguing her stomach wasn't the usual nausea when faced with a male cooking her food. She observed him pouring oil in the hot pan followed by the chopped vegetables. It smelled heavenly.

He set the vegetables on low heat and he did the same to the other pan. "How do you like your steak?"

She swallowed. "Rare."

He tossed her an appreciative look over his shoulder. "Nice choice."

Her chest swelled at his approval. What the fuck was wrong with her? She stood and realized she hadn't a clue where to go. Even if she found her way out of the castle, Eoin still had to drive her home. Unless she called Beth. The poor omega wouldn't want to face an angry dragon and Angie wouldn't place her best friend in such a situation again.

She crossed her arms and glared at his bare back. The muscles slid under his skin as he cooked. It wasn't the smells of the food that made her mouth water. "Why don't you explain what you think I can't understand?"

Eoin set the steaks on the hot pan. The sound of sizzling filled the kitchen. He went to a wall filled with wine bottles.

Not His Dragon

From what she'd seen of the castle, most of the rooms appeared neglected, some of them even exposed to the elements outside. The kitchen must be special to the dragon since it was intact. 'Clean' would have been stretching her description, but she couldn't complain. It would have been the pot calling the kettle black.

Eoin filled two glasses with red wine, handing her one. "I let my guard down." He gulped his glass empty and filled it again.

He was right. She didn't understand. "So?"

"You could have killed me."

She choked on her wine. "What kind of person do you think I am?" Killing hadn't crossed her mind once. Smacking the snot out of him, yes. Not manslaughter.

He stirred the vegetables and turned the steaks. "It's not you, Angie. Don't be insulted. It's hard to explain." He kept stirring, tossing the vegetables with a sauce he'd already prepared. "I don't let my guard down like that."

"Must mean you trust me." She refilled her own glass and tried to hide her smile. Why the hell not have another? She'd need the liquid courage to get through dinner if this was the appetizer. What did he have planned for dessert? She coughed again. Jesus, Mary, and Joseph she couldn't stop thinking about Eoin wearing nothing but his birthday suit. Him being half-naked while cooking didn't help.

Speaking of which, why wasn't she ready to toss her cookies?

He filled two plates with bite-sized food. It smelled fantastic. Either he was the best cook she'd ever met or food cooked by dragons bypassed her neurosis.

In the end, all this meant was she got a free steak dinner. High fives all around. He sat across from her at the counter, since the kitchen lacked a table.

He offered her a fork.

She took the first bite, conscious that he watched her chewing. She must look a mess covered in scale chips and filing dust with his bloody shirt wrapped around her hand. The steak melted in her mouth. "Oh my God." She took another bite.

The smile on his face was pure pride.

Seeing Angie eat the meal he had prepared filled Eoin with a strange sense of accomplishment. It was akin to his first successful solo hunt. Except instead of feeding himself, he provided for Angie.

He leaned on his elbows and sipped from his wine glass. Angie's presence tied him in knots and the alcohol helped loosen them. Feeding *her* in *his* kitchen sated an ancient primal urge. He took another sip so he wouldn't roar in triumph and send her running again.

"Aren't you going to eat?" She pointed to his plate.

"Yes." He ate a piece of steak to ease her worries, but he enjoyed watching her too much to bother with his meal. "Did you grow up in New Port?"

"Uh-huh, in the orphanage off Willobrough Lane."

"Oh." He hadn't even known the city had an orphanage. He'd have to speak with his accountant about donations.

"You didn't know the orphanage existed, did you?" Her tone sounded more amused than insulted.

He shrugged. "I don't involve myself with human things. They tend to scream a lot when I try."

She laughed and the sound eased the empty isolation within his castle. When had he last shared a meal with someone?

"That can be all true, but I heard a certain rumor about a cow."

The more she relaxed and conversed, the more he didn't want the night to end. "I deny those rumors. That was some other sappy dragon." He filled her half-empty wineglass.

"Hey, I'm starting to think you want me drunk."

"If that were the case I would have broken out my collection of whiskey." He raised his eyebrow. "Want some? Not like you have to work tomorrow."

"How do you know I'm not open on weekends?"

"I checked your website."

"So you can surf the web. I'm impressed. I heard the older races usually stagnate in decrepit old castles."

"Must be the same source that told you about the calf."

"A calf? That makes the story even sweeter." Her plate was empty.

He switched his full plate for her empty one. "Finish eating. I'll tell you the story."

"But you haven't eaten."

"Eating in my human form is for fun. I have to hunt in dragon form to be truly fed, which is where the story begins." He stabbed a vegetable and held it to her mouth. "You know you want it."

She took the morsel, running her tongue over her lips. "So?"

He gave her a slow blink.

"The calf?"

"I was flying over the mountains behind my castle, hunting for dinner, when I spotted a speck of black and white curled on a cliff. I hovered next to the area and the spot uncurled." How had this story reached her ears? This happened way before Angie had been born. "The calf had fallen off the cliff and landed on the ledge. A late spring snowstorm had hit the night before so the farmer couldn't search for the babe." The little creature hadn't feared him. It was too young to recognize a dragon. The calf had cried out to him for help in the universal language of animals. "I carried it back home to the farmer, who did a lot of that screaming I mentioned, before realizing I was there to return his calf, not eat his family."

She went quiet in the way that pushed on his skin. She had a few more bites. "Why did you save it?"

He shrugged. "It wouldn't have been a mouthful." Babies were taboo to eat. Not everyone thought like dragons. Even humans, with all their morals, ate them.

Setting her fork on the second empty plate, she leaned back and patted her stomach. "That was a really good meal. Thank you, Eoin."

He sat taller on his stool. He would've thumped his chest in triumph if he thought she'd understand. The urge to ask her to spend the night almost loosened his tongue before he locked it down. He'd made a promise. No seduction. For tonight. "Ready to go home?" Before he did things he'd regret.

Her smile fell. "Sure."

The drive back to her apartment was filled with quiet promises as she leaned against his back, her breasts pressed on either side of his spine, and her thighs squeezing his hips almost daring him to change his mind.

He took the scenic route, prolonging the ride as long as he could. The night couldn't last forever, though, and he parked in front of her building, then walked her to the door.

She faced him, eyelids heavy. "Thank you for dinner." She leaned against the entrance.

He followed, caging her head between his arms. "You're welcome." A kiss wouldn't break his word, right? It would seal his interest in her and make his intentions utterly clear. Angie was tall enough to kiss without cramping his lower back. He normally liked females with long hair but her pixie cut allowed him to admire her fine bone structure.

She unwrapped his shirt from her hand and offered it to him then held up her palm. "See? Almost healed."

He stared at the starting-to-scar wound. "Impossible, even for a half-breed." He grabbed her wrist and poked at the injury. He'd seen it with his own eyes. The cut had been deep.

"Hey." She yanked her hand away. "Watch who you're poking."

Enough was enough. He'd believed her story of shifter ancestry until now. Healing that quickly was impossible for someone with mostly human genes. He'd have to look at Angie with a spell to truly see what she was made of. Cringing, he shifted his eyes from human to dragon. Magical vision allowed him see magic such auras around life forms and spells. In a city the size of New Port the light from so much living energy was blinding. Not to mention the headache he'd suffer. He spoke the spell to open his magical vision. He blinked and almost shouted "*A-ha*." While pointing at Angie.

Definitely dragon. How could she not know, and why couldn't he sense her magic? He should have done this the day they met, but it always left his head pounding for days. He looked closer. What was that? Something surrounded her body like a thin film of oil. This time he did gasp. He'd never seen anything more evil or devastating.

The light from her aura reached out to the natural magic of the world but they didn't connect. This shield prevented Angie from touching magic. No wonder she thought she was human.

He clasped her hand and shook it as she leaned up for a kiss.

She jerked away. "Oh." She stared at their clasped hands and shook back as he bent to return her kiss too late.

He kissed her forehead instead. "Well shit, this is awkward."

She giggled. "I'll take a rain check. We'll try again tomorrow." She opened the door to her building and turned to enter.

He followed on her heels and slapped her ass before the door closed. She gave a surprised yell from the other side.

"Night, toots," he called through the door. Grinning, he returned to his bike. So she already planned to see him tomorrow.

CHAPTER FIFTEEN

Dragons didn't require sleep as mortals did. Eoin could go days without, but like most of his kind, he enjoyed a good nap. Dreams could be as good as memories. The older a dragon grew, the more he retreated from reality. That's why most of his people lived away from human civilization. Too much change too fast.

Eoin found human culture fascinating, though. One moment they were wearing white wigs and the next they were painting flowers on their cheeks, having sex in the fields. Time worked different for them somehow. He envied them. For the last half century, he'd felt stuck in place. How did Angie cope as a dragon who thought she was human? Did time move the same for her? She obviously was young but she always seemed to be in a hurry. Very undragon-like behavior.

He squashed his cigarette under his boot and watched the junkyard dog rush out of his shelter. A fence protected the animal from him. This would be a good time for him to stop obsessing over Angie. She'd already given him a migraine with her aura. He had to put her out of his mind and concentrate on obtaining the material he needed for his sculptures if he was ever going to give this a full-hearted try.

The only thing that had given him solace over the last century was art. He could understand the evolution of an artist's skill. The statue Lorenzo and Roger had fawned over was a new direction in his work. This step could change everything.

Nausea rolled his stomach. This could be the start of new and exciting things, a fresh branch sprouting along the path of his long life. Like most green stems it was fragile and could snap at the wrong move. The urge to vomit struck him hard. Thank goodness, he'd given Angie his dinner and his stomach was empty.

There wasn't anyone around to witness him puking except the dog. It barked at him through the chain link fence, saliva foaming at its mouth. Eoin gave him a small smile and tossed a huge, thick steak over the top. He waited until the animal started gnawing before scaling the barrier and landing next to the creature.

Not His Dragon

The dog gave him a wary glance and whined. Animals always could sense who was the bigger predator even masked by a human-looking body.

Fog had rolled in, clinging to the ground between the piles of scrap metal. It leant the junkyard a mystical feeling, as if Eoin was embarking on a soul-searching quest for treasure, instead of breaking and entering to steal garbage. He chuckled and meandered through the aisles hoping something would give him inspiration. Something he could mold into a reflection of his soul and stir viewer's emotions, like how Angie's aura had moved him. He wasn't asking for a vision of the Holy Mother in a warped bumper. Just *something*…

Anything.

Shoving his hands deep in his pockets, he surveyed the stacks of abandoned vehicles. His view of the world was more two-dimensional, paint and canvas. How did one purposefully create a statue? He'd made the last one using garbage, so it only made sense to create similar objects with the same material.

With the full moon above in the clear night sky, he didn't need a flashlight to see his surroundings. This part of the yard consisted mostly of things either from vehicles or household appliances. Metal things. Things he could melt with his flame.

Now, fire he could understand.

On a whim, he gathered any part that caught his eye—a car door, rusted fenders, a child's bike, an old soda dispenser. He dragged them one by one to the front gate, tossing each piece over the fence. He took one more cursory search of the area and spotted the front end of a motorcycle. 'A death trap,' Angie had called it. Inspiration struck. He pulled it from the pile and added it to his other things.

The dog finished his meal and came towards him wagging his tail. Kneeling, Eoin gave the pooch a scratch behind its ragged ear before vaulting over the fence and stacking the pile of junk in the back of his pickup truck. He pulled out his cell phone from his back pocket and called Roger.

"Eoin?" His agent sounded as if he'd woken from a dead sleep.

"Hey, I'm at the junk yard."

"Good for you. Have you any idea what time it is?" Roger yawned.

"Not really." He'd left Angie on the roof around ten p.m. Eoin glanced at his phone. It was well past midnight. "I've taken some materials to work with."

"I didn't know they were open so late." Roger's voice dripped with sarcasm.

"You know they're not, but I couldn't wait until morning."

"Like the rest of us mere mortals."

Eoin laughed. "You're cranky when you wake up."

"Yes, especially when I was having a good sleep. What do you want?"

"Swing by the junk yard and offer the owner payment in the morning."

"Yeah, yeah. I'll take care of it." Roger was silent on the other end of the line for a moment. "You think you'll have those pieces finished in time?"

Eoin scratched his head. "I'll try my best. You placed me in quite a position."

"Wait a minute. Are you only starting on them now?"

"I had things to do earlier today." Things that mattered to him.

"More important than your career?" Roger sounded much more alert.

"My life doesn't revolve around my art."

"Since when?"

"I had some…health issues to take care of." Eoin didn't like the timetable his agent and dealer had given him. Dragons did not work this way. A day was nothing to him so they should be more than happy if he accomplished anything on deadline.

"I didn't know dragons could get sick. Are you all right?" Roger grew quiet.

"We don't get sick. We do need to do some maintenance and I have been neglecting myself these last few years." He rubbed the back of his neck. The last thing he needed was Roger to start mother-hen-ing him. "Just take care of the junkyard owner, okay?"

"You can count on me. G'night."

Eoin hung up and stuck his phone back in his pocket. Jumping into his truck, he headed home. He'd already set up a space in his castle on the first floor where he could blow his fire without burning down the roof and not have to carry this load of junk to the top of his tower. His stomach grew sourer as he drew closer to home. He hadn't a fucking clue what to do with all this crap in his truck bed. How was he supposed to concentrate on creating something from scrap when he couldn't stop seeing Angie's aura in his mind's eye? What was stopping her from shifting? How could she not know that she was pure dragon? How did human parents get hold of a dragon baby? Angie was such a puzzle.

Eoin shook her clear of his mind. He had so much to do and so little time to do it. Undressing, he tossed his clothes to the far corner, not wanting to scorch them with his flame. He dragged pieces of metal scrap together, separating them in piles, and shifted to dragon form. With a deep breath, he let loose his fire and watched as the middle group changed from dull gray to glowing red.

The statue that Lorenzo was fond of had been created by just the heat in the room, not direct flame. It was too late for him to change his approach and he watched the metal melt into a gooey mass. With his tail, he beat the shapeless blob, trying to mold it as if it were clay.

God only knew how long he worked in this manner.

Fire. More smashing. More flame. Until at last, he stood before a crazy lump of *Megatron* shit. The piece should be titled "Desperation".

His chest ached with each dry breath. He hadn't blown this much flame in ages. Not since his last battle. There'd been so much destruction, he'd almost wept. Dragons, as a whole, sometimes forgot their overall goal during a campaign until things went south. That fight had gone straight to hell.

With legs wide apart, he took another deep breath and blew. Smoke emerged from his throat and nothing else. He coughed and coughed again, choking on his own exhaust. That was disconcerting. He cleared his throat and made another attempt to set his work on fire.

Nothing, not even a spark. Eoin leaned the side of his face against the sizzling hot stone floor and caught his breath. His chest grew heavier and his lungs felt full of sand. Had he lost his flame? He shifted to human form. What would he do now? Maybe he'd over-taxed his system.

He stalked toward the hot watery metal, swung back his right arm, and punched it. The intense heat sizzled against his flesh and he savored the sensation. He was fireproof, so he struck again and again. The molten metal couldn't hurt his flesh even though it stung.

Falling to his knees, Eoin ran his sore hands over the stubble on his head and stared at what he'd done. He'd made his first sculpture out of rage so it only made sense he made the others in the same manner.

Torn and raw inside, he shifted back to dragon and bit the first lump using his teeth until only sharp angry bites remained in the metal. He used tail and claw. Standing, he hit the metal until they had cooled enough to resist molding.

Eoin shifted to human and sat hard on the floor. He didn't know how long he stared at his vicious sculptures. This wasn't what he wanted to share with the world. Anger? Violence? How predictably dragon of him.

Inching his way, he rose to his feet and abandoned the room. Turning his back on what was supposed to be his new medium, he escaped to the top of his tower and his easel. He rested his hands on the cross member under a new canvas and closed his eyes. If Lorenzo and Roger were trying to drive him insane then they'd done it.

Outside the window, the morning sun crested the horizon. Shades of pink bled to dark blue as the light chased away the night. The variance of colors reminded Eoin of Angie's aura. Grabbing his palette, he equipped it with the paint colors he would need and began stroking canvas with loving caresses of his brush. Out of the corner of his eye, he continued to watch the sunrise.

Angie was the new sun in his life. She brought light to his darkness. He continued to paint from memory, but capturing that moment when he'd first glimpsed her aura was harder than he'd thought. He needed another look because it was very difficult to see the details of magic in the city. Whatever kept Angie from shifting, they would destroy it together, even if she didn't harbor the same burning need to be with him. His gaze wandered back to the painting. Now this was beauty. What he'd made downstairs was pure, unadulterated, raw emotion. He obviously couldn't understand what people wanted. Maybe he should just cancel the show and give up on art.

Not His Dragon

CHAPTER SIXTEEN

The morning sun shone bright and the air still held last night's crispness. Eoin stared out the window, wiping the paint from his hands. He'd worked all night yet felt like he hadn't accomplished much—neither sleep, nor inspired masterpiece—but had managed to destroy his ability to blow flame. Only time would tell if it would return on its own. He would wait a very long time before crawling back to his clan seeking assistance. He could almost hear his brothers' laughter already.

His gaze wandered to his latest painting. The colors didn't do justice to Angie's aura but nothing in the natural world could mimic magic. His head still hurt from viewing her with his magical vision. He took a puff of his cigarette.

Cool air breezed into his lair and brushed his flesh, tempting him to follow it out into the sky. He should fly. That would clear his head then maybe he could figure out how to explain the truth to Angie. He traced the black line blocking her magic on the painting. Who would cast such an evil spell on a child? She must have been very young, since she'd never shifted. Their gift to become dragon came early, around ten years old.

Wouldn't it be nice if Angie could fly with him? If he broke this barrier, then she could shift shape. He could think of a few things to try, but they'd need privacy, and he had the perfect place in mind. The media would implode if he dropped in by landing on her roof in full daylight though. They'd be all over her if they discovered he was visiting her. She'd never get a moment's peace. He snuffed his cigarette out against the stone wall and dropped the remainder back in the pack.

He frowned as he made his way to his bedroom two floors down. He'd go in human form again, then bring her back here so he could shift in private. That meant he should clean his skin of his sweat and stink. He didn't have time to fly to the lake and wash in dragon form so he'd shower. The bathroom in his bedroom seemed in better condition than the one by his workshop. He washed and dressed, still dripping water. Didn't he used to own towels? Once inside his garage, he bypassed his bike and jumped into the Aston Martin she had admired yesterday.

Traffic didn't exist on Saturdays in New Port so it took minutes to arrive at her building. Entering, he scanned the mailboxes fixed inside on the wall. Most were unmarked. Two hung open on their hinges. He grimaced. None of them had Angie's name listed.

Approaching the closest apartment door, he knocked until it swung open.

A burly male, dressed only in boxers, glared at him. "Man, do you know what time it is?"

"Six a.m. Do you know where Angie lives?"

"Fuck no." He slammed the door in Eoin's face.

The dragon narrowed his gaze. If he set fire to the idiot's home, Angie's would burn as well. He snarled silently before going to the next door and repeated the process with similar results.

Angie woke to pounding in the hallway. She rolled on her stomach and hugged the pillow over her head. Every few minutes the noise would grow closer with the occasional shout from one of her neighbors. There was a special in hell for those who woke others early on the weekend.

With a groan, she sat on the edge of the bed and stared at her clock in disbelief. What asshole was making that racket at 6:20 a.m.? The weekend was sacred, the only part of the week where all she had to do was care for herself.

Except tonight she would still have to care for Eoin's scale rot, but last night had proven that wasn't much of a chore. She liked hanging with the dragon. Maybe she'd accept his taunt and undress for him. The thought of Eoin watching her undress sent hot pangs of desire between her thighs.

The pounding started again. She jumped to her feet and stormed to her door. Whoever that asshole was better be wearing kneepads because she'd make him beg for mercy. Swinging the door open, her razor words hung on her tongue. She half expected to taste blood.

Eoin knocked on the neighbor's door across the hall. He glanced over his shoulder and the best surprised smile bloomed on his face. "There you are."

She shielded her body with the door. Dirty t-shirt and old boxers were far from lingerie. God, what would he think? "Eoin? What the fuck?"

The neighbor answered the knocking. "What the hell is going on out here?" Mrs. Crane carried her cane two-handed like a baseball bat. Angie had never seen her use it to walk, just to beat people out of her way.

Angie gestured for Eoin to move before the old woman brained him. "Sorry, Mrs. Crane." She shouted so the old woman could hear. "Wrong door."

Eoin strode into Angie's apartment.

She closed the door before Mrs. Crane could follow.

"Are you a hoarder?" He stood in the middle of her kitchen/living room combo assessing her messy home with a critical eye.

"Fuck you, Eoin. What do you want?" She did hoard things and she was a terrible housekeeper. She blamed it on being raised with nothing. Who knew when she'd need a toaster that could set things on fire? What if she wanted to roast marshmallows?

He plucked at the clean laundry on her table until he hung a pair of panties from his finger. "I want to spend the afternoon with you."

She snatched her underwear from his hold. "You're several hours early."

"It'll take some time to fly to our destination." His gaze traveled along her torso, pausing at the curve of her hips. "You look nice." With his fingertips, he tugged at her t-shirt to draw her closer.

A cup of Java couldn't have revved her pulse like Eoin's proximity. She set her hands on his chest. If she drew any closer, she wouldn't be responsible for her actions.

"It's a perfect morning to fly." His voice had gone husky.

"I need a shower."

"Shower while I make breakfast."

Butterflies took wing in her stomach. "Okay, where are we going?"

"Secret dragon place," he whispered.

Nodding, she backed away to the shower. She couldn't believe Eoin was in her craptastic apartment. The paint cracks made abstract designs on every wall and they were so thin her whole floor had probably heard them making plans.

She paused in front of the mirror and stifled a scream. Half her hair stood straight up and the other half was plastered to her scalp. He said she looked good. What a fucking liar. She looked like a crackhead after a hard night on the pipe.

The apartment sucked rotten eggs, but the hot water tank did work as long as Mrs. Crane didn't flush her toilet. She let the shower cascade over her tired body. Flying sounded nice, but how far away would he take her? She didn't have a passport.

"Angie."

She jumped and covered her tits even though Eoin couldn't see through the shower curtain. "Get out!" Thin plastic was the only thing separating them. The air suddenly seemed too heavy with steam.

"You've no food. Are you hiding it?"

She hung her head. She budgeted her food money and hadn't had time to do any grocery shopping this week. It was one of the things on her to-do list. "I have a box of *Pop Tarts* in the cupboard."

"That's sad."

She turned off the water and heard him searching her cupboards. She didn't buy lots of food because the cockroaches were so big they could carry most of it away.

Wrapping a towel around her body, she hurried to the clean laundry pile on the kitchen table and pulled out fresh clothes. It wasn't a workday and Eoin was taking her someplace special. This called for a clean, non-stained or torn outfit.

She tossed him a glance.

He leaned on the counter watching her. His heated gaze pulled on her towel, daring her to drop it.

Temptation loosened her grip.

The toaster popped and she shook free of his spell. On the other side of the paper screen separating her studio in two, she dressed quickly.

"Fuck a duck, these things are hot." Eoin continued swearing under his breath. Pop Tarts could burn like napalm when heated just right. That they could burn a dragon said much of the power of hot sugar.

A setting of paper plates and a stack of freshly warmed prepackaged toaster pastries greeted her return to the kitchen.

Eoin sucked on his finger. "Watch the first bite, they're hot."

The scent of fresh coffee called her to breakfast faster. She waited for her stomach to revolt but it remained calm. Maybe her phobia had gone away. That would be so cool. She could finally go to restaurants.

Things like prepackaged food didn't bother her. The product was made more by machines than by men. Or so she kept telling herself.

She sipped on the cup Eoin offered her. "What should I bring?"

"A sweater. It gets cooler in high altitudes. We'll drive back to the castle and get a riding harness for you."

"I'm surprised you have one. I didn't think dragons would allow riders."

"I'm not a mount, but I'm practical. If I don't want to carry a human in my hands, then they need something to keep them from falling off my back."

"I didn't use a harness the other night."

"It was a short trip. This will be longer and higher."

Her gut clenched. "How high?"

"You'll still be able to breathe."

She felt breathless already. "How high can you fly?"

"The jet streams. Around forty-five thousand feet. That's why most humans can't spot us. We're just a speck in the sky."

"Wow."

He handed her two Pop Tarts. "Eat on the go. We've got lots to do first."

"Like?"

"For one, stop for provisions. I can't be expected to survive on this poison." He flicked her breakfast.

She followed him out of the building. He seemed so animated. The thought warmed her. His mood was infectious. She couldn't imagine what he planned on showing her.

"Eoin?"

He opened the passenger side door to his car. "What?"

"What's at this secret dragon place?"

"It's where we take our young to teach them how to fly."

Not His Dragon

CHAPTER SEVENTEEN

From this vantage point on Eoin's back, Angie could view the world as if she were a giant. She tugged the leather jacket Eoin insisted she wear tighter around her torso. The wind seemed to blow right through her even with her sweater.

They flew over wild lands full of green trees and open fields. She hadn't seen a farm or a road in the last hour. Ahead, a mountain rose from the rolling hills as if something had punched the Earth's crust from underneath.

Stark cliffs formed the sides of the mountain. The peak was flat as a pancake with a piece of the forest still thriving on top.

Eoin did a lazy circle around the summit. "Looks vacant."

The leather harness strapping her to his back creaked as he dove to land. Angie clamped her teeth shut, refusing to squeal in terror. She almost lost her grip on the bag Eoin had packed.

In the center of the plateau a field of wild flowers grew. Eoin chose to glide to a stop here. He patiently laid on the ground as she undid the harness with numb fingers. The air, thankfully, was warmer on the mountaintop.

She made a soft landing next to him with the bag and unpacked his clothes. She also discovered a bottle of wine, a brick of cheese, crusty bread, and grapes.

Eoin knelt next to her. "That corner store we stopped at was well stocked. I have to remember to shop there more often. I hate crowds."

"You have more than I did." She didn't hide her curiosity as she watched him dress. Over the last few days, she'd seen Eoin naked enough times that the effect should have worn off. Nope, the sight of his tight ass still kicked her in the gut. She shivered. What would it be like if she ever touched him?

He pulled a t-shirt over his head and tossed her an inviting smile. The jerk knew exactly what she was thinking.

She whipped a grape at his perfect abs.

He caught it with unnatural speed and popped it into his mouth. "Thanks." Sauntering over, Eoin locked his gaze on her. She noted the possessive nature in that look. She'd seen it enough times on Ryota, except Eoin didn't make her feel owned. "I've never brought anyone here before."

Angie stared over the long grass swaying in the soft breeze. The scent of flowers filled her lungs and not a modern noise could be heard. "It's peaceful."

Lying next to her on his back, Eoin entwined his fingers behind his head. "It's been ages since I've visited." He closed his eyes.

"You said this is where baby dragons learn to fly?" She'd never seen a baby dragon. Heck, the world hadn't seen one. No photos or sightings. "Are there any babies?"

"Sure. My clan has nestlings right now. In about ten years they'll be ready to come here and learn."

"Ten?" That seemed young and old at the same time, depending on a dragon's lifespan. "How old are you?"

"Old enough."

"Fine, be like that. Then answer this. Why am I here? It's not like I'm ready to learn to fly."

"Not yet." He opened his eyes and sat up with a fluid grace she envied. "I want to teach you how to shift."

Her mouth unhinged. They were back to this *again*. He still thought she was a dragon. Just when she wanted to toss caution to the wind and accept his advances, he reminded her why she swore off shifters. All these thoughts tumbled in her head but not a word slipped out of her open mouth.

"Angie." He spoke as if trying to coax a nervous colt to approach. "I know you believe you can't—"

"I can't." She jabbed her finger against his chest.

He wrapped his hand around her finger and held it firm. "You can. Dragons can see magic." Blinking slowly, his eyes changed from human to dragon. "I brought you here so I can examine your aura better."

A breath caught in her throat and she was almost afraid to move or believe. "You already looked?"

He nodded.

She swallowed around a lump in her throat. "What did you see?" Part of her wished he hadn't peeked. She'd come to terms with her fate. She didn't need Eoin raising her hopes for nothing. She'd been down that road too many times.

"It's hard in the city to look at magic in detail. There's so much life that things can blur. Up here, we're isolated." He grinned. "And it's beautiful. No one should disturb us." His gaze unfocused and he studied the air around her.

She squirmed, burning with curiosity. "Are dragons the only creatures who can see magic?" For as long as she could remember, she'd known she was different. She'd wanted to belong but couldn't find a place to fit.

"Your aura is pure dragon." He ran his fingertips over some unseen thing. "We match." His voice cracked and he cleared his throat.

Heavy anticipation settled in her stomach. What did that mean? She glanced at her unnaturally sharp fingernails. Pure shifters weren't genetic throwbacks.

"There it is. I knew I'd seen it last night but I couldn't be sure."

"What?" The question came out sharper than she'd planned. Eoin wasn't the enemy. He wanted to help.

"A shield surrounds your aura and blocks you from touching magic. I think your inability to shift has nothing to do with genetics. All shifters need magic to change shape and you can't touch yours."

She jumped to her feet and paced. "That can't be right." He didn't know what he was talking about. He'd been trying to convince her she was a dragon since the day they met.

Climbing to his feet, he watched her. "I'm not wrong. We can try to break the shield together and then you can shift." He sounded like a child on Christmas who couldn't wait to open his present. Except the paper he'd been tearing apart was her life.

"Eoin! My parents were human." She planted her hands on her hips and confronted him.

"Are you sure?"

"Yes, they died in a car accident. That wouldn't kill dragons."

He ran his hand over his head while searching the ground with his gaze. "I don't know." He shrugged. "All I have to go on is what I see as fact. Let's work on your shifting then we'll figure out the rest."

The cool wind picked up for a moment and shoved Angie's body. She held herself, suddenly feeling very small. "We?"

He moved so fast she blinked when his arms folded around her. "Yes, we. We'll figure this out together. Do you think I'd drop a bomb like this and not help?"

"No one's ever bothered to help before." When her parents had died and her world had shattered, she'd been shoved into one foster home after another. They hadn't cared about dropping bombs on her and abandoning her as a child.

"Let's start by trying to break the shield. As long as it's intact you can't touch the magic." He held her at arm's length and met her stare.

She nodded, the motion jerky and hesitant.

"Clear your mind."

She took a deep, cleansing breath, and did as he asked. Uncluttering her thoughts was akin to chasing cats. It had been years since she'd last tried to shift. Even when Ryota had begged her to try, she had denied him. How had Eoin circumvented her defenses so easily? The process took a few minutes while Eoin stayed quiet.

"What is the first emotion you sense?" He spoke softly.

She'd done this exercise before, so discovering the emotion at her core didn't surprise her. Fear. "Okay, I have it." This sucked. Why couldn't her trigger emotion be anger or happiness? No, she had to think of fearful things to shift.

"Focus on the emotion and—"

"You know I've tried this before, right?"

"No." He sighed. "Either way, I need to watch the shield and see how it reacts to your attempt to change shape."

"Oh." That made sense. She took a deep breath, reluctant to start. She began with her childhood fear of monsters living under her bed. Of being curled under her blankets too afraid to breathe—of needing to pee but not wanting to put her foot on the floor.

Her heart quickened. She moved on to her first night in a foster home. It had smelled funny and she had to share her room with an older girl who had made fun of her fingernails. Small and alone, she'd faced the dark world and realized no one alive would miss her if she vanished.

Cold claws of fear gripped her spine. The nights hiding on the street, a pretty young girl trying to survive… Breathing grew harder.

But worst of all, being in her classroom when the knock came at the door. A police officer asking for her.

Sweat coated her skin. She recalled the sadness in the policewoman's eyes as she accompanied Angie to the principal's office where she sat on the hardwood chair and listened to the empty news of her parents' accident.

She was alone.

Alone forever. After that day, when she'd been sick no one had wiped her brow with a cool cloth. When she'd gotten good grades, there was no one to run home to with the report card. When she'd gotten in trouble, she had no one to bail her out of jail.

"Angie? Angie?" Eoin shook her as his voice invaded her memories.

She opened her eyes. He leaned so close, concern clear in his face. She wiped her face clean and gave him a watery smile.

He gathered her into a tight hug. "Nothing, I saw nothing. Where did you go?"

"Someplace I hate visiting."

"I don't want you going back there again. You scared me."

She buried her face into his chest and melted against his strong body. "Fine by me." Heat enveloped her and she shuddered as the last of her pain faded away. "What did you see?"

"The magic couldn't even sense your call." He stroked her hair nice and slow, resting his cheek on top of her head.

"Are we done?"

"No." He eased his hold as if reluctant to let her go. "I want to try an old way of shifting. Something we use when someone is troubled."

"There's another way?" She tilted her head to the side and retreated from his arms. "No one ever mentioned this before."

"They probably didn't know. The method is an old secret. Dragons and vampires are the longest living creatures on Earth, with a lot of information."

She rubbed her hands together to warm them. "Let's get this over with."

"Picture your dragon."

She went still. "How am I supposed to do that when I've never seen my dragon?"

"Use your imagination."

"Jesus, Eoin." She closed her eyes again. "I'm terrible at these games." What would her dragon be like? She'd be a bitch, just like her, because they were the same person—black scales like Eoin's, sharp claws, and a kick-ass tail.

"Reach out to her and take her hand."

Stretching out a mental hand, she tried to do as he asked. To her surprise the dragon did the same. She laughed and surged toward her dragon-self only to hit an invisible wall.

Her dragon hit at the same time, claws tearing at the unseen surface. The clear image of her dragon blurred until she faded.

Angie screamed. "No, don't go away."

Eoin held her face between his hands. "You saw her?"

She snapped her eyes open and gripped his wrists. "We couldn't touch. Then she vanished. What does that mean?" Had she lost her dragon forever? Was Eoin right? If he was, then who were her parents?

"It means we're close. Let me try one more thing." He pried her hands off his wrists and gave her space.

She clasped her hands to her chest and tried to blow out a frustrated breath but failed in grand fashion. "Eoin." As she backed away, he followed. "I can't anymore." Couldn't he see how much she was hurting?

He loomed with ominous purpose, and she couldn't help but admire the trim definition of his shoulders and the corded grooves between each ripple of muscles in his arms. Compact everywhere. He was a warrior and didn't understand the meaning of mercy. Reaching his fingers toward some invisible force around her, he tried to rip it apart with his bare hands.

Something tugged at her hard and she stumbled. Her pulse jackrabbited in her throat. He was right. Whatever he was doing was affecting her. Searing pain tore through her chest. She arched her torso to relieve the pressure. "Stop!" She shouted into the quiet mountaintop.

Eoin dropped his arms.

Instantly the pain disappeared. She rested her hands on her knees and caught her breath.

"We'll have to reach out to my people. Someone might have a better idea." He touched her hair.

She flinched. "No." Enough was enough. Tears streamed along her cheeks unchecked. She straightened her back. "Don't you think I've tried? Don't you think I'd give anything to shift?" Her throat ached from restraining her sobs. "Some things can't be fixed. Whatever you were doing was killing me." She doubted a strange dragon would care if it killed her in the name of curiosity. "No more, Eoin." Taking a shaky breath, she hugged herself. "No more, okay?" She hated the smallness of her voice.

Eoin wrapped his hand around her wrist. Sparks tingled along her skin where they made contact, lighting her nerve endings with sensation as he stroked her inner wrist with his thumb. Molten desire slid through her body. His other hand wrapped around the back of her neck in a gentle caress. "Okay," he whispered.

Eoin was more than aware of Angie. Mere inches separated their bodies. Her scent coiled around him, calling to his unmated nature. His blood felt thick in his veins.

"I can take care of myself. I don't need your help."

Ignoring her automatic knee jerk response, he began to stroke along her graceful neck. He let his fingers travel over her soft, wet cheekbones, her stubborn chin, the lushness of her lips. He drank her in and she tasted like his. He lowered his head. Gods, those lips were even softer than he imagined.

She thawed and molded her body to his, submitting to his need to care for her. He knew how hard he'd pushed her and was more determined to make things right even if she refused his help. She nibbled his lower lip before sucking it between her teeth. Surrendering in his arms, she opened her mouth. Her tongue touched his for a fleeting moment and disappeared again.

He wanted to explode, to push her to the ground and claim her as his, but not until he healed her from the pain he'd caused. He needed his Angie back. The spitfire, crazed woman who had pepper-sprayed him in the eyes and never apologized. He kissed her again—playful and light—and he sensed the tension in her body relax.

She pushed up onto her tiptoes to deepen the kiss. Her tongue returned and he sucked on the tip gently. Then he followed it back to

112

her mouth where she did the same. It became a game and finally the clouds of fear in Angie's beautiful face cleared as she smiled against his lips.

He drew away. Using his thumb, he forced her chin up so their eyes could meet. He saw the sun and moon and stars in her smile. Such a smile was worth all his protection. "I know you can take care of yourself. You always have." He tried to keep his tone normal, but his heart broke along with hers. He needed her to know something, though. "But you're not alone anymore."

Her smile faded a bit. "You say that now, but in time, you'll leave as well." She retreated from his arms as her damn phone rang. She answered before he could intervene. "Hello? Yes, this is she. Who's this?" Her brows furrowed and she blocked her unused ear with her finger to concentrate on the other voice on the line. "What set off the alarm?"

Eoin gathered their lunch back in the bag. It sounded like their field trip was over. If she thought this conversation was finished, she was in for a shock. Try as she might to shut him out, she didn't realize how good he was at tearing down doors.

Angie returned her phone to her pocket. "That was the alarm company for the shop. They think someone tried to break in. They dispatched the cops. Everything looks untouched but they can't shut off the fucking alarm. I swear that building is going to put me in an early grave."

"You need to go back." He hid his disappointment. Her life revolved around her business.

She nodded. "Can you fly that distance again so soon?"

He snorted. "No problem." His body didn't ache from exertion. It was from sexual tension and constant denied release. "I'll go with you, then we can discuss this over dinner."

She shook her head. "Ryota's pack runs the security company. Your presence will cause trouble."

He scowled. "Contrary to your belief, I can control myself." Not to mention, he didn't want to leave her alone if Ryota showed his face.

She set her hand over his heart. "I'm not worried about you. Werewolves can be so touchy. The last thing I need is one of them thinking he can make a name for himself and attacking you, or worse, calling Ryota over."

"You don't want to see him?" He wished he could swallow his tongue sometimes. But by the all the gods he'd ever heard of, he *needed* to know.

"No, I already have a headache and I doubt a ringing alarm will make me feel any better." She stroked his chest absentmindedly. "Can I take a rain check?"

He gathered her against his thrumming body. Each caress making it harder to let her go. "Fuck, yes."

CHAPTER EIGHTEEN

Eoin sat in his tower workroom, staring at the painting of Angie's aura again. He remembered her cool lips timidly touching his, her sweet flavor, the tangle of their tongues pure aphrodisiac. What was he going to do? Where to begin…a hundred scenarios came to mind, starting with making good use of the bed he never slept in.

No female had ever infiltrated his heart so thoroughly as Angie Weldon. A thin line of smoke trailed from the cigarette hanging from his lip. It obscured his view so he tossed it in the pile of ash left from his bonfire.

Anxiety chewed at his innards. Maybe he shouldn't have kissed her so soon. She'd made it clear that she didn't want a relationship with a shifter, but as said shifter, he didn't give a shit. She was as much a shifter as he was. The arms of the chair creaked under his straining fingers. He'd probably wrecked everything. No, it wasn't his fault. It was Ryota's. *He'd* wrecked everything.

She didn't harbor feelings for the alpha. If anything, she acted like she couldn't stand Ryota. Eoin could understand the sentiment.

The faint scent of death drifted into the room. Only the whispered sound of shoes scuffing against the stone announced the arrival of the vampire. "You missed our appointment."

Eoin grimaced and turned to face his vampire friend. "I forgot." He'd been going to Viktor's tattoo parlor for the past decade. There weren't many people alive that Eoin would trust to ink his flesh.

Viktor strode into Eoin's workroom and stared at the painting. "I like the new turn in your work. It's much more cheerful." He still spoke with a light Russian accent even after living in this country for longer than Eoin.

"I don't recall asking for your opinion."

"No, but you did ask for this information." The vampire held out a manila envelope.

Eoin snatched and set it on his lap. "You work fast."

Viktor shrugged. "I have excellent connections. Why the interest in the girl?"

Stroking the envelope, Eoin struggled not to tear it open. The information didn't belong to him but he had to know where she'd come from. If he wanted to mend things between him and Angie, the best course of action was to help her discover the truth. "None of your business." This belonged to Angie. The least he could do was wait to read it with her.

"Whatever. You'll tell me eventually and I've all the time in the world." Viktor turned his back on the painting and lifted up his shirt. Across his flanks and down his back read a list of names. "I need you to carve a new name into my flesh."

"What happened?" Eoin leaned forward in his chair. "You haven't killed anyone in years."

The vampire wrote the names of his victims on his skin in penance. Some of the names were as simple as *sod behind bar* or *boy unattended*. Viktor had been trying for a very long time to learn to drink without actually killing his victims. He'd been a poor study. It was amazing he hadn't been caught and staked by now.

Viktor hung his head, his long black hair shadowing his face. "I don't know. My date invited me back to her home and things got out of control." He shook his head. "*I* got out of control." He handed Eoin a vial of ink. This special vial was mixed with dragon blood since regular ink wouldn't stain his skin and Eoin's blood burned the color into permanence. Victor also needed something strong and sharp enough to pierce his flesh.

Eoin allowed his pointer finger to shift so his long sharp claw grew. He hissed at the dull pain that radiated up his arm. Partial shifts were slow, which made it painful. "What's her name?"

Viktor approached him pulling his shirt off. "Victoria Smith."

Eoin dipped the tip of his index claw into the vial and scratched the girl's name under the list on Victor's right flank. He didn't bleed and his skin sizzled on contact.

Jaw clenched, Viktor didn't utter a sound during the slow process. Once it was done, he sighed. "Sorry." It seemed like everyone was sorry for something nowadays. The new mark healed before Eoin's eyes. Viktor then threw himself on the floor next to Eoin's chair and leaned against the piece of furniture. "You never miss an appointment."

Eoin concentrated on his claw, retracting it back into his fingertip. "I've been distracted." He grunted in relief as the shift ended.

"What's her name?"

"What makes you think it's a woman?" Viktor was one of the first friends Eoin had made when he moved to New Port. The vampire had shown up at his castle to size up the competition. They had more in common than either would rather admit. Both were artists, both were very long-lived, and both were isolated from their kind. "Her name is Angie."

"So it is the human girl." Viktor rocked with amusement. "How did she get you so tied up in knots? Is she that good in bed?" Viktor twisted to share a salacious grin. "More importantly, are you willing to share?"

Eoin's hand moved as if it had a life of its own and slapped the vampire across the head before either had seen the movement.

"I'll leave that subject alone." Viktor rubbed his head.

"I don't share." Eoin stood up and gestured for the vampire to follow. "My agent and my gallery manager have asked me to expand my horizons. You know how well old races are at learning new tricks." He abandoned the painting and led Viktor downstairs to his sculpting workshop. He opened the door and bowed to let Viktor in ahead of him. The statues still radiated heat but had solidified.

Upon entering the room, the vampire waved his hand in front of his nose. "Smells like sulfur. Who did you barbecue?"

"Neither my agent or manager." There was a growl to his voice. No matter how much he would like to set flame to both of them at present, he knew deep down inside that they were trying to help him in their human fashion. Everything fast and furious—now, now, now.

Viktor paused and assessed his work from a distance. "This is a different medium for you." He strolled around the room and between statues, touching, poking at the material. "What seems to be the issue?"

Eoin tossed his hands in the air and stormed across the room, knocking the prickly statue on its side. Some of the points shattered on contact and skidded across the scorched stone floor. "They're horrid." What was everybody seeing in these abominations? "It has been remarked my paintings are emotionless and cold. I lost my temper and created that thing sitting on my front lawn. Lorenzo loves it and has canceled my painting exhibit so he can show my new statues." He opened his arms out and spun slowly. This would be the end of his career in the art world. He'd be a laughingstock, and worse, his clan would be right. Dragons shouldn't be artists.

Viktor shook his head. "These works are visceral." He fingered the one full of sharp edges and punctured his fingertips. A drop of dark, almost black, blood beaded on his fingertip. "It's almost like a kick to the balls. There's a lot the emotion in this work. Maybe you should try using your new love interest as a model. She may inspire something different. Something not so…" He held up his healing fingertip. "Sharp."

Eoin ground his teeth. "I can't—" He bared his teeth. "I can't blow fire at the moment. I burned myself out, I think." Huffing, Eoin bent forward as if to blow flame.

Viktor dodged to the side. "I'm flammable, jackass."

A cough was all that Eoin produced. No smoke, no spark, and definitely no flame. "See? No danger. It stopped last night and I haven't been able to rekindle my spark." He paced the room, rubbing his head over and over again. His calloused hands barely felt the short stubble.

"Maybe it's stress." Victor shrugged.

Rolling his stiff shoulders, Eoin nodded. "That's possible. I have enough of it." He'd never heard of a dragon losing his fucking flame. If it were permanent, he'd be a dead dragon. His people tended to attack first and ask questions later. Kind of like how he'd met Angie.

A dark laugh echoed in Eoin's workspace and had both of them spinning about face. "I'm not surprised to hear about your impotence, Eoin." The man blocking Eoin's doorway should be the cover model for Stinking Rich Assholes magazine. His black hair looked like he'd only run his fingers through it, but Eoin knew this dragon probably kept a stylist chained in his dungeon. His tailored suit fit him so perfectly that Eoin's sagging jeans wanted to cry in shame. When had the old dragon started wearing modern clothes? Last he'd seen Cedric, the bastard had been still chasing women in his kilt.

So this night could get worse.

Not His Dragon

"How did you get into my home?" The other dragon had been a thorn under Eoin's scales for as long as he could remember.

Cedric crossed his arms and leaned against the frame. "You have no security. No gates, no guards, no alarm system. How can you live in such a dump?" He made a distasteful face. "You don't guard your treasure well." He tsked.

"What I consider valuable, other dragons wouldn't want." Eoin sensed Viktor moving further to the side so he could flank Cedric in case of an attack. The vampire proved to be a better and better friend.

The old dragon shouldn't be in Eoin's city. At least, not without his permission. He hadn't been out to check his perimeter spells since running into Angie. The fucking old dragon must have disabled them somehow. Eoin kept a close eye on the other male. "I don't remember extending you an invitation to enter my territory." New Port was not considered desirable by dragon standards. There were no volcanoes, or glaciers, or oceans. It was also overpopulated, modern, and stank. He couldn't imagine Cedric wanting to take over his territory.

"An unmated female dragon is one of our most precious treasures. If you don't want her, then I'd be happy to accompany her back to my territory, where I can care for her properly. According to our laws, I am neither trespassing nor need an invitation to come to New Port as you have an unmated female in your city." He smirked. "How long did you think you could keep her a secret?"

Eoin's body suddenly felt too hot. Cedric was right. Unmated females were rare among their kind and cherished, but Eoin was still thinking of Angie as human. "When the fuck did you become interested in a mate?" Cedric most likely wanted Angie because she was in Eoin's city.

Females were welcome to travel where they wanted. They usually settled in the territory of their choosing except Angie hadn't known she was dragon until a few hours ago. How had Cedric found out so fast?

Cedric's eyebrows rose and the corner of his mouth curled in a smug smile. "So the rumors are true."

Eoin want to punch himself in the balls. Cedric had that kind of effect on him. The dragon hadn't known for sure she was a dragon until Eoin opened his big, fat mouth. Fuck, Eoin hadn't known what she was until they'd met. He had to think fast to keep the other dragon away from Angie.

"I thought you said that she was human," Viktor added.

Eoin wasn't sure if Viktor had saved his ass purposely, but either way, he'd owe the vampire one. "She's half human." He met Cedric's glare. "She has dragon blood in her ancestry that makes her smell like pure dragon but she can't shift." Eoin's insides were melting from fury, but he somehow managed to keep his exterior cool. This meant he had to postpone fixing Angie's shifting issues until Cedric's curiosity was satisfied. The weird shield around Angie's aura had to be kept a secret until he could figure out how to break it. Otherwise, Cedric would attempt to claim her and force Eoin into a fight, one which he was certain to lose.

Every time Eoin tried to break through her shields, he could see her aura reaching out to the magic but not making contact. It had been so devastating and he wished he hadn't put Angie through that kind of agony.

Cedric gave Eoin a mocking bow. "I will judge for myself, but as custom demands, I declare my presence in your city." He turned his back on Eoin and Viktor as if he considered them not even a threat. Eoin followed him out of his castle and watched as he climbed into a limousine.

So the old dragon hadn't learned how to drive yet. This gave Eoin a small amount of pleasure. He'd take what he could. He suspected the week would become his personal hell.

Viktor set his hand on Eoin's shoulder. "You better warn her. He's an asshole."

"How did rumors spread so fast? Must be that fucking wolf pack." He hadn't told Ryota to keep it a secret.

"Pack animals do gossip." Viktor nodded. "I have a better question. Why are you only finding out about her now? How has she been hiding her nature all this time?"

"She has something preventing her from touching magic. This shields her from detection. The only reason I found her was by meeting her on the street and she smells like dragon." Eoin needed to set something on fire but the heat that should be boiling in his belly remained extinguished. If he had to fight Cedric, he'd be shit out of luck without his flame.

Eoin shook his head. "This is going to get complicated." He glanced over his shoulder at the vampire and scowled. "Do you need my dungeon?" He had killed a human. It was always how it began before Viktor went on a psychotic murdering spree. They'd made an arrangement long ago. Viktor helped him fit in human society and Eoin kept the vampire from becoming a serial killer.

Shifting his eyes away, Viktor nodded.

Eoin grabbed the vampire by the throat before he could change his mind and dragged him to the back of the castle.

"Wait, wait! I have—"

"You know the rules, Viktor." They'd been through this before. Once Viktor asked for the dungeon it was up to Eoin to lock him there as soon as possible before the vampire lost control again. This would be the third time he'd helped Viktor. He was the only one strong enough in the city to do it.

Eoin carried the vampire down to the underbelly of the castle, kicking and screaming, to the far end, where thick silver chains hung from the wall.

Chapter Nineteen

Angie squirmed under the sink in room one at Scratch Your Itch. She'd come in on her day off to clear the fucking blockage. At least she got to sleep in today. Adjusting the pipe wrench to the right size, she tried to loosen the trap. Before opening her business, she'd never owned a tool let alone knew how to use one, but the place seemed cursed with repairs.

It had almost taken a blood offering for her tech guys to get the damn alarm to shut off yesterday. Her ears still rang. Maybe she should take Ken's advice and burn the place down to collect the insurance money. She even knew a dragon who could *accidentally* sneeze a fireball on her place.

All her profits were going back into fixing the building. It was like she had a personal black cloud hovering over her shop— electrical problems, plumbing backups, exploding toilets, for goodness sake. Next the roof would leak. She'd place what little money she had left on that bet.

The pipe loosened and came apart, landing against her forehead with a solid thunk. A gush of cold mucky water splashed into her open eyes. With a noise resembling a dying moose, she scooted out from under the sink and wiped her face on a towel. "I should've called the plumber." But her bank account said no. Not if she wanted to eat next week.

Pulling out the pipe trap from under the white sink cabinet, she peered inside. With her fingertips, she pulled out a clump of what looked like dog hair. Had one of the shifters taken a bath in her sink? Was nothing sacred? She knocked the pipe against the inside of the trash can, while holding her nose shut with the other hand and trying to keep her breakfast down.

She must have been a really, really bad person in another life to deserve this much grief in this one. Nothing would go her way. When she'd made the deal to buy the building, she thought she finally had gotten a break. She could earn a decent living and maybe, just maybe, she could finally afford a decent home. Her throat tightened. Possibly start a family... She squashed that secret dream back inside her heart, not giving it the time of day. She couldn't allow herself the fantasy. If she couldn't take care of herself, she definitely couldn't take care of kids.

With a growl, she put her pity party on hold and crawled back under the sink. Reattaching the pipe was a lot harder than taking it off; the small threads were worn and hard to realign properly over the Teflon tape. She tightened the pipe with her wrench. Her shoulders ached and her neck would have a kink after the way she had to maneuver her body under the sink. She rested her arms at her side and set the pipe wrench on the ground to catch her breath. Gazing up at the sink's underbelly, she spotted something in the corner of the cabinet. She'd been so focused on the piping that she hadn't noticed it. It looked like a bunch of little sticks tied together to form a geometric shape. It was wedged where the sink and counter met.

She heard the chime of the front door opening and pulled the thing free. Crawling out from under the sink, she examined it in the light. The sticks looked like something out of the *Blair Witch Project*, an oddly shaped triangle with a string woven around the small branches. She shuddered.

"Angie?" Beth's voice carried from the front.

Angie jumped and banged her head on the cabinet frame. She rubbed the spot, trying to ease the sharp pain. "I'm in room one."

Beth flounced into the room carrying two cups of coffee. She handed Angie one of them. "Ryota asked me to drop in and check on you."

Biting her tongue, Angie fisted the pipe wrench. "How did he know I was here?"

The omega shrugged. "He drove by and saw you."

"It's your day off, Beth. He shouldn't have done that. If I needed help, I would have called." She was going to need a crowbar to pry the alpha from her life.

"We need to go over the accounts together. Might as well do it today, so we don't have to stay late tomorrow."

Angie sighed. "Fine." She held up the thing and took a sip of liquid heaven, strong enough to make hair grow on her chest. Just how she liked her coffee. "Look what I found."

"You found my charm?" Beth plucked it from her hand and held the bundle in the sunlight. "I hope you don't mind. I didn't know if you would have let me place one in the shop."

"A charm? Like witchcraft?"

"Yes, exactly that."

Angie wasn't sure how she felt about witchcraft. That kind of power could be very harmful in the wrong hands. She usually steered clear of anything to do with witches.

"I had the pack witch make this when we first opened Scratch Your Itch. It's to bring good luck." Beth sounded excited.

"I didn't know the pack had a witch. It doesn't seem like Ryota."

"You'd be amazed at how often we need to use her." Beth shrugged. "Accidents happen and she's very good at cleaning up messes."

"Sounds like something I shouldn't be hearing."

Beth wouldn't meet her gaze. "Do you want me to throw it away?" The omega had only been trying to help in her own way. Witch services weren't cheap and Angie bet the pack didn't pay for that charm.

"If it's for good luck, we'll keep it. I sure could use more." Maybe she should ask this witch to make a set. This time Angie had been able to dodge a plumber's bill. At this point, she was willing to try anything to save money.

"Eoin sent a check yesterday. It should cover this month's mortgage and what we owe the electrician."

Angie flinched. Damn it, she'd hoped for some profit from her evening shifts with the dragon but all of it went to repairs.

Beth played with the lid of her coffee. "Are you finished working on his scales?"

"I think one more session and I should be done. It might be interesting to branch out in this area. I wonder how many dragons live around New Port." Now that Angie knew her origins, she was curious about her people. If Eoin was right and she was pure dragon instead of a throwback, what did that mean about her parents? Had they been dragon as well?

"Dragons are more territorial than werewolves. They live mostly in clans in very isolated areas. Eoin is one of the rare cases who tolerates other races but I'm sure if you advertised, some would fly in for a treatment." Beth gave her a shy smile. "If Eoin gives them permission to enter New Port, that is."

Not His Dragon

"We'd need to rent a warehouse if that were the case. Maybe you should get some quotes." Angie rose to her feet and fiddled with her coffee lid. "He kind of took me on a date yesterday." She had barely slept last night. Seeing her dragon, hearing about magic, and wondering about her parents had left her exhausted yet unable to find rest.

Beth bounced, almost splashing coffee on Angie's shirt. "That's so exciting. Did he kiss you?" She peered at Angie with wide eyes. "What's wrong? He didn't force you to do something, did he?" Beth placed her hand on top of Angie's and gave it a squeeze. "You smell very upset. What did he do?" A small growl escaped Beth's delicate throat.

"Eoin thinks that I'm a dragon. Not just part dragon, but all dragon." She ran her free hand down the length of her body. "One hundred percent pure blood." Would her clients stop coming if they knew she was dragon? Everyone was frightened of Eoin. She didn't want that.

Beth blinked. "But you can't shift."

And there was the kicker. She could be as pure blooded as Eoin wanted but if she couldn't change shape, the rest of the world wouldn't view her as a shifter. She wanted to believe Eoin—being a dragon was more than she could ever dream. It was difficult to understand when he was discussing auras and shields. In everyone else's eyes, even Beth's, she was still human. "He took me to an isolated area so he could teach me how to shift." Angie recalled every detail of her dragon, right down to her glossy black scales. Her chest felt hollow. Would she ever see her dragon again? "It didn't work. I utterly failed."

"Does he have any idea why you can't change shape?" Beth crept closer to Angie, pressing their sides together. As an omega, it was instinctual for Beth to offer comfort to those in need. "That ass shouldn't have hurt you."

Angie tossed her a quick look. "It wasn't his intention to hurt me. He really believes that he can fix me."

"There's absolutely nothing wrong with you Angie."

"Fine, help me. Is that better? He says there is something blocking me from connecting to my abilities to shift. He was trying to break through my block. Since it didn't work he's going to talk to some of the other dragons to see if they have any ideas." She didn't fool herself into believing there'd be a cure. This was a well-traveled route in her life where some shifter would think *they'd* be the one to make her whole. Hope was for romantics, but she wouldn't stop Eoin. She liked his romantic side. "He kissed me." The hollow feeling in her chest faded and the space filled with warmth. Something different and new, something she'd never felt for anyone else before.

Beth gasped. She bounced on her heels again. "Details."

The heat of a blush made Angie's cheeks ache. "It was just a simple kiss."

"You do realize I can smell a lie, right?"

Angie laughed. "It was… It was sweet, and hot, and he's so goddamn sexy, I don't know what I'm going to do the next time I see him." Angie felt breathless.

"Next time?" Beth gave her a knowing smile. "You like him." She said in a teasing voice.

"Of course I do, you wouldn't?"

"I wouldn't. I mean, he scares me too much. Actually, he scares everyone."

"You don't want me to see him anymore?" Beth was the closest thing that she had to a family. Her opinion meant a lot.

"No, that's not my point." An unusual seriousness came over her best friend's face. "I don't know him and haven't smelled him enough to make any judgment calls. I know he's not a player and that he's fair." Those were two qualities that Ryota had failed at and were huge bonus points for Eoin. "Even though he's a dragon, he's still a shifter. If Eoin meets his mate while dating you, he'll drop you in a heartbeat. Shifters can't help but follow instinct." That was another reason why Angie had left Ryota, and a huge negative point for Eoin.

Angie stared at the charm in her hand. Maybe the pack witch had a love potion that she could use? She snorted. What was she thinking? "I need to finish with the sink and I might as well check all the other rooms for broken shit before hitting the accounts."

"Sounds good. I need to eat. Want me to bring you back something?"

Not His Dragon

The familiar nausea kicked Angie in the gut so hard she had vertigo. "No." She clutched her stomach. Damn, she thought she'd gotten over this.

CHAPTER TWENTY

Angie sat at Beth's desk in the shop's waiting room. They poured over the expense account on the computer screen. Angie rubbed the back of her neck. Even though her business was doing well, she would only break even this month. The way things were going maybe she should consider hiring a full time repairman.

Scratch Your Itch was becoming a money pit. She'd be living off ramen noodles and Pop Tarts for a few more weeks or she'd have to dive into her savings account. Her chest tightened at the thought of being trapped in her apartment for another year. That money was supposed to go towards a down payment for a house, not groceries. She would suffer before spending a dime. If she could just figure out how to stop sinking money into repairs, she'd be able to move forward in life.

The door chimed open and closed. Beth must have forgotten to lock it. They were technically closed.

She and Beth glanced up at the same time. A man with a mane of golden hair to his shoulders gave them enigmatic smile. Angie would bet he was a lion shifter.

"Can I help you?" Beth asked, going into receptionist mode.

He sauntered in, tossing his fabulous hair over his shoulder. It should be a sin for men to have better hair than women. "I heard rumors that you service dragons."

Eyelashes too. Men shouldn't have naturally thick eyelashes either. Wait, what? She gave Beth a sharp look.

Her best friend flinched. "I guess what they say about word-of-mouth is true?" She shrugged.

He ignored Beth's outburst since he only had eyes for Angie.

Angie rose from her chair. "I'm offering scale services." She tossed Beth a what-the-fuck look because they had just discussed this a few hours ago. There was no way this dragon heard about her. The wolf pack had to be behind this. Maybe they thought they were helping her drum up more business. This had Ken's name all over it, except where was she going to stuff his dragon ass to work on his scales? The back alley?

Not His Dragon

Beth scooted behind Angie.

"You've nothing to fear from me, pretty shifter." With a flowing motion of his hands, he produced a daisy out of thin air and offered it to Beth. "A gift."

She stared at the stem as if it was full of poisoned thorns before plucking it from his fingers

He turned his gaze back to Angie. "I'm not in need of any scale care. I'm here to have my back scratched. Can you fit me in your schedule?" He sat on the edge of Beth's desk, his body relaxed and at ease as if he were a regular customer.

"I don't have a room big enough for you in dragon form." She couldn't afford to turn away a new customer, even on her day off.

"You can't scratch it while I'm in human form?"

Waving her fingers in front of his face, she showed him her sharp nails. "Only if you don't care if I leave marks."

"My flesh is tougher than it looks." He stood and took off his sport jacket, hanging it on the rack in the waiting room. "It's safe to leave it here?"

Beth nodded and elbowed Angie in the kidney.

She grunted at the sharp pain. "Yes, Beth will watch it." She narrowed her eyes as she turned in the direction of the service rooms and glared at the omega. "We'll use room three, Beth." It was almost a growl. Could they still charge triple rates on just a back scratch? She held out her hand to the strange dragon. "My name is Angie."

The dragon kissed the back of her hand. "My name is Zechariah the Impaler from the Icelandic clan, but you can call me Zech." He ran his thumb over the inside of her wrist in slow seductive circles.

She'd bet what little cash she had that his name didn't come from impaling people with a spear. "Room three is the first door on your right. Undress and lie on the table face down. I'll be there in a few minutes."

"I like a female who can take charge." Zech caressed her palm, let go of her hand, and did as he was told.

Angie faced Beth. "I'm beginning to think all dragons are assholes by nature." She said that for Beth's benefit and it worked. Her best friend gave her a small smile. The worry lines around her eyes eased. "Do not call Ryota. Do you understand me?" Angie jabbed her finger toward Beth's cell phone. "Promise me." All she needed was another scene with the alpha.

Beth clutched the daisy in a death grip. "What if this dragon causes trouble?"

"I can take care of myself. You run."

Angie walked into room three. Zech was lying face down on the table, as instructed, completely naked without the sheet provided. She snatched a fresh sheet from the shelf and snapped it open, setting it over his firm muscular ass.

"Is that sheet for me or you? Because I'm not shy." Zech tossed her a heated look over his shoulder.

She snorted. "I don't know any shifters who are. At least, when it comes to their bodies."

"We are an exhibitionist race." He chuckled. The lines of Zech's well-defined back muscles were softer than Eoin's. What she would call beach muscle, where Eoin's cuts held an edge of violence. Zech's skin was almost as golden as his hair. His scales were probably just as gold. "Iceland is a far journey just to get your back scratched."

"By wing, it's only a few hours. The temptation to enjoy something new was too much. If I had known how beautiful you are, I would have been here sooner."

"Flirt much, Zech?" She began the procedure by running her claws over his smooth flesh. The sharp tips didn't even leave a mark on his skin.

"That feels nice. This is an excellent way to make a living. Doesn't it bother your boyfriend that you are touching other males?"

"Doesn't it bother your girlfriend that you flew hours from home to have a stranger scratch your back?" She bit the inside of her cheeks to restrain her laugh. Zech didn't need any more encouragement. In her heart, she was already taken. One dragon in her life was more than enough.

"Alas, I am still unmated. I know, hard to believe, isn't it?"

She covered her mouth, gaining control of her giggle, but it almost escaped. "Very."

"The traffic is atrocious in this city. It must take you forever to travel to work." He squirmed under her nails. "Right there, Angie. Right there."

Not His Dragon

She put more force into her scratching on the spot he requested. "I walk to work."

Zech relaxed under her nails, his body almost becoming liquid. "So you live in the area. Your boyfriend doesn't worry about you walking alone in these neighborhoods? He mustn't really care."

Caution ran along Angie's spine. Zech seemed too interested in her. Not even her regular customers would have asked such personal questions. She shook her head. He was from out of town and a dragon, so maybe he just didn't know how to act normal.

Eoin parked his motorcycle illegally in front of Angie's work place. She hadn't been at home. This seemed like the next logical spot to search.

Securing Viktor within his dungeon had taken longer than he had expected. The vampire's strength was much improved on fresh human blood and Eoin had lost precious time. He needed to warn Angie about Cedric and could only hope he wasn't too late.

Beth popped onto her feet as he stormed through the shop's front door. The sharp smell of brimstone struck his nose. Dammit, he was too late. "Where are they?" he demanded of the meek female.

She clutched her hands to her chest and wouldn't make eye contact.

"Beth, she's in danger." He did not want to scare the little werewolf but for Angie's safety he would put the pup over his lap and spank an answer out of her.

She pointed to room three.

He clenched his teeth and burst into the room without knocking.

A naked male dragon lay under Angie's attention. Her nails scratched along his bare flesh in his human form. But it was not Cedric.

Bitter bile filled Eoin's throat.

She startled at his loud entrance. "Eoin?" Her lips thinned. "I'm with a customer."

"Not anymore." Before the other dragon could react, Eoin pulled him off the table by his throat and slammed him against the wall.

The drywall cracked and dust poofed over their heads. Wait, this one was blond. "Who the fuck are you? And what are you doing in my territory without permission?" How many male dragons looking for love in all the wrong places were in his city?

Angie made a strangled noise. "I am not paying for that repair."

"You must be Eoin the Charismatic." The strange dragon's words came out strained through his constricted throat.

Eoin clenched his teeth so hard his joints popped. He shook the other dragon and felt slightly better.

"His name is Zechariah the Impaler." Angie still stood on the other side of the table with her arms crossed over her chest, giving him a daggered glare. "Are you done being an asshole, Eoin?"

"I'm trying to keep you safe, woman." He set Zechariah on the floor but kept his forearm across the other dragon's throat, ready to crush it at a moment's notice.

"By scaring off my customers?"

"He's not here for you to scratch his back. He's here for *you*." He returned his attention to the smaller dragon. "Answer my questions or I'm going to disembowel you."

"I couldn't inform you of my presence in your territory because I don't know where you live. It's not like you're listed anywhere."

"Cedric didn't have any trouble finding me." Dropping the older dragon's name might put the fear of the gods into this young dragon enough for him to leave.

Zechariah stiffened. At least he wasn't a complete dumbass. "Cedric is interested in her as well?" The dragon was obviously young, to have the balls to trespass into New Port unannounced. He wasn't worthy of Angie. None of them were.

"Let me make this clear, and feel free to spread the word, but Angie is mine. I'll cut off your wings and leave you earthbound if you ever lay hands on her again."

The dragon cleared his throat. "Technically, she had her hands on me."

Eoin punched a hole in the wall next to his head. "Am I clear?"

"Crystal."

Angie cleared her throat. "I don't remember being asked to be yours."

He released Zechariah and tossed his clothes at him. "Go home." He turned his attention back to his prickly potential mate. The whole purpose of courtship was to attract receptive and compatible mates.

132

Yesterday's kiss had proven to be both and it was too late for her escape.

Zechariah sauntered towards the exit carrying his clothes. He made sure that Angie's eyes were on him before winking. "Catch you later."

Eoin slammed the door on Zechariah then marched to Angie. "No, I didn't ask."

"I don't get a say in this?"

He pulled her into his arms and let his mouth drift along hers. "You can say it now."

She tore her lips away from his.

Chuckling, he trailed kisses over her graceful neckline and inhaled her intoxicating scent. The blood in his veins grew thicker and his heart pounded faster. With a whispered touch, he circled her hard nipple.

She hissed. Not a silly little human hiss, but something a true viperous bitch could make.

"Oh baby, I have all day to wait for your answer. Do you?" He forced his thigh between her legs and rubbed. If she held out much longer, he'd be tearing off his clothes and not so she could scratch his back. He had more demanding itches she could satisfy.

The stiffness in her back softened as she arched against him. "Zechariah was only a client."

It was his turn to hiss. "Don't say his name. He's not worth your attention."

She snaked her hand around his neck and upper back, claws still extended, and dug into his skin. "Kiss me."

Fuck, yes. He bent her backward over the table, stroking his tongue against hers, dominating and demanding. He mimicked with his tongue what he wanted to do to her body with his aching cock, his erection painfully pressed against her hip.

Wrapping her legs around his waist, Angie pulled him against her and rolled her hips. She sucked on his bottom lip, giving him a delightful taste of what she could do with her talented mouth. He could just picture her plump lips wrapped around his—

She bit down hard.

He jerked away, slapping his hand over his bleeding bottom lip. "What the fuck?"

She set her heel against his hard cock. "I'm a person, not a thing. No one can or ever will own me."

Gently, he removed her heel, as if it were a grenade, from his precious, aching package. There was his hellcat. He'd feared she might have suffered damage yesterday when she couldn't connect with her dragon. Not his Angie; she came back biting. A hatchling like Zechariah didn't have the strength to handle a she-dragon like her.

He gave his Angie a crooked smile and leaned over her, pressing her onto the table. "Fine, I belong to you then. Either way, I'm collecting on your rain check and I'll be at your place by six. We could meet on the sidewalk or at your apartment." He wiggled his eyebrows up and down.

She threw back her head and laughed. "You're relentless. On the sidewalk." She hadn't a clue the length he'd be willing to go to keep her in his life.

CHAPTER TWENTY ONE

Angie sat at Beth's desk once more and watched as the omega locked the door behind Eoin. She spun around to face Angie with her back pressed against the door. "You need a dress."

Angie's eyebrows shot up. "For what?"

"Your date with Eoin. All he's seen you in is work clothes. It's time to knock the dragon on his tail."

"I own a dress." Shifter hearing being so acute, Beth had heard their private exchange in room one earlier today.

"I've seen the one you own. Five times." Beth held out her five fingers and grimaced.

"You count?" Angie pressed her hands over her mouth, but the laugh still escaped. When it came to numbers nothing got past Beth.

"It's in my nature. Not the werewolf part, but my fashionista genes cry every time I see you in that yellow frock. If he tears that dress off your body, it would be out of mercy for the rest of us."

"Wow, that's brutal." Nothing Beth said was taken to heart though. Angie knew exactly what she thought of her wardrobe. It was a subject of contention between them, but Beth came from a wealthy family who paid her credit card bills. The omega still tried to bribe her into burning all her flip-flops.

"The accounts are almost done. I can finish things between clients tomorrow." She joined Angie behind the desk and pulled her purse out of the drawer. "My treat."

Angie shook her head. "I don't need your charity. I'm doing well enough to buy my own clothes." If she didn't eat this week.

Beth looked at her long and hard. "Honey, I heard and smelled everything that went on between you and Eoin this morning. He is determined to mate you. I'm not going to let some dress wreck tonight."

"Eoin won't care about what I'm wearing." No, he was more interested in undressing her.

Beth giggled. "But you want to make him sweat before he unwraps the present." She pulled Angie out of her chair and propelled her toward the exit. "Let's shop 'til we drop."

Excitement gave Angie a bounce in her step. She wanted to make Eoin breathless, and beg her to never stop. If it meant a new dress, she could suffer through an afternoon of shopping.

"Oh, and a pair of new shoes." Beth gave her a knowing smile. Angie hated to shop for shoes. Flip-flops were her things. Beth pointed south. "There's a nice boutique a couple blocks down from here that I've been wanting to check out. The dresses in the window are to die for."

Shoes *and* a dress? Maybe she could be late on her rent. It wasn't like there was a line of people waiting to lease her apartment or anything. Angie linked her arm with Beth's. This could be fun if she'd let herself enjoy the moment.

An armload of dresses later, Angie stood in front of the mirror for the hundredth time. Beth was much pickier than she when it came to clothes. The black cocktail dress she modeled was simple yet somehow made her feel like a vixen. The hem fell mid-thigh and didn't expose any of her cleavage, but the silky material flowed over her curves like liquid. It hinted at what was underneath the fabric without revealing much.

Beth whistled low and long. "This is the outfit. If things don't work out with Eoin then I'm going to date you. Those shoes cry out *fuck me all night long*."

"Beth." The omega didn't use that kind of language. Maybe some of Angie was rubbing off on her. She laughed at Beth's blush. Angie hadn't looked at either price tag yet. She wouldn't let Beth pay for them and she really couldn't afford to spend more money. But Beth was right about the outfit. This was a date with a dragon of her heart. She turned and looked over her shoulder at her reflection. Eoin seemed obsessed with her ass, the way he kept slapping it. In this dress, he wouldn't be capable of keeping his hands off her. She sighed. This was why credit cards were invented.

Beth looked at her cell phone and gasped. "We're going to be late." She opened up her purse and pulled out a small makeup bag. With a few swipes of a comb, Beth cleaned up Angie's short hair and applied some mascara and lipstick. She waved at the clerk. "She's going to wear the dress and shoes out. Ring her up."

Not His Dragon

Angie slowly made her way to the exit after paying, trying to forget the dollar amount.

"You look like you're walking on a tight rope." Beth shook her head. At this rate Angie would reach her apartment tomorrow morning.

She grimaced. "I don't have much practice in heels." The stilettos felt like stilts.

"It's all in the knees and the hips. You have to pretend that they're shock absorbers. Focus your weight on your toes, hold your head up high, look straight ahead and take long smooth strides."

Thankfully, Beth's car wasn't too far. Angie made it by following her advice. She was still wobbly at her ankles but at least she didn't have to hold out her arms for balance anymore. She got in the car and breathed a sigh of relief. She could imagine spraining her ankle tonight if she wasn't careful.

Beth drove to Angie's apartment. Her friend gave a chagrined smile. "Just try to stay seated as much as possible." Beth pulled up behind a limousine parked in front of Angie's building. "Looks like Eoin isn't going to be pulling any of his punches." She winked at Angie with a knowing smile. "Leave your clothes in the car. I'll bring them to work tomorrow."

Angie could only nod. Her palms were sweating. She'd never been in a limousine before. From the state of his castle and his clothing, she just assumed Eoin struggled financially like she did. Then again, there were all those cars in his garage. Maybe he just wasn't as materialistic as humans. On wobbly feet, she stepped out of the car and slowly made her way to the limousine.

Beth honked before she took off.

The sudden loud noise startled Angie and almost made her fall flat on her ass. She gave Beth the bird and could almost hear her laugh.

A chauffeur jumped out of the driver's side door and opened the back door. She peered inside and met a stranger's curious gaze. Backing away, she blushed. "Sorry, I thought you were someone else." That had been pretty presumptuous of her and Beth to assume the limo belonged to Eoin. Awkward.

The stranger followed her out of the limousine, looming over her. Thick, dark hair and piercing black eyes were all she could focus on. Power and age oozed off him. Time slowed as he circled her with deliberate steps as if assessing her from head to toe. "Very nice." He traced his fingertips along her neck and over her shoulder.

She shrugged him off. Her pepper spray was in her jeans pocket on the backseat of Beth's car. The fine hairs on her nape and arms rose as she edged toward her apartment building. She didn't need shifter abilities to know this predator wasn't human. His movements were too smooth, his grace unnatural. She took a quick step toward the door.

He blocked her way. "I am Cedric of the Alaskan Pacific Rim clan." He bowed and kissed her hand just as Zechariah had.

She blinked rapidly. Another fucking dragon? Was there a convention in town because this seemed out of the realm of normal?

"Do you have a title?" From her limited experience, dragons enjoyed titles and she hoped his was long. So long that it would give Eoin time to arrive. Cedric gave her the impression that *no* wasn't in his vocabulary.

He drew closer as he rose. "I think modern shifters like to use the term alpha."

Yes, shifters did like to use that term, but Angie hated it. "What do you want?" She backed away but he snaked his hand around her waist and kept her almost pressed to his chest.

Lowering his face near her hair, he inhaled slowly. "Yes, there it is. Unmated female."

Her heart stopped. Was that why these dragons were showing up on her doorstep today? "I'm not in the market for a mate."

"How cute. You think you have a choice." His hand ran along her waist and lingered there for a moment before he retreated, giving her space. "I came to see if you were worth the effort of courting."

"I'm already seeing Eoin. I'm not much for dating different men at the same time."

"That's nice. Courting has nothing to do with dating. It's a drive bred into our cells much like breathing. Dragon instinct will end up choosing your mate, not your heart. And I like a challenge." He strolled to the limousine and gestured for her to enter.

Something inside her stirred. This instinct wanted her to follow. She shook her head and retreated until her back hit the gritty brick of the building.

He raised his eyebrow and tilted his head as if reassessing her. "We can do this the easy way, Angie, or the hard way."

"I'm a big fan of the hard way." If she got in that limousine, she suspected she'd never see her home or friends again.

"So am I." He gave her another small smile before sliding inside the vehicle and closing the door. The limo sped off, leaving her breathless and alone on the sidewalk. She wasn't sure how long she'd been frozen there, when a silver sports car parked in front of her.

Eoin jumped out of his car and hurried to Angie. "I saw Cedric's limousine. Did he hurt you?" He ran his hands over her arms, concern clearly in his voice. "You look so pale. Do you need to sit down?"

She shook her head and met his concerned look. "Do you know who that was?"

"Yes, Cedric was the reason why I showed up at your shop this morning. I got so caught up with Zechariah that I forgot to mention that Cedric was in the city as well."

She rubbed her aching stomach. "They're both here for me." She felt numb inside. Almost as if in shock.

Eoin hung his head. "Yeah, and more will arrive as news of your presence spreads. An unmated she-dragon can cause quite an uproar among our kind."

"But it's your territory. They're not supposed to trespass."

"I wish that were true but during the courting process all bets are off, unless I fight every single male who comes to the city." He gathered her in his arms and cradled her head against his chest. "Dragons like Zechariah are not much of a concern but Cedric is more than capable of killing me."

"He made it sound like I didn't have a choice when it came to courtship."

He rubbed her back and muttered something in an unknown language. "There are a lot of stages to a courtship but the most important is the mating dance. That's when our base animal instincts take over. What makes us sentient has very little control at that point. That's why most of us choose to do the majority of the courtship in human form and create a relationship first before the mating dance begins. Cedric is old enough and strong enough that he could probably skip all that and just go straight to the dance."

"Why?"

"Because females always gravitate to the strongest and most fertile of males for the future generation." With his thumb, he lifted her chin so their gazes could meet. "Do you want to cancel our date tonight?"

She straightened her spine. "No, I'm not letting him wreck our first date." Inside, all she wanted to do was to crawl into bed with a bag of cookies and pretend this never happened, but she doubted the bolts on her door would keep out a dragon like Cedric. She never let fear rule her life, and she wasn't going to start now. She allowed Eoin to escort her to his car and assist her into the passenger seat. She finally noted the earth-toned formfitting suit that he wore and his upbeat purple tie and running shoes. The combo should have been a fashion disaster but Eoin pulled it off beautifully. She ran her hand over his thigh and cupped his ass. "You look nice tonight."

The dragon's gaze darted to her and he blushed.

He helped her with the seatbelt and brushed the back of his fingers over her nipple. It hardened at the slight touch as if seeking more. His gaze traveled to the little nub protruding through the thin material of her dress "God, I can't wait to have you, Angie."

She laughed long and hard. "You're that confident?"

He rose to stand outside the car and gave her a smug grin. "Not after your bite this afternoon." She knew he'd done that on purpose just to make her laugh and the effort was much appreciated. Cedric had really shaken her. Eoin closed the door and jumped into the driver seat. He took her out of the city to a quaint little restaurant along the river. Before he exited the car, she placed her hand over his. "Don't they understand that I can't shift?"

"If they looked at your aura like I did, then they'd know it's only a matter of time before you do. All you need is a little help to figure out how to break this magical shield."

CHAPTER TWENTY TWO

The hostess settled Eoin and Angie at a secluded table in the darkest corner of the room. Eoin pulled his chair from the other side of the table and sat next to her, sitting so their sides brushed against one another as he rested his arm on the back of her chair.

His luxurious heat enveloped her. Angie could only hope that her phobia of eating food possibly cooked by a male was gone. This would be a test. If she failed? She gave Eoin the side-eye. She'd make sure not to puke on his suit. God, it was as sexy as lingerie.

Eoin took both menus from the maître d' and set them on the table. "I want to speak with your head chef."

To the hostess' credit, she didn't even raise an eyebrow at the request. She just nodded and went to the back of the restaurant.

Angie, on the other hand, did raise her eyebrow. "What's that all about? Most customers wait to eat before they complain." Eoin was full of surprises. Life with him would never be boring.

"You'll see." Trailing his fingertips in small circles over her bare shoulder, he gave her a lazy smile. The heat of desire sparked in her lower abdomen. Dinner had better be short. She wanted to do naughty things with this dragon.

A tall woman in a white jacket approached the table. "Monsieur le Dragon, how nice to see you again." The way her gaze narrowed as it landed on Angie gave her the impression that she was not as welcome.

"Angie, I'd like to introduce Margaret. She is the head chef, the only chef, of the restaurant. She will handle all your food. Isn't that right, Margaret?"

"*Bien oui*, Mademoiselle. I own and run this restaurant, but I do have two sous chefs helping me."

"Who are both female?" Eoin asked

The chef looked puzzled. "Oui."

"Angie was skeptical of a completely female run restaurant."

Heat flooded her cheeks, right to the tips of her ears. What was he saying? The cook would poison her now.

"May I take your order while I'm at the table?"

"We'll take the house specials with a bottle of your finest red wine." Eoin handed her the menus.

"Very good." The chef nodded to Angie and left her table.

She poked Eoin in the ribs with her sharp nail. "You made her think I'm some kind of chauvinistic woman." She playfully gave him a pinch. How did he know about her phobia? She'd never voiced it to anyone, not even Beth. How could he possibly know?

"Don't look so concerned." He gave her a small kiss on the tip of her nose. "I've never known of any unmated female capable of eating food cooked by a male."

"I ate the meal you cooked."

His gaze grew heated and possessive, his eyes changed to slitted dragon pupils. "Trust me, I know."

"What does that mean?" She leaned forward, closing the gap between them.

He ran the back of his fingers over her cheek. "It means instinctually you trust me, and I would never take that for granted. Any potential mate cherishes the moment that his female of choice eats the meal he provides. It's part of the courting process."

She smoothed his unwrinkled jacket, looking for any excuse to touch him. So firm… "So you're courting me now officially?" She smirked as his eyes went wide.

"I guess I am." Eoin scratched his chin in thought. "Looking back, I guess I have been since the day we first met. It's a very instinctual process for dragons. Just like the way that you are responding to me."

"I would like to think I had some choice in the matter."

"Of course, you have a choice. You could have refused my scale care or rejected my food. Or you could have chosen to get into Cedric's limousine." He kept her face within his hands and pressed his lips against hers in a light, chaste kiss.

Someone cleared their throat. "The appetizer." The waiter looked at them with a weary smile and set a small plate filled with roasted vegetables and assorted cheeses in front of them. He also filled the glasses with a dark red wine and left the bottle.

"You have a thing for getting me drunk."

He clinked the edges of their glasses. "To many more bottles to share."

Angie enjoyed every morsel of their meal and she wasn't plagued by any nausea. Setting her fork by her empty plate, she pushed away from the table and rubbed her full stomach. "This is the first time since I was a child that I've been able to eat in a restaurant." Not to mention the best meal she'd ever had. This blew her casserole surprise out of the water.

Eoin leaned on his elbows. "I can't express the visceral pleasure I get feeding you."

"What about cooking for other female dragons?"

"I've never had the urge to feed another she-dragon." He gave her a shy smile. "You're my first."

"But you didn't know I was dragon."

"No, I didn't, not consciously. Instinctual drives are almost impossible to ignore. It seems the drive to court you snuck up on me subconsciously." From the moment she'd met him, he'd been nothing but a huge flirt—all slapping her ass while opening the door for her and cooking for her half-naked. He stretched, leaning in close enough that his breath brushed her over-sensitive skin. "Let me settle the bill, and I'll take you home."

"By home, you mean yours?" She raised an eyebrow at him in a challenge.

He rose from his seat, straightened his suit, and gave her a knowing smile.

Eoin assisted Angie out of his car. He had parked in front of the castle's entrance where he had left the light burning. He ran his hand over the vehicle's hood. This was the car he found most suited Angie's needs. "I have a gift for you." He handed her the car keys.

She blinked at the dangling keychain. "Are you out of your mind? I don't need a car." She crossed her arms.

He frowned. From the movies he'd watched, it seemed women reacted differently when given a car. Eoin had expected at least a smile. "Everyone needs a car nowadays. It would make it easier to travel back and forth to the shop." And safer. He'd breathe easier if he knew she wasn't walking the streets by herself, especially in the evening. "It would make it easier for you to travel to my castle, as well, or to Beth's, or shopping. Anywhere you want to go, it's available." He pressed the keys into her hands.

She glared at the metallic object, then at the vehicle. She chewed her bottom lip before moving her daggered stare in his direction.

He was surprised to see tears.

"I can take care of myself. I don't need your charity." She whipped the keys at him. If he hadn't ducked with his supernatural speed, she would have left a dent in the middle of his forehead. When he straightened, Angie was already halfway to the road stomping wildly on her high-heels.

He ran after her, scooped her up in his arms before she broke an ankle. "I don't know what's going on inside your head. But the only reason I gave you this car is that I don't like you walking alone, especially in that part of the city. That's it. Nothing more." He had to hold on tight as she squirmed, swinging her elbows. Then again, maybe he should worry about any idiot who tried to attack her. He chuckled. She had taken care of him in short order the first time they met.

"If I wanted a car, I would have bought one."

He squeezed her against his chest, let her legs drop to the ground and kissed her hard.

She beat her fists against his shoulders until the hits turned into caresses and she responded with as much demand. Cradling his head, she pulled him closer, opening her mouth in invitation.

He hesitated, remembering her sharp teeth. Fuck it, living with Angie would always have an edge. It's what drew him to her. He slid his tongue against hers, savoring her spicy flavor. Her body fit his perfectly as he ran his hands along her waist until he cupped the ass he planned to worship all night.

She withdrew from his lips and pressed her hands to his cheeks. "I'm sorry. The car is a kind gesture. I'm just very sensitive about my finances and my independence."

"A car will give you even more independence. You wouldn't need anyone to drive you around." And she could come see him all the time. Every night, maybe.

She gave a small self-conscious laugh. "Sure I would. I don't know how to drive."

Not His Dragon

After a couple of centuries, things didn't surprise Eoin often, but he stared at Angie with his jaw open. He didn't know how to respond to that. He thought after the women's rights movement that they all learned how to drive. Obviously, he'd missed something. "I could show you how." Inside he cringed. He was never sure how Angie was going to react. It was part of her allure.

She bit her bottom lip and eyed the sports car. As if walking on a tight rope, she approached the vehicle and ran her hands over the smooth surface. "Are you sure?" With her eyes wide and still moist with unshed tears, she appeared so vulnerable.

He'd seen this side of her on the mountaintop. He suspected that she kept this part of herself well-guarded and he was one of the few people she allowed a glimpse. "Of giving you the car, yes. Of teaching you how to drive, definitely."

There was a longing in the way she touched the vehicle. "I'll have to think about it."

He strode towards her, arms extended. "Angie—"

She pressed her hand over his lips to silence him.

"I didn't say no, but you're rushing me. It's only our first date and you're giving me a car."

He kissed her palm. "I guess this isn't a normal gift." Maybe he should have discussed this with Viktor first. The vampire understood human dating customs better than he did.

"Would this be normal for a dragon you were courting?"

"A she-dragon would be capable of flying. She wouldn't have a use for a car. But diamonds, on the other hand…" He gave her a sly grin. "Would you like gems instead, Angie?"

She threw her head back and laughed, flinging her arms around his neck. "Sometimes, I forget you're not human until you say something like *would you like diamonds* so nonchalantly."

He took a deep breath, pulling her scent into his lungs, enjoying the fragrance. "And sometimes I forget you still think of yourself as human."

She sighed and relaxed into his arms. "I'm getting more accustomed to the idea every day, especially with strange dragons showing up on my doorstep."

A growl rumbled in Eoin's chest. He would have to take care of those assholes soon. If he didn't make an example of them then others would be on their way as word spread. He wished she hadn't brought them up. It would only put him in a foul mood.

She tugged at his hands, pulling him towards the castle. "You didn't bring me here to discuss dragon things and cars."

He scooped her up in his arms and carried her inside his home. One day he would like to call it their home. As they entered, a faint beeping noise was going off in a distant room. His timer. Shit. The heat flowing in his blood turned to ice. He'd forgotten to feed the fucking vampire.

He set Angie on her feet and pointed in the general direction of his bedroom. "Umm…can you wait a moment? I have to take care of something." What would he tell her? That he forgot to feed his vampire friend chained in his dungeon? "That alarm is to remind me to—to water my plants." He struggled to keep his face straight and not laugh at the ridiculous lie. He gave her quick peck on the cheek and a little push in the right direction, before he raced to the kitchen and pulled out a bag of blood from the fridge. God, he hoped Victor hadn't gnawed through his arms. It was gross and messy when he did that. Taking the steps two at a time, he hurried into the dungeon and was greeted by a vicious snarl.

The vampire sat in his cell, chains slack as he leaned against the wall. He wasn't as far gone as Eoin had feared, thank goodness. He lifted his head, eyes completely black with blood lust. "That alarm has been ringing forever." He lifted his nose and inhaled as if smelling a sweet bouquet. "You're with the girl."

Eoin tossed the blood bags he'd purchased from an employee at the local blood bank.

Victor caught them midair and crouched over his meal like an animal. He tossed Eoin a challenging glare. "Are you going to stand there and watch?"

Shaking his head, Eoin backed away. He wished he knew what triggered Victor into these blood frenzies, but the vampire never wanted to discuss it. He just wanted to be kept from killing. That was something Eoin could offer him.

He pulled off his coat as he climbed the stairs and tossed it on the closest chair. Entering his bedroom, he came to a halt. It was empty.

146

CHAPTER TWENTY THREE

He did a slow circle and backtracked to the entrance with no sign of Angie. He called out her name and it echoed within the mostly empty building.

A distant, "I'm here," answered back. It came from his workshop area where he worked on his terrible sculptures. Inside the room, where he had blasted the metal scrap, he found Angie strolling among the statues. At his entrance, she spun around with a huge grin on her face. "I got lost but I found this wonderful room. I didn't know you collected art." She ran her hands delicately over a mass of clawed gashes. The statue looked like a wounded animal.

His chest constricted. He'd never been shy about showing his work to anyone but now with Angie standing among his new medium, he felt stripped of all his defenses. He couldn't bear any criticism, especially from someone he cared about. He carried enough self-doubt that he didn't need to hear it from anyone else. "They're mine." The emptiness of the room allowed his whisper to travel to her ears clearly.

She didn't seem to notice him standing on the precipice of self-loathing. "I didn't know you were an artist." Tiptoeing on her high-heeled shoes, she moved to the next statue with careful steps. She fingered something. "It's a Dodge Ram emblem. You're recycling material. That's eco-friendly."

It was? He had used scrap metal because it was easier to melt and more available in abundance within the city. There wasn't a mine close by where he could just pick up raw ore. "My preferred medium is paint but my agent and gallery manager have been pushing me towards this new endeavor. They say my sculptures invoke more visceral emotions."

"So you're a professional artist? You show and sell your work?"

"I have a tour making its way across Europe. It's not doing very well. In a couple days, I'll have a show in New Port that will debut this new series." He stuffed his hands in his pockets and shrugged. "If the gallery manager likes it."

"Are you finished?" She strode toward the window, the glass pane having been broken long ago. The night air breezed into the room. She fingered the old stone windowsill with the stars haloed around her shape. The more she leaned forward, the higher the edge of her dress rose on the back of her thighs, until it raised high enough to give him a small glimpse of the curve of her ass.

He licked his lips. The teasing flash imprisoned his attention. His cock throbbed in time with his heartbeat as if he'd never seen a naked woman before. The anticipation was killing him. The heat in his groin spread higher and reached his chest. He moved to an Angie-sized lump of raw scrap metal and blew a thin stream of flame over the middle until it was pliable.

His fire was back. He was back.

Viktor had suggested Angie as a muse and he was right.

If Cedric stole Angie, he would pound on her personality like Eoin did on his sculptures until nothing remained of what made Angie special. The ancient dragon wouldn't relent until he'd molded her into his own vision. Eoin couldn't allow this to happen, no matter the consequences.

As if sensing she was the center of his thoughts, she glanced at him over her shoulder. Her stare moved to his hands, where he had caressed the soft metal to match her shape. She twisted to face him and slid one of her spaghetti straps off her shoulder. "Do you need inspiration?"

Oh yeah, baby. He needed her like a pulse. His heart would stop without her. She stoked his flame. The soft metal slid under his heated palms like silk as he shaped in the form of the person he desired like no one else.

She slid off the other strap.

His hands refused to move as he waited, heart in his throat. Through the thin fabric, he could see the pearls of her hard nipples. Her breasts were the perfect size not to wear a bra, which he whole heartedly appreciated, yet big enough to bounce a little when she walked in those heels.

Turning her back on him, she returned to the window. Was she waiting for him to tear the dress off her body?

The liquid-like material pooled at her feet and she leaned forward to gaze out the window once more.

Not His Dragon

All the air left Eoin's lungs. If Cedric burst in the room right now, Eoin would be flameless. The way Angie's waist curved out to a perfect heart-shaped ass with two delicious dimples at her lower back. It was art made in flesh. As if having a mind of their own, his hands moved over the cooling metal until this moment was captured forever. No matter what the future held, he'd always have this statue.

The edges of his shirt smoked from being singed by the hot metal. He tore it off his back.

Angie spun around at the sudden ripping noise, eyes wide and innocent.

He wiped his hands on his shirt and strode toward her with nothing innocent on his mind.

Angie froze. The dragon stalked toward her, bare shoulders rolling as he moved. Every muscle in his body defined him as a predator and she was his prey. The hunger in his heavy, lidded glare sent her heart racing. He looked like he wanted to devour her whole.

"Turn back around," he snapped before he reached her.

She did as he ordered without a second thought. This was one of those moments where she recalled that Eoin wasn't human. The heat of his body enveloped her as his hard chest pressed against her back. A pleasant rumble rolled within his chest and vibrated along her nerves as their skin touched for the first time.

He ran his nose along her neck and inhaled deeply. Snaking his hand around her body, he fondled her right breast, pinching her nipple into a hard, aching peak. "How do you want me to do this?"

She leaned her head against his chest and closed her eyes. "Oh God, what are my choices?"

"I can pretend I'm human and do my best to make love to you." He bent close to her ear, his breath hot. "Or I can be myself and fuck you like a dragon." His whispered words sent a flood of desire through her veins.

"You've never bothered to pretend to be human with me before."

"I don't want to scare you." Now, he fondled both breasts. "Decide fast." He pressed his hard cock against her lower back.

"I'm not scared of you." She'd be lying if she claimed to feel no trepidation, but she never wanted Eoin to be something he wasn't. When she agreed to this date, it was to a dragon. "I want you, Eoin."

He fell to his knees behind her and cupped her ass in both hands, pushing her stomach against the stone windowsill. "Thank fuck." Then he nipped her ass.

She squeaked at the sharp yet playful bite.

"I've been dreaming of doing that since the day we met." He kissed the spot and proceeded to leave a trail of them to the dimples on her lower back where he slowly traced each one with his tongue.

She shivered and arched into his strong hands. The cool breeze against her aching nipples contrasted with the heat on her ass, leaving her body confused and wanton.

"Spread your legs."

She complied, clinging to the windowsill. Her balance in the heels was precarious at best.

He wrapped her thong around his hand and with a sharp jerk, tore it off her hips. The slick touch of his tongue slid between her folds.

She gasped at the trail of wet heat he left behind.

He moaned, then pressed his mouth greedily to her tender female parts. Sucking, tasting, thrusting…

She dug her nails into the stone, her body bent forward out the window. Thank God, he didn't have neighbors. They'd get an eyeful. She rocked her hips with need. "Eoin." She moaned his name as he latched onto her clitoris and sucked the sensitive bud. Her knees wobbled and she couldn't catch her breath.

Oh God.

Eoin held her thighs apart, keeping her from moving away from the intense pleasure. He was relentless. Without mercy.

She gasped for air and cried out as an orgasm exploded along her senses, leaving her blind to anything but Eoin's mouth. Nonsensical noises tumbled from her lips as she rocked her hips, helpless to sensations Eoin created within her body.

He released his hold on her.

The sudden vacancy between her legs left her breathless.

He spun her around, his eyes slitted in dragon form, and he let out a throaty growl. With one hand, he unzipped his pants and with the other he lifted her so she could wrap her legs around his hips until his cock pressed at her entrance. Pushing her to the wall, he thrust deep inside her with one ruthless stroke.

The burn of stretching had her crying out. Pleasure bordering on heavenly ecstasy made her shiver. She clung to his shoulders, digging her nails into his back.

"Harder, Angie." His voice sounded inhuman and deep with desire.

She scratched into his flesh, meeting his demanding strokes with her own. "Fuck me." She bit his ear lobe.

His roar echoed out into the forest and he pounded into her as if out of control. Each stroke was accompanied by his grunt. "You're so tight." Perspiration slicked their flesh.

Angie licked a bead that trickled along Eoin's corded neck.

He hissed and changed the angle of her hips so she could feel his cock run along her clit as he moved inside of her.

"Oh, oh, oh…" She flung her head back as the second orgasm grabbed hold of her body. She sensed the heat of Eoin's climax inside her.

He buried his face in her neck and bit her. Not a soft nip like on her ass, but a possessive bite as if marking her forever.

CHAPTER TWENTY FOUR

Somebody had a death wish. They were pounding on Eoin's front door. The sound echoed through his castle and ricocheted against his skull. If it was another group of damn tourists, he was going to flambé them. Damn the bad press. He rolled out of bed and flinched as his feet hit the cold stone. Angie was right; a few throw rugs would be nice. He glanced at her sleeping in his bed. It would give him a reason to skin Ryota.

She moaned and buried herself deeper into the bed, pulling the blankets over her head. "I'm going to find something sharp to poke whoever's knocking." That was the most romantic thing he'd ever heard a woman say.

He completely agreed with her sentiment and kissed her bare shoulder. "I've got something I want to poke you with."

She snorted and whacked him in the head with a pillow.

"Stay here. I'll be right back. I've got someone to maim first." He whistled as he took the long, curving staircase to the foyer. With a little elbow grease, he could polish the black and white tiles of the room to their former glory. Or hire someone else to do it. He wanted Angie to desire his home as much as him.

The knocking was joined with a shout. The voice sounded familiar but he couldn't imagine who had the courage to visit uninvited. Eoin rubbed his naked stomach and blinked the sleep out of his eyes as he made his way across the foyer. The tile wasn't any warmer than the stone. He released both locks and swung the door opened.

"Whoa." Zechariah covered his eyes with his hands. "I don't need to be greeted like that. Put some clothes on, dude."

Eoin glanced down at himself. Good thing it wasn't a bunch of tourists. "What are you doing here? Didn't I make myself clear yesterday?"

"You told me I had to declare my presence in your territory." Zechariah held out his arms and twirled. "I'm here." He took off his jacket and tossed it at Eoin. "Wrap that around your waist before you poke out someone's eye."

Not His Dragon

Zechariah made as if to push into the castle.

Eoin blocked his way with an arm to the doorframe. "Where do you think you're going?" He was beginning to think this dragon had been born out of a soft shell.

The young dragon bounced off his arm and stumbled back. "I thought we'd have breakfast together." He scratched his head as if confused. "You're not very social, are you?" Zechariah crossed his arms, leaning his weight on his back foot.

"No shit." Eoin was beginning to remember why he'd stopped living among his kind.

"You know you don't need to be such a dick." Zechariah's gaze darted over Eoin's shoulder and his eyes went wide.

"Zech?" Angie asked.

Eoin shut his eyes and rubbed the bridge of his nose.

In Eoin's moment of distraction, Zechariah squeezed past him and entered the castle. "You lucky jackass, she chose you."

Eoin followed him inside. Where he found Angie dressed only in the bed sheet with her bare shoulders exposed. Sunlight streamed through the window behind her, leaving very little of her body's contours to the imagination.

Zechariah bent over her hand and kissed the inside of her wrist. He took his time to sniff her skin. "But you're still not mated?" He gave Eoin a searching look as if sizing him for a fight.

"We just met." She sounded almost scandalized. Withdrawing her hand, Angie approached Eoin and fingered the jacket around his waist. "Nice look," she whispered.

Zechariah's gaze followed Angie's body and rolled over every delicious inch. He licked his top lip and took a step in her direction.

Gritting his teeth, Eoin grabbed the annoying dragon by his arm and dragged him out the front door.

Zechariah dug his heels into the worn tiles and struggled against Eoin's superior strength. "If she's in your bed then why haven't you bonded?" The younger dragon's eyes changed form and widened as his gaze fell upon Angie once more. He elbowed Eoin under the chin and broke loose. "What is that around her aura?" He sounded in awe.

Without a second thought Eoin punched Zechariah, knocking the younger dragon to the floor. He stepped on his throat, pinning him to the ground. "Do I need to explain what will happen to you if this gets out?" More male dragons would show up in his city if they realized the truth. The more of them who thought Angie was human, the better.

Wrapping his hands around Eoin's ankles, Zechariah made strangling noises yet managed to shake his head slightly.

Eoin pressed harder. "Are you sure? I don't mind going into detail." Maybe he should make an example of the pest.

"Eoin." Angie pushed against his hips. "Stop it."

He waited another second before releasing his hold. Killing Zechariah would only draw more attention to his territory and in turn, Angie.

The stupid dragon coughed and crawled onto his knees. "What is that around her aura?" His question came out hoarse.

Eoin paced around the other dragon, letting him catch his breath. "I don't know." It was the truth. "And you should forget about it and Angie."

Zechariah bowed his head in submission under Eoin's glare. "I'm just curious."

Eoin narrowed his gaze. He didn't trust the younger dragon any further than he could—well, he could toss Zechariah pretty far if he wanted. Maybe he had the resources to help Eoin figure out this problem? He wasn't above demanding information. "It's some kind of curse that prevents her from shifting."

Zechariah sat up with a surprised grunt. "Is that right, Angie?"

She stood glaring at them with her arms folded. Not a good sign. "Oh, I'm in the room now? For a moment, I thought I'd gone invisible. Yes, Zech, I can't fucking shift."

Eoin kept forgetting how sensitive this was for her. All the brownie points he'd scored last night were going to vanish fast if he kept choking on his foot.

Zechariah continued to stare at her with his dragon eyes. "She's definitely dragon and from her colors I'd say she's from one of the older clans."

Eoin blinked and resisted the urge to shift his eyes to dragon. "You can tell the difference?"

"Sure, I've been studying auras most my life." Zechariah rose to his feet. It hadn't occurred to Eoin to analyze her colors.

She scowled at both of them.

He still had the manila envelope to share with her once they were alone. This might turn into another pepper spray kind of day.

"So maybe you can help me—" Eoin cleared his throat. "Help her. Until we break the spell, we can't mate." He grabbed Zechariah by the throat and pulled him close enough to smell the coffee on the younger dragon's breath. Their gazes locked. "And I will mate her, so stop sniffing around. She's made her choice. She's eaten my food and slept in my bed. So get the fucking idea of stealing her out of your head." He pressed the younger dragon toward the exit. "Let me know if you have any ideas. And, Zech, if any of this gets out I know who to hurt. Your clan doesn't scare me." He slammed the door shut on Zechariah's face.

"After everything we've shared, I'm still not good enough to mate?"

The question stabbed Eoin like a blade between the shoulders. Angie did not know how to hold back her punches.

He spun around. "What? No! That's not what I meant."

"Funny, because that's what I'm hearing. Is my supposedly pure blood not good enough for you?" She turned away, her head hung low and her arms wrapped around her in a hug. He hated seeing her spine bent in defeat.

"How many times do I have to tell you?" He slid his hand under her chin and lifted her face. Her clear glare challenged his, even when hurt. She was the strongest person he'd ever met. "Sorry." He had never apologized to one single person so many times in his life. Maybe one day he would learn to stop screwing up around her.

She sighed and her gaze softened. "I'm sorry too."

He grinned. "All right." Entwining his arms around her, he tried to pull her closer.

She knocked his hold loose with her forearms. "Back off." Her bared teeth bit off her words.

He raised his hands in the air. "We're cool." And he circled away from her, giving her space.

"Not in the slightest. You got what you wanted from me last night."

Eoin wouldn't make any kind of commitment to her unless she could shift. He'd said it right to her face. She'd known he was too good to be true and she fell for him anyway. If she was ever going to find somebody to share her life with, she would need to get away from the shifter community. That meant closing up shop and cutting all ties. The only humans she knew were her neighbors. That said a lot about her.

"You didn't even get a glimpse of my appetite last night." He yanked the blanket off her body and dropped Zechariah's jacket. His skin seemed like silk as his hard muscles slid underneath. He stormed towards her, his grace fluid, his gaze dark. He countered her retreat. Caught within his intense stare, she witnessed his eyes change from human to dragon. The slit pupils dilated as if taking in every detail of her body. Something inside her didn't want her to run. She should stand her ground and claim Eoin as hers. But she didn't know how or where these urges came from. He circled her slowly, as if waiting for her to make the next move, but she wasn't familiar with his needs.

"Eoin?"

He flinched and shook his head. When he lifted his head, his eyes had returned to human form.

She retrieved the sheet from the floor and rewrapped it around herself. Whatever trance he'd been under was gone. "What was that?"

He stood dazed, rubbing his head and taking in their surroundings. "Wow, I never expected it to be that intense." Without another word, he left the room, turning in the direction of his bedroom. Suddenly, the castle seemed too big for Angie and too empty.

She swallowed the lump in her throat and followed Eoin to the bedroom. Sitting on the edge of the bed, she watched him dress. Was this when he would give her the breakup speech?

Eoin tugged on his jeans and shirt with sharp jerking motions. "I think I was initiating the fucking mating dance." He fastened his jeans, crossed his arms, and loomed over her. "I can't believe you inspired the urge so soon."

"Why, because I'm still considered human?" The edge of her voice was sharp enough to cut.

Not His Dragon

He grabbed her by the shoulders and pulled up so their noses almost touched. "No, Goddamn it. I would've mated you right there in the foyer. You are mine forever. Don't think just because you can't shift I'm ever going to let you go."

"Then why don't you mate me?" She hated the way her voice quivered. *Stupid girl, get a grip and ignore his fancy words.* They were just intangible things to keep her from running. If she really meant something to him, he would have finished.

"Because you didn't continue the dance. The mating between two dragons is magical, Angie. It's a spell that's created instinctually between a mated pair. Don't you get it? I'm not the one who stopped the binding. It was you. Without your dragon, you can't respond and complete our mating." His voice sounded so raw it made her eyes water. She'd hurt him.

Shrugging out of his grasp, she pulled him down next to her on the bed. She cradled his head against her shoulder and rubbed the soft fuzz on his scalp. "That wasn't my intention. You know that, right?" God, she loved the feel of him against her.

He gathered her onto his lap and squeezed her tight against his chest. "I'm never going to let you go." If her heart swelled any more, it would burst. She'd only known Eoin for a week but already she knew she'd spend the rest of her life with him. "It felt like you dumped me, kicked me in the balls, and slept with my best friend all at the same time."

She gasped. "But none of that's true." She cradled his face within her hands and made him meet her stare. "If I knew what to do, I would've finished the mating dance with you. I need you to understand that."

He nodded and broke his gaze from hers. "But you have to understand my dragon nature feels rejected, even though I know that's not your intention."

"Then we need to fix my shifting problem."

"That means we're going to have to delve into your past. Are you prepared for what we might find?"

No, spoke her younger self inside her mind. Would the truth change the way she felt about her parents? Not in a million years. She knew they had loved her. Whatever she found out, that wouldn't change. If Eoin was going to be her future, she'd have to learn to let go of the past. "I'm ready."

He rose, setting her on her tiptoes. "There's a bathroom through that door where you can shower. Meet me in the kitchen. I'll cook breakfast. Then I have something to show you."

CHAPTER TWENTY–FIVE

The food on Angie's plate vanished quickly as she cleared a track through the scrambled eggs and bacon. Eoin purred in pleasure.

They sat in a small sitting room he hadn't used in…forever. He'd discovered an old wooden table with some chairs in the room and he had set them close to the fireplace.

Her gaze wandered to the bare walls and the crackling fire but never on him. The silence stretched and he waited for it to snap like an elastic band. Beads of water dripped from the tips of her wet hair, leaving a small puddle by her plate.

"I forgot about towels." He grimaced. "You have need for those kinds of things." It shouldn't take long for him to order a few online and have them delivered, but what else would she need?

With her fingertips, she shook out some of her short hair. "Don't worry about it. My hair dries fast."

"I know it's rustic here. I don't use this place like humans would. It's just shelter. With some guidance, I could make it better."

She chuckled and pushed her empty plate away. "The place definitely needs a woman's touch." Leaning back in her chair, she rubbed her stomach.

The motion trapped his gaze. She wouldn't understand how such a simple gesture would affect him. Feeding her meant feeding his future young. It was protecting possible progeny, survival of the fittest, and fucking, all rolled into one. The mating dance, the need to own her, to drive his cock into her—fought just under the surface, pushing under his skin, waiting to get out.

She wasn't ready. He could dance his heart out but she wouldn't know how to reciprocate. He took deep breaths and pushed the instincts from his forebrain.

He needed a distraction. His gaze darted to the manila envelope sitting on the mantle. It was the same one Viktor had hand-delivered two nights ago. He hadn't had the courage to open it yet. "I have something to confess." He stared at his clenched hands resting on the table. When he'd hired Viktor to delve into her past, he hadn't thought through the consequences. Now, he would have to admit trespassing into her past without her permission. "You have to promise not to get angry."

"Well, you know that won't happen. And Eoin, that's the worst way to start a conversation with me." She had a point, but experience made Eoin wary. If this woman had a chance to get angry, then she would. No matter how much forewarning he offered.

He pushed his chair back, rising to his feet, and made his way to the fireplace. Snatching the manila envelope off the mantle, he spun around and held it out to her straight-armed. "I hired a detective, of sorts."

Angie leaned against the table to face him and she crossed her legs. "To do what exactly?" She raised her eyebrow. Eoin recognized the expression enough to know that she was not amused.

"You have to understand, after we met, I had to know who you were. I mean, a human girl who smells like dragon doesn't cross my path—ever."

"What's in the envelope?" She wouldn't take it, as if almost afraid to touch the package.

"Your past." He drew closer to her, offering the envelope again. "I haven't opened it."

"Why not?

He shrugged. "You're not the only one apprehensive about opening Pandora's box. I'm not sure what we're going to find, but I'm pretty sure that whatever is inside, we're not going to be happy."

She crossed her arms and turned away from him. "How long have you had that thing?"

"Two nights." He stared at the envelope in his hands. When he first met Angie, his desire for this knowledge had been so strong, he'd been willing to pay anything. Now, he'd pay anything for it just to vanish. Some things were just better not being known. He moved closer to the fire and held the envelope over the flames. "If you ask, I'll drop it."

"No!" She shoved her chair back so hard it fell as she rose to her feet and snatched the envelope from his grasp. "Stop teasing." She crumpled the envelope within her fist, aiming a daggered glare at him as if she wished he were in the fire. "The answers that we need might be in here." She shoved the envelope under his nose. "Who else knows about this?"

"Besides the person I hired? No one."

She deflated then rushed him with a hug, pressing her face against his chest. "God Eoin, I don't know if I want to kiss you or strangle you."

He released a sigh of relief and rested his arms around her fragile shoulders. He kissed the top of her head. "Kisses only, please. My list of stranglers is too long."

"Will the person you hired talk?" Her voice was muffled against his chest.

"I've known him for a very long time. He can be trusted." There was no way Eoin was going to tell her about the vampire in his dungeon. They'd crossed enough bridges for one day and he was serious about the list of people who want to strangle him. He never wanted to add Angie to that list. Out of them all, she'd probably succeed.

Until this very moment, Angie had not believed everything Eoin had told her—being dragon, magic, this curse… Not until she held the envelope did she realize how heavy the truth weighed. If she had let him burn the envelope, she might as well accept being a throwback and walk away from him forever. She couldn't do that. She couldn't imagine spending the rest of her life without Eoin.

Opening the envelope and reading the contents meant she accepted that her parents had lied about her life. Until today, she had lived a lie. A knot formed between her breasts and made it hard to breathe. What if she opened the envelope and the information confirmed she wasn't a dragon? What if she really was a genetic fallback? She chuckled. That would be more probable. Fate always made her life harder. She wasn't the type of person who got breaks.

"I need you to know, no matter what you find in the envelope, you will never chase me away." Eoin rubbed his chin in the top of her head as he hugged her tighter. She knew he meant those words but it was based on what he believed in now.

"Mated or not?" He obviously wanted to mate with her but what if she couldn't respond and complete the ritual? Eoin deserved more.

"Mated or not."

She withdrew from his arms and sat back at the table, gesturing to the chair across from her. "We do this together."

He joined her, refilling both of their coffee cups.

Sliding her finger under the sealed lip, she tore the envelope open and pulled out a handful of documents. She separated and lined them up between her and Eoin—birth certificate, fingerprints, her arrest record, her adoption papers.

The tight knot in her chest dropped into her gut like a cannonball. The pain was so sharp and sudden that she couldn't make sense of the words on the paper work for a moment. She'd known this was possible. She'd known, but fuck, here it sat in front of her in reality. "I'm adopted." Saying it out loud didn't make it any more real. Why hadn't her parents ever said anything?

Eoin's fingers gripped her hands from across the table, anchoring her. His concerned gaze melted into sadness. "The supernatural community would never have let human parents adopt a shifter, let alone a dragon. We're just too different."

She pulled the papers from his grasp and reread them slowly. It never mentioned anything about her race, human or dragon or otherwise. "Maybe my parents thought I was human." This envelope didn't answer any questions. It just delivered more. "I don't know what to do with any of this."

Eoin shuffled the papers and shoved them back in the envelope. "Well, I do." He moved around the table and pulled her to her feet until she was cradled within his arms. His lips found hers and he kissed her gently. "This information only confirms my claim on you. Nobody else has any rights but me."

CHAPTER TWENTY SIX

The shop door closed behind Jessica Brown. She turned and waved at Angie before heading home. That was her last customer for today. Jessica was one of the rare panther shifters living in New Port. Angie loved running her sharp claws through the female's thick glossy fur. But there were no potential mates for the panther shifter in the city and she was talking about moving. That would be a shame.

Beth cleared her throat behind her and held out a piece of paper.

"What's this?" She plucked the note from her best friend's hand and read the list. "You have got to be kidding me. I just cleared that sink yesterday. I've changed more light bulbs in this last month than I have in my whole entire life. And Eoin is paying for the dent in the wall of room three." She paced across the waiting room, waving the slip of paper over her head. "The electrician said that we were up to code, that there are no electrical surges or malfunctioning sockets." She crossed her arms and faced Beth. "I'm beginning to think that those charms you bought from the witch are actually curses."

Beth lowered her gaze and folded her hands on top of her desk. "You could throw them away if you want," she whispered. "I can change the lights for you." The omega's posture deflated Angie's frustration.

Shuffling to Beth's side, Angie rested her arms over Beth's shoulders. "I'm not blaming you, sweetheart. I'm just frustrated by all this. I can't keep shelling out money for light bulbs and sockets and pipes. One day, I'd really like to move out of my craptastic apartment." Not to mention buying decent groceries.

Beth's expression brightened. "I can go without pay for a few weeks."

Angie dropped her head. "No. You deserve every penny you make." And probably more. "I don't think I have any bulbs left anyways. Can you add that to your shopping list for tomorrow? I'll deal with the sink now."

"Sure, Angie. The pack has a plumber. Maybe you can barter some scratching in exchange for his expertise."

It was an excellent idea, but Ryota had finally given Angie some space ever since she'd started seeing Eoin. If she kept relying on the pack resources, he might get the wrong idea and come knocking on her door again. "No, it's okay. Beth. I'll handle this myself." If her shop went bankrupt maybe she could start apprenticing as a plumber.

Angie grabbed her tools and went back to the same Goddamned sink and crawled underneath. Her gaze made contact with the same little charm Beth had planted in her shop. She plucked it from under the sink and sat staring at it. She'd moved this last time her sink was plugged. "Beth, can you come here?"

Beth poked her head around the doorframe. "Yes, boss?"

Angie winced. She hated it when Beth used that title. She held up the little stick figurine. "Did you put this back under the sink?"

The omega nodded her head. "I thought you said it was okay to keep the good luck charms."

Angie nodded. "But why under the sink?"

"Well, originally to keep it out of your view. I put it back there because I really didn't know how our customers would feel about witch charms within the shop. Some people are very sensitive."

Fingering the little sticks that formed a triangular shape held by string, Angie reconsidered her position on superstitions. "Do you think it's possible that this witch made a mistake with her charms? Is she reputable?"

"She's been the pack witch for as long as I could remember."

"Why does a pack need a witch?" No one from the pack had ever mentioned the witch to her before. There were times when Angie felt like she was drowning in pack politics and others, like now, that made her feel like an outsider.

"Sometimes there are messes that need to be cleaned up or hidden." Beth rubbed her arms as if cold. "They help keep the human police out of pack business. Could you imagine the reports that would pile up if the humans could hear some of the hunters fighting challenges within their homes?"

To be honest, Angie had never really considered it.

"I could take you to see her. You can bring the charm and she could re-examine it. I'd pay."

Not His Dragon

Angie ground her teeth. "You won't pay but I'd appreciate it if you can take me to her. I will never stop doubting these charms until I speak to her myself."

They closed the shop, went around the corner to Beth's sports car and climbed in. It reminded Angie of the car that Eoin had gifted her. "Do you think you could teach me how to drive?" She fiddled with the zipper on her jacket, making adjustments that weren't needed.

Beth gave her a quick side-eye. "I'd love to." She couldn't hide her excitement. "We could start this weekend. And I can take you to lunch and maybe catch a movie after." What with her breakup with Ryota and her new relationship, Angie hadn't realized how much she'd been neglecting her best friend.

"It's a date." Even if she couldn't eat at the restaurant that Beth chose.

They pulled up to a cape-style house. The white picket fence had seen better days and leaned in a drunken fashion to the left. Opening the front gate required brute strength as Angie both unlocked and lifted the wooden structure to push it forward without dragging it through the dead grass.

"Seriously, has she ever heard of stereotyping?" Angie mumbled under her breath. Guess the witch market didn't pay any better than back scratching.

Beth rushed past, her heels clicking on the uneven cobblestone pathway that led the front porch. With dainty steps, the slim omega climbed the front door and rang the bell.

Angie hurried to her side as the door opened. She'd expected someone to match the house but the woman who answered the door could have been Mrs. Claus's twin sister, right down to the cheerful apron and rosy cheeks.

"Good to see you again, Beth." The witch cleaned her hands on her apron. What came off was a rust-colored substance that smelled somewhat like blood. "Come in, come in. And who are you?"

"I'm Angie." She made a half-hearted wave.

"You're not pack."

"We work together." Angie elbowed Beth in the side.

"Angie's my boss." That didn't help the awkwardness.

The witch eyed her up and down. "I'm Sabrina. What can I do for you girls?"

Angie's stomach rolled and she glanced back at Beth's car.

Beth grabbed Angie's hand and tugged her inside. "You remember the good luck charm I purchased from you a few months ago?" She held up the charm that Angie had pulled out from under the sink.

Angie plucked the charm from Beth's fingers and handed it to the witch. "I've been having nothing but bad luck. I wanted to check to see if we were using this thing right."

The witch examined the charm in her hand and led them to what Angie could only call the kitchen, but it really belonged on a movie set. A fire pit was the focus of the room where a cauldron sat upon the flame, its contents boiling. All manners of dried plants hung from the rafters and on the far wall a large wooden shelf held many different-sized jars with questionable contents.

Next to Beth was a table where it appeared the witch had been rolling out cookies. A plate with the finished product sat within Beth's reach and the omega plucked a cookie off the plate. Angie slapped it out of her hand and gave her an *are you out of your mind* look. It didn't seem smart to be stealing cookies from a witch.

Sabrina held the charm up in the light, nodding to herself. "Someone's tampered with it." Her declaration had Angie and Beth moving in opposite directions, with Angie getting closer to the witch and Beth toward the exit. "Someone removed a piece of my charm. See how these threads all match color?" She showed Angie the off-white thread holding some of the sticks together. "They shouldn't be. This one should be red." She raised her eyebrow at Beth. "Do you know anything about this?"

Angie did a slow turn to face her best friend.

Beth stared at her shoes. "I didn't think that changing the thread colors would harm the charm. It looks prettier when the threads match." She glanced up at Angie and gave her a sad smile. "I didn't do it on purpose. You have to forgive me. I'll pay for all the damages that I caused."

"The charms didn't cause the damage, Beth. It just means that the good luck charms didn't work. Right?"

Sabrina gave the werewolf a stern glare. "She made them into hexes. You know better than to fool around with witchcraft untrained, Beth. Your alpha will be very displeased about this."

Angie massaged the bridge of her nose, trying to ease the headache that was forming. "Are you telling me that these charms have been the cause of all the things breaking in my shop?"

"Unfortunately." The witch took the curses—hexes, whatever!—to her table and began reassembling it. She waved Beth to come closer. "You may as well observe so you don't make the same mistake again." Was Beth dabbling in witchcraft or was it just her sense of fashion that had made her change the thread colors? They had lots to talk about on their date this weekend.

The witch handed Beth the charm. "Did you alter the other charms I gave you?"

The pretty shifter nodded.

"Then fix the other ones like I just did." She glanced at Angie. "You can bring them back here for me to double check her work. Things should improve at the shop now." There were more of these hexes in her shop? Sabrina tapped Beth on the nose with a sharp fingernail. "All is forgiven, little wolf. Now go to your car while I have a private word with your friend."

Beth left without question.

Angie's heart drummed as she watched her friend leave. What could the witch want to talk to her about?

Sabrina seemed to be looking at the air surrounding Angie. As she drew closer, she waved her fingers through something unseen. "We've taken care of your bad luck, but what about this personal curse that surrounds you?"

Angie didn't think her heart could have beaten any faster. She swallowed with a throat gone dry. "You can see it?" It hadn't occurred to her or Eoin to seek out advice from other magic practitioners. Well, maybe it had occurred to him but he hadn't mentioned it.

"Your aura is not human. It's actually quite blinding. Something surrounds it and holds it close to your body. If it were flame, you would be cremated within seconds." Sabrina blinked, rubbed her eyes. "I can remove it." She gave Angie a knowing smile. "For a price."

Chapter Twenty Seven

Sunlight gleamed off the lump of metal that Eoin had dragged to the middle of what he thought of as his statue room. The surface of the sculpture was warmer, but not from his flame. He rubbed his hands together, braced his feet, took a deep breath like the big bad wolf and blew.

Nothing happened.

Well, that was not true. He managed to coat the surface with spit. If he'd been from the Trigog clan, then the spit would have eaten through the metal like acid.

He wiped his mouth and paced around the lump of trash then kicked it. Fucker. People used to tremble at his flame. He could burn down a barn with a sneeze. Roast a marshmallow with his control. He roared at the material and triggered his flame. All gone. Coughing, he leaned against the metal and caught his breath. Eoin, harbinger of smoke and darkness, was no more.

His gaze rested on the metallic version of Angie's ass. From here, even the solid material seemed soft like her skin. It cried out to be caressed. Damn, he could be good with the right drive. Just last night, he'd flamed while sculpting her curves. Hell, he'd been so hot he hadn't needed to blow flame. The heat from his hands had softened the material. He had burned with desire.

Now he was dead cold with concern. He'd given her a lift to work this morning, but she'd insisted he leave her alone for the rest of the day to think about the information he dumped on her at breakfast. Did a phone call cross the line? He respected her independence, but not when it came to them. Had his invasion into her past pushed her away?

Viktor was Eoin's guide to human behavior. He'd been human once. In his present state, though, Eoin couldn't trust anything he said.

It hadn't occurred to Eoin that Angie would still go to work after finding out about her adoption. If he had his way, she'd never work another day in her life. She could keep him company instead. He had enough wealth to provide for her every need. But she had insisted, saying something about appointments and customers and keeping schedules. Things that had never concerned him in his long life until recently.

His agent would be by sometime today to pick up his new displays for the gallery. Unfortunately, Eoin didn't even know if any of the statues were finished. Angie's statue definitely was, but that one was for him; it wouldn't be going on any display. Rubbing the back of his neck, he paced the room.

Stress. Viktor had mentioned something about stress being the cause of his flaming issues.

His potential mate was in distress and wouldn't see him, other males were in the city wanting to steal her and she had a curse preventing her from shifting. He shouldn't be in the castle while Angie was in the city dealing with her own emotional crisis. He should be at her side, helping her fight these personal demons. Every cell in his body was crying out for him to begin the mating dance the moment she crossed his threshold.

Eoin wiped a thin sheet of sweat off his forehead.

Angie couldn't respond, though. It was like dancing with a partner who couldn't hear the music. It wouldn't be long before these urges drove him insane.

The solution lay in Angie's past. How had her parents gotten hold of a baby dragon without knowing? It was true that dragon offspring didn't manifest true shifting capabilities until about ten or twelve years old. Yet, there should've been other signs, like her claws. If he couldn't convince her to dig further into her past, then he'd have to do it on his own for both their sakes.

A distant voice called hello from his foyer and caught his attention. Who had the audacity to enter his castle uninvited? Again. Maybe he should get an alarm system. He stood in the middle of the room with his arms crossed as he listened to the approaching footsteps.

Roger stuck his head into the room and rapped his knuckles on the doorframe. "Knock, knock."

Eoin relaxed his tense muscles. He'd expected another dragon. Fuck, what if one of those other two bastards were at Angie's shop talking her up right now? She'd agreed to be his mate but Cedric owned more gold than most countries and Zechariah had that full head of hair. He was sure that if she had been able to shift she would have continued the mating dance. But she hadn't, and that left her susceptible to other male influence.

His agent wandered into the room, gaze darting to the statues in different phases of completion. "Love it, love it." He stopped by the work that was filled with spiky imprints of his claws. He ran a finger against one of the points and gasped. A drop of blood dangled on the tip. "Sharp." He sucked his finger. "We'll have to post a warning on this one." He spoke with his mouth full. His eyes widened as his gaze fell upon Angie's statue. He dropped his hand and made a beeline for it.

Eoin cocked his head to the side and lowered his brow, following the agent's direction.

"Wow this…this—" Roger held out his hands toward Angie's torso. "Wow, this just makes me want to touch it." He ran his hands over Angie's perfect ass.

A growl tore from Eoin's throat.

The sharp piercing noise made his agent jump from the statue. "What the fuck?" He eyed Eoin as if he'd shifted to dragon form.

"Don't touch her." Eoin strode between the statue and his agent. "This one is not for display. It's for my private collection only."

Holding out his hands in front of him, his agent backed away. "Okay, take it easy, buddy." He continued retreating until he winced. "Ouch." He jerked his left shoulder away from one of the sharp points of another statue. There was a fresh bloodstain on his shirt. "Fuck, Eoin. You don't have to go all dragon on my ass. I'm on your side, remember?" He pressed his hand to his wound.

"Of course I do. It's what I am." He grabbed his agent by the arm and guided him into the kitchen where he pulled out the First Aid kit. "Sit on that stool and take off your shirt." He pulled out disinfectant and gauze. "I am a dragon. It's the only way I know how to act. Just don't touch that statue. It's personal."

His agent sat where he was told and removed his shirt, glancing over his shoulder at the wound. "Can't believe how sharp that sculpture is."

"What did you expect? I made it with my claws." Eoin poured the peroxide over the wound.

His agent hissed. "That stings!"

Not His Dragon

Eoin had kept his hand on Roger's shoulder so he wouldn't escape the chair. "No shit." He applied a bandage after inspecting the wound. "It's just a flesh wound. Girls like scars." He slapped his agent on the injured shoulder and put way the First Aid box.

His agent tried to hide his wince of pain. "Four statues makes a poor show. Do you have any other things I can bring to the gallery?"

Eoin shook his head. "I can't work like this." He paced the kitchen. He couldn't help the need to move when pressured. It was the animal in him. "I'm preoccupied with some personal issues and it's really fuckin' around with my control. You have to cancel the show."

His agent jumped to his feet, pointing back toward his workroom. "That's the best damn work I've ever seen you make. That sharp statue, whatever you call it, is so full of violence and rage it makes me want to scream looking at it. Don't get me started talking about the ass one… I kind of want to keep my organs inside."

Eoin darted glare in his direction. "Smart."

"If I cancel the show it's going to be impossible for me to book any others when you backed out at the last minute on Lorenzo. Contrary to popular belief, galleries don't want to work with difficult artists. It's do or die, man. This is it. The statues." He pointed back to the workroom. "We just need two more."

"I can't focus. Period." Eoin wasn't going to tell Roger he was flame impotent. "I need to take care of my personal life."

"Have you ever considered that the turmoil in your personal life is inspiring you to make these fabulous pieces of work?"

Eoin rubbed his eyebrow and stared at his feet. Roger was the closest thing to a human friend he'd had in years. "No." He needed the contact to keep in touch with the species. They changed so fast, he couldn't stay informed on his own. How could he explain how shredded his insides were, to a creature who didn't have similar mating instincts? Humans had a choice to follow their heart or not. They didn't know what a blessing that could be. "Look, I can't explain in terms you'll understand. It's a dragon thing."

Roger rubbed his injured shoulder. "Try me."

Eoin had signed with Roger as his agent because he was relentless. It was ironic that his agent would turn those skills on him. He chewed the inside of his cheek. "I lost my ability to blow flame a few days ago."

"Oh."

Crossing the small space between them, Eoin pinned the human to his chair. "This doesn't leave the room."

Roger's face drained of color. "Never." He made a zipping motion across his mouth. "I like living. It's better than dead."

Eoin nodded. He'd also chosen Roger because he was a smart man. "Without flame, heating the material enough to work with it is impossible."

"I can get you a blow torch." Roger waited through Eoin's silence before adding, "What about a flame thrower?"

The dragon snorted. "I need time." Focusing on Angie and finding a way for her to shift was his priority. With other males chasing her tail, he couldn't afford the luxury of art. Until he mated Angie, nothing in the universe mattered. "Cancel the show."

"Eoin, you're making a mistake."

"It's time for you to leave. I'll contact you when the work is done." If it was ever done.

CHAPTER TWENTY EIGHT

Beth seemed caught within her own bubble of quiet as she drove from the witch's house.

Angie glanced at her from the corner of her eye. She had hexes to fix at the shop. Maybe Beth was thinking on what she had to repair? Angie had her own concerns to worry about. The witch had offered to remove Angie's curse. Could it be so simple? *Simple* being a relative word. She hadn't asked the witch for details. Maybe she had to sacrifice her first-born child or something crazy. Or maybe not. The price was steep, so the risk could belong all to the witch.

Beth pulled up to the curb in front of Angie's apartment building. "I'm sorry for causing you so much trouble, Angie. I want to help pay for the damages."

"Is that what you've been worrying about? It could all be just coincidence, Beth. All of those things could have been broken with or without those hexes." Beth would be up all night if Angie didn't nip her guilt in the bud.

"I'm responsible." She clutched her hands in front of her chest. "I should have asked you first before buying those charms."

"You were trying to help. Look, if you want you can pay for lunch this weekend and consider the driving lessons payback." She held out her hand to her best friend. "Deal?"

Beth grinned and shook her hand eagerly. "Deal."

Angie exited the car and hurried to her apartment. Once inside, she pulled out her smartphone and checked her bank account balances. Her meager savings didn't even come close to covering the price. Sabrina would laugh in her face. If she withdrew her limit on her credit cards, she could gather maybe half. Noodles would become her dietary staple.

She'd spent the past year saving every dime so she could move. Each time something broke at her shop that savings account grew smaller and smaller until it hardly existed. The only thing that she'd ever wanted was a home, but now those dreams had changed. Whose dreams wouldn't change after finding out they were a full blooded—holy crap!—dragon?

If she could shift, she would never have to drive a car. She would fly everywhere, like Japan and Africa. Then what? It's not like she had a clan waiting, but she didn't need a clan. She was sure Eoin would be right at her side, helping her every step of the way. Her life was finally coming together after all the other disappointments and neglect. She had something positive blooming in her future. The hexes in her shop would be changed to lucky charms, so things should stop breaking and she'd save money on repairs. Now this, a possible cure.

She could borrow the money. Her stomach cramped. Ryota was rolling in it. Eoin might have the funds—she just couldn't be sure with the dragon because of the state of his castle. Beth could afford to lend her the cash. What was Angie still doing sitting in her fucking apartment? She should be making calls, begging on her knees so Sabrina could remove her curse.

Doubt, that's why. Part of her still believed that she'd wake from this dream. No matter how much Eoin insisted she was a dragon, she still felt…human.

She dropped onto the kitchen chair and rested her forehead on the table, closing her eyes. She'd seen her dragon. They'd been so close to touching. She tried to picture her in her mind again with the dark, black, glossy scales and the sharp claws. She slowed her breathing until she sensed something click within her head. There in the distance—faintly, she could see the outline of her dragon, except now she wasn't black. She seemed pale of color and the shapes of her scales seemed longer, more rounded in shape. The darker dragon was really a figment of her imagination. What she pictured her dragon shape would look like since she'd never actually shifted. Was this dragon her true form? She raced towards her other shape. The closer she drew, the more distant the dragon seemed.

Shoving back from the table with a screech, she stood. As long as she had the shield surrounding her aura, she couldn't touch magic. She wouldn't be able to make contact with her dragon shape. She ran her hands over her short hair, her palm brushing against the ruby stud Eoin had given her. Her heart skipped a beat.

Rubies were valuable…

And her neighborhood had many pawnshops.

Not His Dragon

Screw her apartment and her dreams to move. Nothing would stop her from achieving her true self. She stormed from the apartment building and strode to the closest pawnshop. Pushing inside, she inhaled the stale air. Filled shelves with knick-knacks and electronics crowded the store. At the counter, a familiar pock-marked face grinned at her. "Long time no see."

In the past, before she opened her shop, she'd used to pawn her garage sale findings frequently to help ends meet. "Hey." She grinned back. "Been busy with a job." She set the ruby stud on the counter. "I want to pawn this."

The owner blew out a long whistle and raised the jewel up to the light. "It's not a pair?"

"No, just the one."

He frowned. "Will be hard to sell."

"I don't want to sell it, just pawn."

"Yeah, but if you don't pay me back then I'm stuck with a single stud."

She ground her teeth and bit back a sharp retort. "What's it worth?"

He led her to the jewelry counter and placed the ruby under an ultraviolet light. "It's not lab grown so that's a plus." He set an eyepiece over one eye and examined the ruby. "It's clear and an excellent shade of red. Where did you get this?"

She bit her bottom lip. "It was a gift." Would Eoin be hurt? She planned on paying back the pawnshop loan and keeping the earring. She just needed the money *now*. If it broke her curse, she was sure he wouldn't mind.

"You do realize if this proves to be stolen I have to report you." The shop owner pinned her down with an expert's glare.

She gave a nervous laugh. "I'm no cat burglar." But a dragon had given it to her. Most humans wouldn't touch dragon treasure. Bad things tend to happen to those who did.

He frowned but set the earring on a scale. "It's a little over a carat with the setting. I'll give you fifteen hundred for it."

Her heart sank. That wasn't enough. She needed five hundred more. "I need two grand."

Shaking his head, he held out the ruby. "Find another pawnshop."

She glanced at the time on her phone and wanted to scream. With her bank account and credit cards, she could manage the rest but she had to hurry. Her savings account wasn't linked to her debit card so she needed to see a teller. "Fine but we need to fast track this deal in cash. I have to make it to the bank before they close." She already was in his system so the transaction was quick.

With long strides, she ran the five blocks to her bank, flip-flops and all. The locals must think she was training for sprints the way she ran at least once a week for some stupid reason or another.

Reaching her destination, she slipped into the bank just as the manager strolled toward the entrance with the key. Angie made it to the teller without need of CPR. "I'd like to withdraw everything from my savings account." She had to stop between words to catch her breath.

The teller eyed her.

Sweat beaded her skin and she shook from the exertion. She looked like she was in withdrawal. She giggled and clapped her hand over her mouth. That wouldn't help.

The teller asked for ID.

Angie did as she asked and filled out all the proper paper work. "Large bills, please." It would be easier to carry.

It didn't take long for the teller to gather the cash into a neat envelope and bid her goodnight, obviously in a hurry to go home.

With more grace, Angie exited the bank's main lobby and hit their ATM machine with her credit cards. She withdrew the balance to make the witch's price. God help anyone who tried to mug her. Able to shift or not, she would go dragon on their ass.

The witch did not live within walking distance, so Angie had to catch the bus. Sitting on the hard plastic seats, she stared out the window. The shadows grew darker and longer as she traveled. Maybe she should have called Eoin? He had been instrumental in the discovery of her true nature but she suspected he would insist on paying or refuse to let her work with the witch. He could be pigheaded. This was her decision, her dragon and her life. She needed to see this through on her own.

When the time came, she got off at her stop and walked the rest of the way to the witch's house. By then the sun had set and the creepy house was veiled in darkness.

Not His Dragon

Half expecting to see zombies creeping from the ground, Angie quickly made her way to the front door.

Sabrina answered just as Angie rested her knuckles against the wood. The witch still wore her apron and smelled of gingerbread cookies. "Angie, did you decide to accept my offer?"

Angie held out the envelope of cash. "I have the money. Take this curse off me."

Sabrina gave a surprised laugh. "That was fast." She led Angie back into her kitchen and began to pull ingredients off the shelf and set them on the cutting board by the boiling cauldron. "It's not as easy as that. If I knew who had cast the spell, or at least why the curse was cast, this would be much easier."

Dread settled heavily in Angie's gut. With heavy feet, she crossed the kitchen closer to Sabrina. "I don't know any of those answers." It seemed like her whole life was filled with unanswerable questions. "I've always thought of myself as human until a few days ago. A dragon told me he could see that I was shielded from magic. Does that help?"

"Somewhat." She opened some jars and lined them up in front of her. As she leaned her hands on the cutting board, she stared at Angie. "Why would someone want you to think you were human?"

Angie rubbed the familiar ache in her chest. "So my parents could adopt me." Why had her dragon parents given her away? Had she been defective? She had no childhood memories except those of her human parents.

"Good enough. We will work with that and I'll prepare you a counter-spell." With fast fingers, she pulled out ingredients and threw them in a bowl, grinding the ingredients to dust. She poured the powder into a dissolvable capsule and handed the pill to Angie. "There you go. The answer to your prayers."

Staring at the pill, Angie was reminded of the wicked witch who had poisoned Snow White's apple. How desperate was she to trust this perfect stranger? Without a second thought, she swallowed the pill. Pretty desperate. "How long will it take to work?"

"As soon as your body digests it. But don't shift here. Not inside my house." She shooed Angie out of the kitchen with her hands. "Go out into the country and try shifting there. By then you should have absorbed my cure. You'll also have space for your dragon body and you won't accidentally eat anyone on your first shift."

The advice seemed sage. Angie hugged Sabrina. "I can't thank you enough." She hurried out of the door and back to the bus stop. Screw that, she'd take a taxi straight to Eoin's house and he could guide her through her first shift.

CHAPTER TWENTY NINE

Eoin crossed his arms and inspected his work. He gave it a nod of approval. The bathroom fixtures gleamed and the room smelled much fresher than when Angie had last visited. Folded towels sat on the edge of the deep bathtub. While looking for clean rags in his garage, he'd found a storage bin of candles. He had filled the wall candelabras with them.

As a prospective mate, it was Eoin's job to provide her with a home. The apartment she lived in was much worse than his castle and he wanted her to have more. Maybe they should just start over. There must be something big enough for two dragons in the country.

The distant sound of tire treads crushing gravel reached his sensitive hearing. He tensed. He wasn't expecting anyone. If it was another fucking male dragon, he would start rolling heads. Cracking his knuckles, he made his way to the front door and yanked it open before Angie's fist could knock. "What are you doing here?"

She smiled so wide she glowed. "Are you busy?" She glanced around his shoulders and pushed her way inside his home. "I've got great news." She grasped his hands and squeezed them tight.

Her mood was contagious and he found himself returning her smile. "I'll never be too busy for you." He'd never seen her this happy and he liked it. The way her presence immediately warmed his hollow heart and lifted the burdens of the world from his shoulders could be addictive. Making her smile this way seemed like the perfect future goal.

"I found somebody to break my curse." She pressed herself against his body and bent her head back to meet his stare. "Let's find someplace outside and you can help me shift for the first time."

He forced his smile to remain on his face but inside he went cold. "Wow, how did this come about?" He didn't know of any practitioner of magic within the city who would be powerful enough to break the curse.

"The pack witch was able to see the curse and made me a concoction to swallow that should break it." She pulled at his hands and led him outside. "Do you know taxis will only come up here if I paid them double their rate? What a scam. Beth said that she would give me driving lessons this weekend so I can borrow your car to travel back and forth." She tossed him an amused glance over her shoulder. "But I'm only borrowing it until I can afford to buy my own."

"Okay." He furrowed his eyebrows. The pack witch? That old hack? "I would have come to get you if you would have just called me." Concoction? She'd taken a risk ingesting some unknown substance.

"I couldn't wait. I'm so excited. I can't wait to be one with my dragon form." She spun around, her smile even wider. "When can you start teaching me how to fly?"

He quickly smoothed his expression and chuckled. "One step at a time, wild girl." He shoved his doubts to the back of his mind. Angie deserved his support. Who knew? Maybe it would work. Or maybe it would kill her. He frowned again.

"Stop worrying so much." She playfully poked his stomach. "Should I take off my clothes?"

He sat on a boulder in his yard and pointed to the center of his lawn where she would have the space needed to expand in size. "If you're giving me the choice, I'll always choose naked."

She tossed him a salacious smile over her shoulder. "If I shift in my clothes, they'll be torn apart?"

He nodded. "So either way you'll be naked." He leaned back on his arms and crossed his ankles.

When she was a little further, he shifted his eyes to dragon and peeked at her aura. Shit, the curse was still visible. He chewed on his thumbnail. Even if he told her, she would still want to try to shift.

Angie stripped and tossed her clothes in a crumpled pile at her feet. Shivering, she wrapped her arms around herself. "Chilly." She closed her eyes like he'd taught her, probably to commune with her dragon shape.

With Angie's nipples perked in the cold air, Eoin couldn't complain about the view. He'd never had a favorite body type, but everything about Angie was perfect. Right down to the little dimples over her ass. He recalled sucking that spot last night and how she had laughed.

Her eyebrows furrowed and her smile slowly changed into a frown. Even from this distance Eoin could see sweat forming on her brow. She was trying too hard. He could sense the magic building around her but there was no release. This wasn't going to work.

He pushed himself to his feet and approached her. "Angie," he whispered.

Her shoulders drooped before she opened her eyes. "What am I doing wrong?"

He gathered her sweet form in his arms and lifted her so he could cradle her against his chest. "Absolutely nothing. I don't think the witch lifted the curse."

"But she works for the pack. Her spells work for them. She really sounded like she knew what she was doing." The despair in her voice broke his heart. He'd find this witch and eat her whole. Crunch her bones and spit her back out.

With Angie still in his arms, he bent and gathered her clothing with his fingertips then carried her back to his castle before she caught a chill. "I know of the pack witch. She's not strong enough to break your curse. I've touched this barrier with my bare hands, I know how strong it is."

She struggled out of his arms and tugged on her clothing. If fury had a scent it would smell like Angie. "You don't understand. I paid her."

Foreboding filled Eoin's gut. "How much?"

She glared at him with the determination of a she-dragon on the hunt. "I pawned the ruby earring and paid her every last dime I owned."

He ground his teeth. "We'll take the bike. If there's traffic, we can weave through it and move faster." He led her to his motorcycle in the garage and followed her directions to the witch's home.

The house had seen better days. Obviously the pack didn't pay her very well and she was most likely strapped for cash. The front door swung loose in the wind, swinging back and forth against the frame. The darkness didn't affect Angie's vision but he took her hand anyway and guided her over the uneven walkway stones toward the front door. He pushed it open and didn't bother calling out as he entered. He could already sense the house was empty.

Angie pushed past him and stared, open mouth. "What the…"

"She moved. She must've known it wasn't going to work and left town."

"But…" Angie moved from room to room quickly with him close on her heels. She stopped in the kitchen and turned in a slow circle. "This house was full of stuff. How could she possibly move that fast?"

"Magic."

She slammed her fist on the counter and the thump echoed within the house. "I can't believe I was that stupid." She squeezed her eyes shut, her breathing ragged. "She took everything. I have nothing left. I can't afford to hire anybody to find her."

He came up from behind and hugged her against his chest, leaning his chin on top of her head. "Why did you trust her?"

"She worked for the pack." Angie shook her head and leaned her body against him. "That's not it. I was desperate." She broke away from his hold and paced the room. "Because of you. You dangled this dragon thing in front of me, just out of my reach and I wanted it so bad." Tears streamed down her cheeks. "I want to be with you but I can't. You want to do some kind of mating ritual and I can't respond to you the way you need." She stopped to face him. "The way I need."

Angie's insides were more than raw. She'd been gutted and left out in the sun with fire ants. That's what the witch had done to her. She wiped her cheeks dry on her sleeve.

Eoin crossed the room and helped her with his own shirt. Cleaning her face, smoothing her short hair. He added kisses to her forehead and nose and cheeks as she continued to cry. She just couldn't stop.

"Screw our people. Screw instincts and customs and laws." He grabbed her chin and forced her to meet his stare. "I'll marry you. Just like the humans do and—and we'll move into one of those middle class neighborhoods and pretend to be human."

Her sobs turned into a laugh as she tried picturing them living in a middle-class neighborhood with a white picket fence. Him with his punk-rock look and her with her ghetto style. They'd fit in perfectly. "No."

"No, what? You won't marry me? I'm not good enough?" There was a growl in his voice. "All that matters is that we're together."

"Being dragon is who you are and it's who I fell in love with." A twang ran across her soul as if God had strummed it like a guitar. She jerked in Eoin's arms from the sudden sensation.

"You love me?"

"I'm feeling a little weird. And dizzy. When I said those words something happened."

"Once you say them, you can't take them back, Angie." He held her at arm's length and she saw his eyes change to dragon form. "Let me check your aura." His eyes wandered around the air surrounding her. "It's smaller. The shield looks like it's almost gone but I can still see a shadow. Try to shift."

"I'm inside the house."

"Who gives a shit? We'll tear this place apart. Who's going to care?"

She gave herself a hug and attempted to connect with her dragon for the third time this evening. On this attempt her dragon came to her call right away. She stood so close Angie could almost feel the softness of her scales. But they didn't connect. She took a deep shaky breath and met Eoin's disappointed stare. "I think this is the part where you need to take me home." She followed him back to his bike but he bypassed her neighborhood and took her on the interstate back to his castle. She was too worn out to argue with him and just absorbed the heat of his body as they rode as one toward his home.

He parked his bike by the entrance and helped her dismount.

She tucked her frozen fingers in her armpits while her teeth chattered. She hadn't dressed for a motorcycle ride and nights were getting cool.

Eoin gave her the once-over. "Do you remember how to find my bedroom?"

She nodded, too disappointed to talk.

"Why don't you go and draw us a bath while I make us something to eat?"

She raised an eyebrow at him, recalling the state of his bathroom yesterday.

"I cleaned." He raised his hand up by his head. "Scout's honor."

She gave him a weary smile as she tried picturing him scrubbing the bathtub. "Sure." She did as he asked and she sat on the edge of the large tub, watching the water. What now? Did they continue as they were? Could he love her when she was stuck between worlds?

Eoin returned with a tray filled with strawberries, cupcakes and popcorn with a bottle of wine tucked under each arm. He set the tray down by the tub and offered her a bottle. "One for you and one for me." He gave her a wink. "It seems like tonight should be a two-bottle night." It sounded like a perfect idea.

She popped a piece of cupcake in her mouth and undressed. "After the bath, I can finish working on your scales."

He made a purring noise. "They just need oiling to protect my skin while the scales grow back. It can wait until morning." He popped another piece of cake in her mouth, watching her lips intently.

She licked the icing off her mouth, taking her time. "I could model for you while you work. I had fun the first time."

He ran his hands over her bare shoulders. "No need to model."

"Are you finished?"

"I've decided to put my art on hold until we solve our mating problems. It's difficult for me to concentrate when inside I'm a mess."

"But what about the show you were telling me about?"

"I canceled it."

Stepping into the tub, she watched as Eoin undressed and slipped in behind her. The tub was large enough to hold them easily with the water up to her chin. All this time, she'd been so focused on how her being a dragon was affecting her life, and had never considered how she was destroying his.

CHAPTER THIRTY

The streets were quiet this time of the morning as Angie watched Eoin drive away. She yawned so hard her jaw cracked. At the butt crack of dawn, she'd dragged him out of bed and finished working on his scales. She felt better knowing his hide would heal.

No doubt Eoin would spend the rest of the day trying to make contact with somebody who knew what to do about her curse. While he did, she had to return to work before she lost her mind.

She entered the shop and smiled at Beth, the last person she wanted to see. She couldn't mention how the witch had conned her out of all her money. Her best friend already felt guilty about the luck charms. It wasn't Beth's fault that Angie was a dupe.

Her first free moment, she was going to burn those damn charms.

Beth looked half-asleep with her chin in hand. "No appointments for the next hour." She yawned so wide her jaw cracked. "Ouch."

Bending over the desk, Angie examined her face. "Late night?"

"I had nightmares. That witch gives me the creeps and her vibe clung to me the rest of the evening." She shuddered.

"Then this calls for fresh coffee." Angie's card should have just enough credit to purchase the drinks. She didn't need Beth's order. She knew her coffee preferences by heart and took off before Beth could offer to pay again. Angie understood Beth's natural instinct was to please others but she needed to grow a backbone. Luckily, Ryota prevented any assholes from abusing her giving nature, but the alpha didn't have eyes on the back of his head.

Their usual coffee hangout was busy. While Angie stood at the counter waiting for the barista to finish the orders, she spotted a poster on the building across the street. Eoin's face was featured. She eased away from the counter and closer to the window for a better view. Was that the gallery? She'd never really paid attention to the building before. Art wasn't really her thing, not until she met Eoin.

The barista shouted her name.

Angie paid for the two coffees then crossed over to the gallery and checked out the announcement.

The poster declared that Eoin's new work was going to be shown in two days. She ran her fingertips over the surface. This had been a major part of his life and he was giving it up because of her. She loved the way his face softened when absorbed in the production. His heart went into whatever he created. If stopped, what would happen to the dragon she was falling in love with?

She squared her shoulders. They hadn't canceled his show yet. She knew about sacrifices; she'd made them all her life. Eoin didn't need to sacrifice his art for her. They would eventually solve her shifting problem. It was flattering he wanted to make her the center of his life, but how long before he started resenting her for it?

With her hands full, she managed to open the gallery door and paused just past the threshold. Ceilings melted into shadows overhead and small bright lights shone on the paintings hanging on the wall. The floors and walls sparkled white as if freshly painted, nothing like Eoin's home.

The first painting caught her attention and she paused under its illumination. Multi-shades of red and orange flamed over the canvas in passionate heat. She read the information written on a slip of paper pinned under the painting. *Pepper Spray by Eoin Grant*. He had a last name? She hadn't thought to ask. Trailing her fingertip over the frame, she sighed. He'd done an excellent job of portraying something burning.

She turned her back on the painting and could picture his recent statues standing on the pedestals in the middle of the room. The visceral figures would drastically contrast with the gallery's modern decor and exhibit Eoin's true dragon nature. She edged deeper inside the room and noted that some of the spaces on the wall were blank, with Eoin's nameplates underneath. In the far corner were pallets and half-packaged paintings. She hadn't realized how much work he'd put into this.

"Sorry, the gallery is not open. I must've forgotten to lock the door behind me." A tall thin man with a goatee came out from an office in the far back of the room. He waved his hands, showing her the way out.

"I saw the poster outside about Eoin's art show. I was wondering—"

Before she could continue, he scowled. "Canceled, canceled, canceled. Sorry, you'll have to see the dragon's artwork on his next tour."

"I was wondering if there was any way I could get you to change your mind about canceling." Eoin sure had pissed him off.

"Honey, I wasn't the one to cancel the show. So far, I only have a few pieces to exhibit. Without the artwork, there is no show. But since you seem to be a fan of his, I'll let you see his latest venture in sculpting." He led her around the corner where one of the metallic statues stood mounted on a pedestal.

"I haven't seen this one." She circled around, noting the sharp edges and deep grooves. They almost seemed like bite marks as if Eoin had used this as a chew toy in dragon form.

The manager edged closer to her. "What do you mean by this one? You've seen others?"

Turning slowly to face him, she raised an eyebrow. "You haven't?" Eoin's workroom was filled with statues. Why hadn't he sent them here for the show? "What exactly is going on between the two of you?"

The manager folded his arms, evidence of chasing her out of the gallery gone. "Exactly, who are you? Don't tell me you're his agent. I know his agent personally." That was good, because Angie hadn't even known Eoin had an agent. She was sticking her nose deep in the dragon's business. He'd be pissed. She would be, if Eoin tried to take over her shop, but she wasn't trying to take over his artwork, she was trying to save his career.

"I'm his girlfriend and I think there's been a misunderstanding. He's created other sculptures to exhibit but I think he's feeling…a little insecure about them." Eoin was going to kill her. She'd better pack a double handful of pepper spray next time they met.

"Insecure? Are we speaking of the same dragon?"

She laughed. "Yeah, don't tell him I said that. We may both regret it."

"I need to see them." He grimaced. "I can't make any definitive decisions until I know what I'm working with. I mean, I understand that working with metal is a new medium for him, but the emotion that this statute evokes is exactly what he needs to breathe new life into his art career."

She glanced at the coffees in her hand as an idea struck her. "Do you have time right now to take a look?"

He startled. "Are you talking about going up to Eoin's Castle? Right now? Uninvited?"

She nodded. "I have to drop these off at my shop down the street and then we can go together if you have a car."

"What about Eoin?" The manager's voice rose an octave or two.

"Leave him to me." Famous last words.

"My name is Lorenzo. Seems like the person who's holding my life in her hands should at least know my name."

She laughed again. "I'm Angie. I own the back-scratching shop a couple blocks from here. Pick me up there." She left Lorenzo to lock up the gallery, and hurried back to the shop. Handing over the coffee to Beth, she gave her a huge grin. "What would you say if we took the day off?"

Beth rose to her feet and felt Angie's forehead. "You don't feel feverish."

"Call all my appointments today and reschedule them, make any excuse you want, but I have a small emergency I need to take care of." A grey sedan parked in front of the shop and honked. Angie waved to Beth before the omega could stop her, and left.

Lorenzo shifted his car into drive and started towards the interstate. "How many pieces has Eoin completed?"

Angie took a deep swig of her coffee. "How many do you need?" She was way over her head. She hadn't even considered if any of his work was actually finished. They seemed to be to her.

He eyed her. "Never mind that question. We can do a combination of statues and paintings that should be enough to fill the show. We're lucky that Eoin's name causes a buzz in the art community, because we don't have much time for any more publicity."

She gulped the hot coffee and stared out the window. She'd been on a roll of making mistakes, so she may as well keep tumbling along with it.

They pulled up to the castle and exited the car.

Lorenzo followed on her heels like a second shadow as she cracked the door open and peeked inside. No sign of Eoin so far. Thank God.

The gallery manager cleared his throat behind her and almost sent her into the ceiling rafters. "I assume by your tiptoeing that he'll be angry to catch us here."

"You assume correctly so keep your fucking voice down."

His eyebrows shot up but he gave her the thumbs up.

Quiet as church mice, they crept into the castle and she led him toward Eoin's workroom. She hadn't a clue how good the dragon's hearing was or if he was even home, but from his words last night she didn't expect him to be working on his sculpting.

Lorenzo gasped as he spotted the first of Eoin's statues.

She hung back by the workroom door and let him experience them alone. Most of Eoin's work expressed a lot of anger and violence, all except hers. It was like he poured his desire into the scrap metal, making it and her look dang sexy. Her ass never looked so good.

"What is Lorenzo doing in my home?" Eoin whispered in her ear. Not the seductive kind of whisper either, more like the kind that serial killers say right before they slaughtered their victims.

She shouted in surprise and tossed her coffee straight into the air. Spinning around, she witnessed him catch it midair before the cup hit her in the head. "Hey there."

"Hey." His lush lips thinned as his gaze followed the gallery manager's movement. "No point in hiding, Lorenzo." He turned his narrowed gaze on her. "Explain. Now."

She plucked the coffee cup from his hand and drank the remains. Her thoughts had scattered like a bag of dropped marbles when he'd startled her. "I met Lorenzo this morning. You came up in our conversation. He mentioned that he hadn't seen any of your latest sculptures so I offered to show them to him. Now you don't have to cancel your show." She playfully poked him in the stomach and caught her breath.

He glanced down at the gesture. But when his gaze returned to hers there was no amusement in his eyes. "You've had enough coffee." He snatched the cup from her hand and drained it.

"These works are exquisite, Eoin." Lorenzo still remained on the far side of the room, keeping the statues between him and Eoin.

"You're saying that because you're frightened. Go home, Lorenzo." He pointed at Angie and her heart jumped into her throat. "You and I have to have a little chat."

Angie ground her teeth. The dragon could be so pigheaded. "Well, if you want an honest opinion from him maybe you should be less intimidating." She bumped her chest against his. Well she tried; he was considerably taller than her. "And terrifying."

A small growl rolled in his chest. "Why aren't you at work?"

Angie pushed Eoin behind her and ignored his question. "He won't hurt you, Lorenzo. Not while I'm here and can draw breath." She elbowed Eoin in the gut. "Right?"

He grunted. "I won't harm you." The *yet* was silent but present in his tone.

"Are the statues good enough to exhibit in your gallery?" She wanted to smack some sense into Eoin. Hadn't anyone taught him it was better to use honey than vinegar when he wanted something? It was like he wanted Lorenzo to reject him.

Lorenzo ran his hands over the smooth surface of her metallic ass. "These three most definitely." He gestured at two others in the room as well as the one he was touching. "We'll add them to the sculpture we already have and showcase some of your paintings."

"Take your hands off of her." Eoin took a step towards the gallery manager but Angie dug her heels into the floor and body-blocked him. "That is not for sale and I don't want it exhibited."

"Why not?" Angie grunted with the effort to keep Eoin from strangling Lorenzo. "I think it's your best one."

"I won't share you with anyone."

She sighed and flopped against him, forcing him to catch her instead of taking violent action. "That's just the statue of me. You've got the real thing."

He pulled her tighter within his arms, the place that he eternally seemed to want to keep her. She didn't have any complaints. "You never said why you're not at work."

"I told Beth to reschedule my appointments for the day. This was more important."

Eoin gave her a slow blink. All the anger in his face drained. "You did that for me?" He glanced at Lorenzo. "Make the arrangements to retrieve these sculptures. Keep the show scheduled." He kissed her forehead tenderly. "Thank you." He turned his back on her and left the room.

Lorenzo joined her. "That was awesome, Angie."

"No, he's awesome."

Chapter Thirty One

Angie walked Lorenzo out of the castle and watched him leave the grounds. He'd be back later this afternoon with movers to get the three statues for Eoin's show. She smiled to herself and did a little happy dance. Now she had to face the cranky dragon.

She searched the kitchen and found it cold. The bedroom and bathroom were just as empty. She scratched her head and returned the workroom. Well, fuck, had he shifted and flown away? Could he be that upset? The castle was so big. She didn't want to lose her way. It might take days for Eoin to find her. She bit her bottom lip. Was there a basement in his castle? He'd never shown her, but he had taken her to the uppermost part of the tower on the first night she came to work on his scales. She returned to the stairs and climbed two at a time until she reached the top. Leaning against the wall, she tried to catch her breath. She shouldn't have bothered.

Eoin stood on the edge of the railingless balcony staring at the bright blue sky. He spun around, crossed the space with a few long strides, captured her face between his hands and stole her breath once more.

He claimed her mouth with a smash of lips and clash of teeth.

Sandwiched between him and the wall, she clung to his shoulders, absorbing his passionate assault. She preferred Eoin heated with desire over anger any day.

His kiss possessed her, marking every part of her as his. He pulled away with a more chaste peck before leaning his forehead against hers.

Between gasps, she asked. "What was that for?" She'd thought for sure he'd be furious.

Nose to nose, his gaze never left hers as he stroked her cheeks. "I love you."

She threw back her head and slid to her knees as a searing white-hot pain sliced into her back muscles and gripped her spine. Her lungs forgot how to work. She reached out to Eoin with shaky hands.

Not His Dragon

In the distance, she could hear Eoin shouting. Asking what was wrong and why she was screaming. She was screaming? She squeezed her eyes shut and clenched her teeth, fighting the pain. Suddenly she could sense a large shadow coating her, shielding her from the agony. Her dragon? She focused on the presence, seeking out support and help. Angie sensed her body coiling around her just before all the pain eased away.

She panted on her stomach with her face pressed to the cool stone of the floor. She cracked open her eyelids.

Eoin stood in front of her, eyes wide and jaw slack.

"Eoin?" She sounded hoarse.

He sank to his knees and crawled towards her. "Oh my God, Angie. You're the most beautiful she-dragon I've ever seen." He ran his hands over her... Muzzle?

She moved her hands and sensed claws digging into the stone. Her heart pounded, but the beat was louder, heavier. Trying to stand, she wobbled towards the edge of the roof on four unfamiliar legs.

"Wait, stop. Don't move!" Eoin shifted to his dragon form, tearing through his clothes in an explosion of rags, as he moved to block her fall. He gripped her body with dragon strength and scooted her from plummeting over the edge. That could have been a flight lesson she wouldn't have recovered from.

She spread her wings and gazed at them over her shoulders. "Are th—those feathers?" Narrowing her eyes, she quickly examined her body. Covered in pearly white scales edged in delicate white feathers, Angie appeared...part bird? The membranes of her wings ended with long narrow feathers. She'd recalled seeing pictures in the Natural Science Museum portraying fossils found in China. They had similar feathers. "Why do I have feathers?" She'd never heard of a dragon with them.

Eoin ran his hands tenderly over the arch of her wing. It sent a shiver down her spine. "I don't know, but I love it." He was still much bigger than her and was capable of cradling her against his body. He ran his muzzle along her sleek neck. "Just like I love you." He let out a tremendous roar that rattled some of the loose stones from the castle, sending them tumbling to the ground far below.

She nestled even closer. "I want to see myself. Do you have a mirror big enough?" She could hear the birds singing in the distant forest and see them flying above the clouds. She could smell the sizzling musk of Eoin as his scent wrapped her in a possessive blanket. Power surged in her veins as she finally connected to magic. It rushed through her limbs and she wanted to burst into song.

Now, that would put a tragic spin to the day since she couldn't sing a note without breaking eardrums.

"I don't have a mirror here in the castle but I know of a place where you'd have a great view. Are you ready for your first flying lesson?"

She jumped to her feet and knocked his chin with the top of her head. "Ow, am I ever." She shook the stars clear of her vision then licked the spot where she had knocked him good. "Sorry."

Even in dragon form, Eoin managed to give her a wary look. He rubbed his chin. "I still have my teeth." He gestured for her to follow. "Stand on your hind legs and face the edge of the roof, but not too close."

She did as he instructed. Her heart skipped beats as she stared at the ground far, far below. How big of a hole would she leave in the earth if she fell?

"That's good. Now spread your wings."

Her long throat went dry and her tongue stuck to the roof of her mouth. "This is a bad idea." She retreated from the edge. Wouldn't it be her luck to die on her first day as a real dragon? She sensed Eoin pressing his stomach to her back, blocking her escape. "If you know what's good for you, you'll move your scaly ass."

With gentle hands, he petted the feathers on her underbelly. "So soft."

She elbowed him in the gut. "Stop that."

He chuckled and wrapped his big, brawny dragon arms around her torso, just under her wings. "I won't drop you." He inched her closer to the edge. "Ever."

"Eoin." She clung to his hands. "Can't I be a ground dragon?"

"I'll be the one flying and you'll be just testing your wings. Don't squirm, bite, or hit me." He knew her so well. He gave her a little nip on the back of her neck and then launched them off the roof of the castle with his great wings extended.

194

Not His Dragon

The wind caught Angie's wings and tugged her new delicate membranes open. The land below rushed past her so quickly the trees and grass blurred.

"Relax." Eoin spoke close to her ear. "Let the air speak to you." The hardest thing in the universe to do was give up control. Technically, she hadn't given it up. Eoin had taken it from her. Otherwise, she'd still be on that damn roof pretending she was human in dragon form. She needed to embrace her true nature. She wasn't human and shouldn't act like it.

She stretched out her new neck and embraced the wind with her wings. She mimicked Eoin's motions with her own wings trying to learn from example. He made it look so easy.

Eoin flew them over the mountain and below into a green valley with a long, crystal clear lake. The surface was smooth as glass and as they flew over it she finally could see her reflection.

He hovered over the water so she could have a good look. She was an ivory color with golden eyes. The feathers covered more than just the edges of her wings. They covered her limbs and her long thin tail. She was only half Eoin's size. Opening her jaw, she stared at the transparent needlelike teeth. She might be small but she'd have one hell of a bite. From the reflection, she saw Eoin's great horned head hovering over hers. The look of adoration in his eyes swelled her heart. They could truly be together.

"Have you had your fill of looking?" His great dragon voice rumbled above her.

"For now." She rubbed him under the chin with her nose and it felt right.

With a few strokes of his wings, he brought them to the shore and landed close to the water. "This is where I usually bathe. In dragon form, of course." He ran his side along hers as he circled around her body. "You should join me from now on."

"Why do I get the impression that bathing is the last thing on your mind?" She dipped her claws in the cold water and shivered. She didn't know if she could give up her human habits of hot showers. The important word being *hot*.

Eoin brushed his jaw along hers in a very cat-like act and made a happy rumbly noise. "You're so soft. I don't know of any clan with feathers."

She sighed and sat by the lakeside, leaning her full weight against him. "Another mystery to add to my list." She'd hoped once she shifted to dragon she'd be able to find the answers to her past, but she had more questions. Eoin sheltered her with a wing over her back, pulling her next to him. "I'm kind of relieved."

She tilted her head back to look at his strong-jawed face. "What do you mean?"

"I don't have to share you with anyone."

She ran a clawed hand along his muzzle. "You're very sexy when you're possessive."

"That's just the dragon in you talking." He winked at her before shifting back to his human form.

She admired his tattooed, muscular back. He had the body of someone who knew how to use it. A cooing noise escaped her chest and she blinked at the odd sound.

The corner of his lips lifted in a smug smile. "I like you too." He entwined his fingers in the small, downy feathers on her body. "Are you going to change shape so I can fuck you already?"

"Oh, is that how it's going to be?" She smirked and whipped the end of her tail at his firm, fine ass. "Maybe I'll be the one to fuck you." She calmed her mind, like Eoin had instructed her to do on the mountaintop the first time she had tried to shift with him, and pictured her human form. Nothing happened. She shifted her position and tried again. Her heart raced a little faster. "Eoin? I can't seem to become human. What am I doing wrong?"

CHAPTER THIRTY TWO

Angie rose to her hind legs and struggled to find balance. She flapped her wings uselessly and cantered to the right. Her wings struck something solid and she heard Eoin grunt. What if she was trapped as a dragon for the rest of her life just like she'd been trapped in human form? At least as a human she'd been able to hold a job and have a life. As a dragon, she couldn't even fit in her apartment. She'd be dependent on Eoin for the rest of her existence. That was not acceptable. She tripped over something and slipped in the mud. Landing flat on her back, she knocked the wind from her lungs.

"Are you done yet?" Eoin stood a few feet away, hand pressed to his eye as he bent over, resting his other hand on his knee.

"I—I can't shift." She flapped her wings against the ground and did her best to roll on her side, but she'd gone from having four limbs to six and none of them were hands. "Eoin, help me."

"I will once you're calm down and won't trample me again."

She went still. "Did I hurt you?"

As he approached, he lowered his hand. His right eye was already beginning to swell shut. "You have a strong right-wing." He smiled to take the sting out of his words. "I'm going to help." He raised his hands as if trying to calm a wild animal before resting his palms on each side of her dragon face. Warmth spread from his touch into her flesh.

"What is that?"

"My magic touching yours." He spoke softly. "Concentrate on it and follow the path I'm taking. Eventually, this will come naturally to you."

Closing her eyes, she relaxed into the sensation as it spread deeper within her body and then she sensed another pop. She opened her eyes and once more she was human. "You'll teach me how to do that?"

"You shouldn't even have to ask." He took a step toward her and cupped her cheeks with his calloused hands.

Angie sucked in a breath as his electrified touch sent tingles along her nerves. Right now, Eoin looked nothing like the furious dragon that had confronted her on the street. His anger and mistrust had been replaced with desire and love. She stood on tiptoe to meet his lips halfway, curling her fingers over the rough stubble covering his head.

A sexy growl rolled from his throat as he crushed his mouth to hers. He tasted of cinnamon and firecrackers all rolled in a fireball of *holy cow*. His kiss was firm and demanding. He pulled her against his chest until her feet left the ground.

She wrapped her legs around his narrow hips and rubbed against his growing erection. Odd how only a week ago, she'd have cut off her own arm to avoid becoming some shifter's mate. Now, it seemed like the best idea ever invented and she couldn't wait to make him hers.

Eoin set her on the cool, soft grass along the lakeshore. He prowled over her, skin brushing over skin. His muscles bunched and released with controlled movement as he skimmed her curves. Fierce craving shone from his pale blue eyes as they caressed every mound and dip of her body. His gaze returned to hers and he started another breath-stealing kiss.

Running her hands over his arms and shoulders, she memorized every hard detail of his form. She moved to his back and stretched her reach along his flank, needing to touch, lick, and nip every inch of him.

He pulled her left leg up around his hip and with the head of his cock he stroked over her clit. With just the tip, he started slowly pushing against the sensitive area, but soon they became longer strokes until the underside of his cock slid against her, using her own moisture as lubricant.

The pressure built steadily until she could barely breathe.

Breaking off the kiss, he stared between their bodies at where they met and groaned—the sound so raw and primal. His body trembled as if in terrible need. The angle of his cock shifted slightly so the tip no longer hit her clit but press in a little at her entrance before he withdrew.

Her hips rose of their own accord, following his retreat.

He repeated the process of rubbing his full length against her clit then dipping in a little bit farther, bringing slickness and fiction and heat.

Not His Dragon

She landed a flurry of kisses on his neck, jaw, and shoulders, clinging to his hips so he wouldn't withdraw, but he was too strong. "Fuck me." Inside, the pressure built to unbearable pleasure but he wouldn't let her go over the edge in release. "Oh God, Eoin." Sweat slicked their skin and her hands lost their purchase.

On this dip, he thrust deep inside her until he couldn't go any further.

She cried out at the sudden and intense pleasure.

He hovered over her, suspended by his arms, and he rolled his body from hips to abdomen as he moved inside her. Deep, strong thrusts followed by his own rumbled growls. He dug his knees into the ground as he pinned her under him. "Mine." He repeated by her ear in a raw voice. "Mine." Over and over.

She arched into his body, repeating yes to his every claim. Unable to keep her eyes open any longer, she dropped her head back as her climax burst through her body in long, wild sweeps leaving her in a shivering, spine-tingling mess.

Eoin pulled her tighter into his embrace and rolled onto his back so she lay limp across his chest. He nuzzled her cheek as if they were in dragon form and laughed.

She loved that sound. She loved the feel of him against her. She loved his patience with her crazy, especially when trying to teach her about flight. They had so much to share and a whole dragon lifetime ahead of them, except something still bugged her. And Eoin still hadn't voiced the question she knew must be burning in his heart. "Why do you think that the spell suddenly broke?" Angie lifted her head. "I mean, one moment I was me, and then pop, suddenly I'm a dragon. I didn't do anything. I didn't even try to shift."

He traced her collarbone. "Can you recall what I'd just said before you shifted?"

She paused and searched her memory. He'd said he loved her. Could it be so simple? "Did you mean it?"

"Every word."

Was Eoin's love what broke her curse? "The key to undoing the curse is to understand the reason why it was needed in the first place."

"Where did you hear this?"

"The witch who stole all my money. It's what she said when we were discussing the source of this thing shielding me from magic. Except at that time, I had thought whoever had abandoned me had placed this curse on me before I was even given to my parents."

"That has nothing to do with love. If anything, it's the opposite."

"Exactly, but the truth had been staring me in the face all this time and I never wanted to admit it. My parents, my adopted parents, were the ones who placed the spell on me. Otherwise I never would have developed the sharp nails or the fast healing or other mild shifter traits when I was ten. It's when I began developing these things that my parents pulled me out of school and were fearful whenever I spoke about my differences. They must have been the ones who placed the spell on me." She hugged herself, suddenly going very cold. If they had loved her so much, why would they hide such an important thing from her?

"That makes sense." Eoin rubbed her back in soothing circles.

"What? That my parents were ashamed that I was a shifter."

"No, that's not it at all. If it were found out that humans had adopted a shifter child, then you would have been taken away by the supernatural community. Humans are not equipped to deal with a child just learning to change shape. It's very dangerous."

"So, they did it…"

"Because they loved you and couldn't stand losing you."

"Why didn't they ever tell me?" Angie flung her hands up to the sky. "I would've gone the rest of my life living as a human if I had never met you."

"They died when you were young. They probably wanted to wait until you were older and more stable so you could control your shift better and make your own decisions."

"So this is an accident." She leaned into Eoin's embrace.

"I think so, but they had foresight. They set a failsafe in case you met a dragon—"

"And he fell in love with me?" The world seemed very big all of a sudden, even for a small white dragon. She'd been alone for too long and Eoin's love was filling all those empty, hurtful places in her soul. "Can we go to your home now?"

He lifted her chin with his finger and stared into her eyes. "Yes, let's go to *our* home."

With Eoin's guidance, she shifted back to dragon form.

"But there's one last thing we need to do before leaving." Eoin spread his wings and began to circle Angie. He beat his feet against the ground to a primal rhythm that only he could hear. Swinging his tail back and forth, he began to dance.

She sensed his magic once more caressing her feathers, and in turn, her own magic flared. Only then did she hear the music. Unable to resist, she drew closer to him, spreading her wings, ready to join.

Out of the corner of her eye, she spotted something burnt orange diving from the sky. She cried out as it landed upon Eoin was such force that the wind caught her wings and blew her back toward the forest. With more grace than the first time she had attempted, she rolled back onto her feet and faced the destruction.

Another dragon stood upon Eoin's back, his talons scraping against Eoin's new-grown scales. Burnt orange in color, he was much larger than Eoin in bulk. His muzzle ended in a sharp beak like an eagle's instead of teeth. With lightning speed, he darted in to snap Eoin's neck.

Eoin moved out of the way just in time and shouted, "Run, Angie. It's Cedric."

CHAPTER THIRTY THREE

Pinned to the ground by Cedric, Eoin tried rolling the bigger dragon off but his weight was too much. Body tense, muscles quivering, he snaked his head around and blew fire. A familiar burn rolled in his stomach, spreading up his throat and out his mouth. His flame bloomed like hungry death. It was back. Eoin was back.

The force of the blow sent Cedric rolling off. Angie was vulnerable. They'd started the mating dance but hadn't finished. This left her open for any males to take his place and bind her. He had to protect her.

Eoin regained his feet and caught a glimpse of white in the corner of his eye. His gut clenched. Angie still stood by the lake. Why hadn't she run? He set himself between her and Cedric. She didn't know how much danger she was in. He should have taken the time to explain the details to her instead of impatiently rushing to possess her. "Angie, you have to go."

"I'm not leaving you."

Her heartfelt words only made him more determined to protect her.

Cedric had recovered from Eoin's fiery strike. His scales steamed from the heat. They were not of the same clan and Cedric was somewhat more vulnerable to fire. But that also meant that Eoin was vulnerable to Cedric's power.

Eoin stood his ground. "You could have had any mate in the world. Why did you wait for her?"

The ancient dragon tilted his head to the side as if not understanding the question. "Because I want her. She's of an ancient bloodline as old as mine. My claim should come first."

Eoin wanted to take this fight into the air—he was younger and faster—but there was no guarantee Cedric would follow him to the sky. He might just grab Angie and run, even though Eoin doubted the aged dragon would be so cowardly. "She's mine." Cedric was bigger and more experienced, but was he willing to fight to the death for Angie like Eoin? "She loves me."

Not His Dragon

With a snort that set sparks off around his nostrils, Cedric shook with laughter. "That's because she's known no other dragons." Cedric used his wings to leap high in the air with his talons extended toward Eoin's chest.

The only choice Eoin had was to deflect the sharp talons. If he dodged, then Angie would take the hit instead. With all his strength, he shoved Cedric away but was left with a deep gash in his side. Blood streamed from the wound and would sap his strength if he didn't put an end to Cedric soon.

Angie cried out and raced to Eoin's side. She'd been raised human and wasn't accustomed to the violent ways dragons used to settle their differences.

He swung around and extended his claws to stop her. "Stay back." She was going to get trampled. He'd rather give her up than see her killed.

Angie crouched low to the ground and circled the two male dragons. What were they fighting for? She'd made her choice. Nothing was going to make her leave Eoin. That asshole Cedric might hurt her wonderful dragon. She wasn't one to back down when someone she cared about needed help.

Cedric's gaze caught hers, and of all things, he winked. "By the gods of thunder, you're tiny." What would happen to her if this jerk won the battle? She sure as fuck wouldn't mate him. She suspected a mating with Cedric would be more the akin to prison than marriage.

Whipping his head back toward Eoin, Cedric opened his mouth, but it wasn't flame that he blew. Jagged lightning bolts snapped and crackled from his throat. Static electricity tugged at her feathers.

"No!" she shouted as Eoin curled into a ball, his mouth open with no sound coming out.

With what grace Angie could manage on four legs, she hurried toward Cedric. When she reached his side she slid on her stomach and bit his ankle with her new needle-like teeth. It seemed like the only place on his body where her mouth would fit properly.

A startled cry from Cedric stopped his electrical attack. He swung his hand, hit the side of her head.

The world spun and she landed on her side, crushing one of her wings. She whimpered at the sharp pain. The taste of blood coated her tongue and she probed her teeth with her tongue to see if she had lost one.

Cedric hovered over her, concern apparent on his beaked face. He stroked her head as he gently lifted it from the forest floor. "You startled me. Are you injured?" He gathered her in his front arms like a child and took flight. "Let's get some ice on this bump." He didn't even look back at Eoin.

"Let me go." Her feeble attempts at struggling were ignored. "I don't want you as a mate."

"You don't even know what I can offer you. You haven't given anyone else a chance but this reclusive bore of a dragon. I will take you home to my clan and you can learn what it is to be a proper she-dragon."

Icy dread gripped Angie's spine. She'd never see her friends or shop again. Cedric was stealing her life and thought she'd be fine with that? She flexed her new claws and searched for a weak link in his exposed under-neck. The dragon was built like a tank, though. "Fuck." She screamed at the top of her lungs.

He startled and paused in his flight. "Did I break something when I hit you?"

Not when he'd hit her, but her heart was shattering with every stroke of his massive wings. She lashed out with her claws, aiming for his eyes. "Put me down." Over Cedric's shoulder, Angie spotted Eoin in pursuit. Her heart soared.

He lived.

Eoin tackled Cedric mid-air.

The impact jarred her against the bigger dragon's chest and she bit her damn tongue. She probably pierced it with her new razor-sharp teeth. Blood filled her mouth and she choked. The ground spun far below in a dizzying swirl of browns and greens.

The three of them fell in a tangle of wings and claws.

Her stomach suddenly traded places with her brain. Cedric had dropped her. She spun out of control and tried to spread her wings. The wind snapped them back, pulling her young muscles and tendons. She tried to flap them and ease her impact. Could she survive such a fall?

Not His Dragon

As the ground grew close enough for her to see the details of her crash site, a set of strong arms caught her around the chest. "Got you," whispered Eoin, his head bent close to hers.

He back-winged to slow their speed and spun so she was cradled against his chest as he took the brunt of the blow. They slid in the mud into the shallows of the lake, causing a small tsunami. Helping to her to her feet, he half-dragged, half-carried her out of the water.

She caught sight of her wings. They were more beige now than white. She shook and fluttered her feathers, spraying muddy water everywhere. It was such an odd, instinctual sensation. She'd seen the wolf shifters do a similar motion but never imagined how good it felt.

The bloody gape in Eoin's hide still oozed as he scanned the sky. "Are you okay?" The question was aimed at her.

"I'm much better than you are." She hurried to his side and examined his wound. "You need stitches."

"This isn't over." He shoved her toward the forest. "Hide, damn it."

Cedric landed with a thunderclap. The shock wave of power ruffled her feathers and she squinted against the wind.

"Eoin…" She'd never felt so helpless in her life. Even when she'd been alone on the streets, she'd always been faster and stronger than her assailants. Cedric made her feel like an ant.

"You made me drop her. She could have died." Cedric crouched as if preparing to pounce. "If it's to the death that you want, then to the death it will be."

This was getting out of hand. Angie's head still spun and she fought the urge to lose her breakfast. She hurried between the two larger dragons. "Stop. I'm not some piece of meat to be fought over. I get to choose my mate."

Eoin pushed her gently out of his way. "It's the way of dragons, Angie. The law of nature extends to dragons as well and only the strong shall survive."

"And breed." Cedric smirked.

Eoin snarled and faced his opponent. Blood dripped from his deep wound and he limped. "I can't fight him and defend you. I'll die for sure." Suddenly he swung his head around and spoke in a rushed low voice. "Run and I'll keep him busy!"

CHAPTER THIRTY FOUR

Angie gave Eoin a slow blink as his words sunk in to her dazed brain. He was right. She was just in the way and causing him to get hurt more than he needed to. He had to win this fight.

Eoin struck Cedric with a very human-like undercut and both males fell to the ground.

Angie dragged her horrified gaze from Eoin and took the most direct path into the forest, since she couldn't fly. She was slim enough that with her wings tucked against her back she was able to squeeze between the tree trunks. Mostly. The low-hanging branches proved more a hindrance than anything.

There would be a trail of loose feathers for the victor to follow. She swallowed a sob. What a time for her to become a crybaby. Why couldn't she and Eoin get a break? They just wanted to be together. She'd finally fallen in love and found a good man—dragon—who loved her back.

The more distance she placed between her and the lake, the less panicked she felt. Her brain stopped spinning its wheels and she took a deep breath. She shouldn't have left him. She should have fought at his side. If he died, she didn't see how she could ever return to a normal life.

She paused by a stream and took a quick drink to ease her parched throat. Working dragon lips to sip wasn't much different than using her human ones. Something still strummed in her body like a distant song she couldn't quite hear. Her heart wanted to beat with the music but couldn't keep time.

The magic that she and Eoin had created as they had started the mating dance still sang in her body. She'd been so focused on surviving Cedric's attack, she hadn't sensed it until now. Uncomfortable pressure built within her body. Her skin seemed too tight and she fought the urge to rub against the rough bark of the trees.

She needed release but she didn't know how to achieve it. The scent of dead leaves and earth filled her sensitive nose. She searched the sky between the treetops for any sign of Eoin but to no avail. If she headed up the valley side, she might spot the towers of Eoin's castle and find some direction toward safety.

Something flew overhead.

She instinctively crouched low to the ground, tucking her tail against her body. It had gone so fast it was a blur. Should she hide? What if Eoin was hurt and needed her help? Goddamn dragon bodies didn't have pockets for cell phones. Even if he was dying, who would she call?

With a grim growl, she followed in the direction that the blur had flown until she came to a clearing. Trying to stay unseen was almost impossible with a white hide. She couldn't shift back to human form without a little guidance from Eoin. If she had time and not a possible concussion, she could probably do it on her own.

In the clearing, she spotted a metallic blue dragon standing in the midst of wild flowers.

He stood on his hind legs as he angled his agile neck to see her. "Angie? It's Zechariah."

A rush of relief flooded her system and she raced from her hiding spot, tripping over her own wings. Before she hit the ground, he caught her in his hands. Zech would help. He'd been pretty cool about her and Eoin mating. She rubbed her face against his arm.

"Hey, dragons don't cry." He stroked her head gently. "Or have feathers. What the fuck is going on, Angie?"

"Cedric is going to kill Eoin. Can you stop him?" She clung to his arm for support.

Zechariah was shaped more like her and Eoin, except he had great ram horns growing on each side of his head and his tail ended in a spiked ball. "Your aura is freed. Eoin finally broke that shield that was blocking you from magic. Did you and Eoin just mate?"

"We were interrupted by Cedric."

Zechariah stroked his clawed hands over the arch of her wing. It was an intimate act. "Before I help Eoin I have to get you to safety. Can you fly?"

Retreating from the blue dragon, she shook her head. "No, I just learned how to shift a few hours ago. I haven't had time to learn to fly. But I need you to help Eoin now. I don't know how much longer he can last."

208

"It's too dangerous for you in this state." Zechariah gathered her in his arms like Cedric had. Angie was fed up of these dragons treating her like a glass doll.

She shoved Zech away. "I can take care of myself."

"I don't doubt that. But when a female has not completed the mating dance with her chosen, then any male can step in and finish it, binding her against her will. If I take you back, Cedric can do this to you. That's probably why he waited to attack when he did."

Angie spun around and made a frustrated noise. The last thing she wanted was to end up mated to that asshole.

Zechariah cradled her within his limbs like Eoin had and leaped into the air, flying over the treetops.

Her wings ached from the abuse she'd suffered when dropped midair by Cedric so she didn't bother to practice flying. She twisted her neck around Zech's broad shoulders and caught a distant glimpse of the lake. Her vision blurred. Eoin had to win.

Please…

The lake vanished from her sight as they crested the mountain and Angie's hope vanished with it. She returned her gaze forward and spotted the towers to Eoin's castle and she sighed in relief. As soon as Zech landed, she'd encourage him to return to the lake and help Eoin, then she'd call every shifter who owed her…

Zech flew past the castle, heading further south.

"Hey." She shouted over the wind and pointed toward the towers. "The castle is that way." How could miss the huge stone structure?

He nodded and hugged her tighter, but didn't make any adjustment to his direction.

Angie squirmed in his arms, trying to get his attention. Maybe he couldn't hear her? "You're going the wrong way." She shouted even louder, but he continued to ignore her. What the fuck? She escaped a kidnapping attempt by Cedric to run into another one by Zech? How could she be so stupid?

She snapped at his hands with her new needle-like teeth.

"Ow." Zech shook out one hand and laughed, yet he still managed to hold onto her as she kept trying to bite him. "That's enough." He pinched her slender jaw closed. "I don't want to drop you." Flying over a different stretch of forest, they hovered over a wide clearing. "This will do." He lightly landed and let her go.

Angie pushed from his arms and stumbled over her own limbs. He was going to force her to mate him and Eoin wouldn't think to look for her here. She had to fight this dragon on her own. She ran toward the dense forest where Zechariah would be too big to follow. She had no misconception of what he wanted from her. She recalled what he'd said about her state of unfinished mating and the reason why he'd come to the city in the first place.

Her.

He flew over her head, landing to block the away. His wings extended and the light reflected off of his metallic scales as he began to weave to the faint beat inside Angie's head.

"I don't understand. There's nothing special about me. Why can't you and Cedric find your own mates?" Angie tried to back away, tripping over her fucking tail again. She needed a belt for that thing.

"Of course you don't understand. You have only been a true dragon for a few hours. What you don't know is that there are more male dragons born than female. It's one of nature's ways of ensuring that only the strongest or smartest breed." He pointed to himself when he said 'smartest.'

"So you think you have outsmarted the others?" She knew he did, but she had to buy herself some time to figure out a way to escape. But he continued to dance and the music grew louder. The pressure in her body needed release and her hips rose. She had to resist, she had to revert her gaze before she started yowling like some cat in heat.

"You don't see me getting my head pounded in, now do you? I can make you a very happy she-dragon, if you would only let me try."

"I've no doubt of this, Zech. But I've already fallen in love with Eoin."

He circled around her, fluttering his wings on the ground and snaking his neck around closer to her.

She found it hard to breathe. The pressure inside her head and chest from the magic urged her to join in his dance. "Stop, please."

Not His Dragon

With Angie safely away, Eoin focused on defeating Cedric. The other dragon was bigger but Eoin was fast and his heart was in this fight because without Angie he didn't care to live. Blood dripped from multiple wounds now. How much more could he lose before he passed out?

Cedric took another dive, trying to tackle Eoin underneath his weight again.

Throwing himself to the side, Eoin landed hard on the lakeshore as Cedric grazed past. His solid *thunk!* vibrated through the ground and Eoin gathered his waning strength to face Cedric one last time. He dragged himself to his feet and found the great dragon lying on his stomach.

Cedric's chest rose and fell, but everything else remained unmoving. A trickle of blood oozed from Cedric's ear.

Eoin approached carefully. His limp would prevent him from deflecting an attack if Cedric was faking. If this was not a ruse, Eoin didn't want the ancient dragon dying on his watch. Like it or not, his mother had taught him to respect his elders.

He knelt next to Cedric and lifted his eyelid. It drifted back closed. Well, fuck, he was unconscious. It appeared that when the old dragon passed Eoin, he'd slammed his head against a boulder hiding behind a large bush. To be on the safe side, Eoin poked the dragon's underbelly with his claw and limped in retreat.

Cedric rumbled but didn't move.

Eoin's eyes widened. He'd won. Then he glanced down at the multiple wounds in his hide. Sort of. He limped in the direction of Angie's escape. She couldn't have gone far without flying, but it would be difficult for him to follow through the dense growth of the forest.

On sore wings, he leaped into the air and flew close to the treetops, trying to follow her scent. Another smell mingled in the wind with hers and seemed fresher than the ones he was getting from the ground. It seemed a familiar male musk. His talons extended to their fullest.

Zechariah.

Eoin winged in the direction that this new scent led him. It flowed in the wind so it was thinner and much more difficult to follow, but he was dragon. He knew how to follow the flows of air.

The direction took him toward his castle. Had he misjudged the younger dragon? He couldn't imagine that Zechariah would have traveled all the way to New Port to court Angie only to help her mate a different dragon. Goodwill was not a strong trait within his people.

When the scent went past his castle, he had the answer to his question. The little bastard wanted to steal Angie. He put more effort into his flight but he'd burned up most of his reserves with Cedric.

CHAPTER THIRTY FIVE

The forest blurred below him until he came to a clearing where a metallic blue dragon swayed in the grass caught in the grip of the mating dance.

Angie crouched, shivering among the wild flowers. The intense drive to mate must be physically painful by now. That she had been able to resist Zechariah this long spoke of her love for Eoin.

Taking a page from Cedric's attack strategies, Eoin dove from the sky and tackled Zechariah. With his claws, he dragged the blue snot across the field and away from his Angie. He'd pound the little fucker into the ground until only his tail stuck out. Wait until the tourists took a picture of that.

Zechariah snapped at Eoin's throat, but thankfully the angle was wrong, and the younger dragon inexperienced. They landed in a twist of arms and wings and tail, rolling to a stop against the far wall of trees with grunts.

"Did you think you could steal her from me?" He grabbed Zechariah by the horns and slammed his face into the ground repeatedly.

In between slams, the blue dragon shouted his response. "Not. Really."

Eoin hesitated and twisted Zechariah's head to look at him with a raised eyebrow. "What did you say?"

"I said," Zechariah spoke with a lisp since his lips were swollen. "I said, not really. But she just showed up out of the blue in the throes of the mating bond. I'm not as much of an idiot as you think I am." He swatted at Eoin's hands holding his horns. "Let me go. She's yours. I'm not stupid enough to fight you even when you're half dead. Fuck you, Eoin. And the horse you rode in on." He shoved himself to his feet and glanced over Eoin at Angie. "You'd better finish the dance soon. I don't think she can take much more magic." Zechariah took off on his wings and flew wherever.

Eoin didn't give a shit as long as he left him and Angie alone.

As he approached her, Eoin could sense the bonding magic within Angie. Her feathers trembled as if stirred by the wind, but the air was still. She crouched low to the ground with her neck and head curled around her body. Her eyes closed tight.

"He's gone." At the sound of his voice, her eyes snapped open and her golden eyes almost glowed with power.

She rose to her feet. "Eoin." She sounded breathless and he wanted this moment to last forever. "I waited for you." With a snap of her wings, she extended herself to her glorious beauty and continued to dance where they had left off by the lakeshore.

Angie's heartbeat was the rhythm that the mating dance followed. The music was internal and instinctual, as were the moves. Her soul rose in spine-cracking joy that Eoin had found her. She'd buried herself deep inside while Zech had done his best to seduce her from her true mate.

Injured and obviously having some trouble moving, Eoin joined her. They danced as one. The magic burned her from the inside out, finally releasing, and she could see its flow from her to Eoin binding them together. The song faded and the urge to dance followed, but she still heard the beat.

Eoin ran his muzzle along her neck. He drew her hand onto his chest above his heart. It beat in time with what she could hear. "Can you hear it?"

"Yes," she said with a touch of awe.

"I hear yours as well. No matter how far apart we are, I'll always be able to find you by listening for your heartbeat."

"So you can never run away from me?" She smirked and nipped his jaw. Part of her was joking but she'd been abandoned so many times that the insecurity was palpable.

"Why would I want to? I love you so much, Angie." He cradled her jaw in his large clawed hand and lifted her gaze to meet his. "I can't believe that you resisted Zechariah for so long."

"How could you doubt me? I love you just as much." He'd fought two dragons for her. Nothing would ever make her uncertain of Eoin's loyalty. She ran her hands over his side and they came back covered in blood. Her stomach rolled. She didn't want to experience throwing up as a dragon with this long-ass neck. "We

214

need to take care of your wounds. Are you capable of flying back to the castle?" It hurt to see him injured. He'd taken these wounds for her. For them.

"Yes, but I wouldn't be able to carry you." He leaned heavily on his left side and a small pool of blood was forming under his body.

"You need to go then. Just point me in the right direction and I'll meet you there." Nine-one-one responded to human emergencies, not to supernaturals. The hospitals wouldn't know how to take care of an injured dragon, let alone have enough space for his huge body. "Is there someone I can call for help?" The only person that she could think of was Ryota and he'd make her pay. She cringed at the imagined conversation.

"No, Angie, I'm not leaving you here alone." His eyelids looked heavy and he seemed to struggle to keep them open.

"Shit, Eoin. Stop being a hard-head. If you pass out here, I can't drag your ass back to the castle." He was twice her mass and she hadn't a clue where home was. She blinked. "Shift to human form."

He gave her a confused look. "Why?"

"Because I can carry you in that form."

He ran the back of his claws along her jaw. "That's my girl." He changed form quickly, but his injuries still remained serious.

She had to lie on her stomach and lower her wing to help him climb onto her back. Bright red smudges stained her new, muddy feathers, and that concerned her because of the amount that Eoin was losing. "Point where I need to go." Angie ran to the forest as fast as she could. Ignoring tree limbs getting caught in her wings and scraping her scales, she finally spotted the castle towers above the tree line. "I see the castle."

He didn't respond.

She glanced over her shoulder at the still form on her back. "Eoin?" Silence answered her. "Fuck, fuck, fuck..." Panic gave Angie's feet new grace and speed. She raced to the castle. When she arrived, she used her shoulder to crash open the front door and searched for her cell phone in Eoin's bedroom. All this time, Eoin remained on her back nestled between her folded wings. With claws too large to handle the small instrument, she finally got her phone out of her purse and used the voice command to call Ryota.

It went straight to his answering service. God, where was the alpha when she was ready to sell her soul to save Eoin? Maybe Beth knew of a shifter doctor who could take care of a dragon. "Eoin?" She couldn't stop herself from calling out to him again. Her ear strained to hear his heartbeat. The sound was faint. She was going to lose him all over again.

Abandoned.

Someone cleared his throat behind her.

She spun around and bared her sharp, little teeth. "Cedric."

The older dragon was in human form and dressed in a three-piece suit. He held an ice pack to the large lump on his forehead. "Peace, Angie. I see that you have both mated. The front door was…broken so I didn't bother to knock." He moved to have a better view of Eoin. "How is he?"

"Why would you care? You were trying to kill him not long ago." She was no match for Cedric but she would go down with teeth and claws before she'd let him continue to hurt her mate.

"I don't care. Not about Eoin, but no one should have to see their loved one die on their mating day. Besides, Eoin could have killed me, but he left me to live. Let me return the favor and I can clear my debt to him." He pointed to the bed. "Lay him there." The other dragon obviously was used to everyone following his commands without question. It irked her to comply, but he was their only hope.

She angled her body to the bed, slid Eoin off her back and let him roll onto the mattress.

"You can shift back to human form now." Cedric eyed her.

She wasn't going to admit to this ass that she couldn't do it without a little guidance. "I'm fine this way. If you do anything stupid, I can bite you in half."

Cedric chuckled. "I knew you would have made a good mate." The other dragon took off his jacket and rolled his sleeves before sitting next to Eoin. He set both his hands on his chest and closed his eyes, speaking a few words. Angie couldn't see the magic like during the bonding, but she could sense it flowing from Cedric to Eoin.

The wounds marring Eoin's tattooed skin mended together without a scar and his breathing grew much easier.

Cedric wiped his hands on the bed sheets and gave her a low bow. "It's all done. Let him sleep and he'll need to eat when he wakes." He unrolled his sleeves and put his jacket back on before strolling towards the bedroom door.

"Cedric?"

He hesitated at the threshold and glanced at her.

"Thank you."

He nodded and closed the door behind him.

Angie melted to the floor in a quivering mess of tears and snot. She couldn't catch her breath. Oh God, she'd come so close to losing him. She crept to the edge of the bed and with a pop stumbled against the mattress as she shifted form to human. Jesus, Mary, and Joseph, she needed to get a handle on this. What if she'd done that while carrying Eoin? He would have surely died. She wiped her face on a dirty t-shirt on the floor and crept into bed next to Eoin, pulling the blankets over them.

Nestling his head on her chest, she stroked the velvet stubble on his head.

He made a pleased noise and cupped her bare breast. "I want to wake up like this every morning."

She flung her head back and laughed. "Of course, you would."

CHAPTER THIRTY SIX

The gallery was making more sales than Eoin had expected. He tugged at the bowtie constricting his throat. Angie had insisted on the tux. He didn't understand why, since he'd attended all his other art shows in jeans and a t-shirt, but the way her eyes had heated when he'd tried it on convinced him to comply. He'd pick up a jar of Nutella she'd been teasing him about last night and see how much this tux was worth.

He'd been standing in the same corner for the last hour, nodding and smiling to the spectators. No one had been brave enough yet to shake his hand. That was perfectly fine.

Angie mingled with the populace. He stared at the form-fitting red dress that caressed her curves so tightly that it should be illegal. She chatted with his agent on the other side of the room. They both turned toward him at the same time and laughed. Great. He didn't want to know. Somehow he had survived the fight with Cedric, so he'd survive this night. He still didn't understand completely why the old dragon had saved him. Maybe there was a heart beating in that hollow chest after all. Even though he'd eaten a dragon-sized meal prior to the show, his stomach growled once more. It was past time to go home.

He crossed the room toward Angie. The crowd parted before him like the Red Sea.

"Eoin, I was just telling Angie how well you're doing tonight." Roger raised his glass of champagne to him in salute. "We've sold all your statues and there's a bidding war on that piece that you called Angie."

The hungry feeling in Eoin stomach vanished. "I told you that piece wasn't for sale."

His agent held up his hands. "I know, I know. That's been explained to them but the bids still keep coming in. There are now five zeros following the last bid."

Angie slid her hand within Eoin's and she leaned against him.

He gave her a small smile. "That statue is priceless. It belongs to me and only me. They are lucky that I let them see it in the first place."

Angie squeezed his hand. "Lorenzo said he has a list of commissioned work for you. I think we can call this show a success."

"Commissioned? I've never done anything commissioned before. I better talk to Lorenzo before he gets me over my head in work."

As Angie watched Eoin search for the gallery manager, she spotted Beth having a drink with Ryota. She excused herself from Roger and joined the two shifters.

Beth greeted her with a big smile. "You'll be happy to hear that nothing has broken in the shop today and your schedule is full for next week."

Angie returned her best friend's high-five. Things were finally starting to look up at Scratch Your Itch. If her business kept rolling this smoothly, she'd make back the money she lost to the witch in no time.

Ryota cleared his throat.

Angie held her breath. She didn't want any more trouble with the alpha. She just wanted to be friends.

He held out his hand. "I hear that congratulations are in order."

She shook his hand hesitantly. "Thank you."

"I want you to know that I am truly happy that you have found your roots and your mate, Angie. Nobody deserves happiness more than you." She suspected Ryota was being sincere. She half expected to hear *Twilight Zone* music in the background.

"That means a lot coming from you."

Eoin slid in next to her, wrapping his arm around her shoulders possessively. "Ryota." He nodded to the alpha. "Angie, I think it's time to go home."

She sighed in relief and leaned against the strong body. "I couldn't agree more." She couldn't wait to peel him out that tux one torturous button at a time. They took one of Eoin's sports cars back home. Angie was looking forward to her lessons with Beth tomorrow.

Eoin held her hand after they parked the car in the garage and walked to the front door. On the front steps, they found a letter sealed with a wax stamp. Eoin picked it up and led her inside the castle.

She tried to glimpse the name over his shoulder. "Who is it from?"

He lit a lamp so he could examine the seal. "It's from Cedric, but it's addressed to you." He held it out for her.

"Cedric?" She stared at it. "Is it safe?"

"Would I have handed it to you if I didn't think so?" He quirked an eyebrow.

Curious, she broke the seal and read the precise and elegant script out loud.

"Dear Angie, I hope all is well with both you and Eoin. I have taken the time to research possible clans that you may have descended from. Not many have feathers in their gene pool. I have narrowed it down to three."

She stared up at Eoin.

He blinked. "And?"

She folded the letter and set it back on a side table. "I don't want to read anymore. I've been doing fine without a clan. I don't see why I need one now. Not when I have you." Eoin completed her.

He yanked her against him, pulled something from his pocket and held the ruby stud earring between his fingers.

She gasped and hugged him. "Wait." She pushed him away. "You paid off my loan?"

He shrugged. "*Our* loan. Mated now remember?" He rested his hand over her heart.

"How could I ever forget?" She plucked the stud from his fingers and slipped it into her ear.

He pulled another thing from his pocket and held up a jar of Nutella.

She purred. "Oh baby, you know what I like."

Thank you for taking the time to read Not His Dragon. If you enjoyed it, please consider telling your friends or posting a short review. Word of mouth is an author's best friend and much appreciated. Stay up to date with my new releases, giveaways, and news by joining my newsletter. As a thank you, a link to a free novel, Ravenous, will be sent to you via email.

Annie Nicholas

Annie Nicholas

Did you enjoy your read? Want to try a similar series by Annie?

Vanguard Elite Series

You can start with **Bootcamp of Misfit Wolves** at only 99 cents! Or free with KU.

Ian's alpha tosses him out of his car at a training camp for worthless and weak wolf shifters run by a crazy vampire.
His only choice is to escape and go lone wolf.
Until he runs into Clare...
She actually volunteered for this gig.
Her wolf is all alpha but it's crammed into a petite package, and she definitely has no mercy when it comes to him.
The work is hard.
The training dangerous.
Surviving is optional.
Clare can't stand Ian's disregard for her authority and he hates her driven ambition.
Sparks fly and teeth are bared. Opposites attract they say.
If they don't kill each other first.

About the Author

Annie Nicholas writes paranormal romance with a twist. She has courted vampires, hunted with shifters, and slain a dragon's ego all with the might of her pen. Riding the wind of her imagination, she travels beyond the restraints of reality and shares them with anyone wanting to read her stories. Mother, daughter, and wife are some of the other hats she wears while hiking through the hills and dales of her adopted state of Vermont.

Annie writes for Samhain Publishing, Carina Press, and Lyrical Press.

Made in the USA
Columbia, SC
06 February 2022

55597771R00136